MOLLY SINGS
FOR THE
Devil

MARTIN O' HANLON

authorHOUSE®

AuthorHouse™ UK
1663 Liberty Drive
Bloomington, IN 47403 USA
www.authorhouse.co.uk
Phone: 0800.197.4150

Published by AuthorHouse   10/06/2016

ISBN: 978-1-5246-6424-4 (sc)
ISBN: 978-1-5246-6425-1 (e)

CHAPTER ONE

THE TOWN OF MULLDISH IN 1941 was a quiet and friendly place in which to grow up, and a far cry from today's industrial buzz. Agnes McGinley, a woman who had just turned thirty, was left devastated after losing her husband Frank in a freak accident while working on a harvest mill. Frank was a hardworking man from the traveller community, and the father of six children ranging in age from twelve year old Cissie down to six month old Joseph. Frank had set off, as he did every morning, looking for work, and didn't mind where or what it was to be. He was what would be described in football terms as a sweeper; in other words he could turn his hand to anything - be it working at the docks or on a farmyard or in a harvest field. It was on a Saturday afternoon in Jack O'Toole's 16 acre field that Frank met his fate. The labourers were flinging the corn into the threshing machine, singing and joking as they worked in harmony, when doom struck. Frank slipped into the thresher and was crushed almost to death. The men got the machine stopped, dragged Frank out and rushed him to the nearest doctor - five miles southbound by horse and cart - but the damage to both of Frank's legs and left arm was far beyond repair and Frank died within the hour.

The news reached Agnes shortly after when Frank's workmate, Tommy Murphy, turned up on horse and cart at their little whitewashed cottage situated on the outskirts of the town. Agnes knew immediately by the expression on Tommy's face that something was seriously wrong - the sort of gut feeling one gets, you could say, just like that of a seasoned poker player who gets reads on the hands his opponent is holding. She dreaded instantly what Tommy was about to reveal. Just as she suspected, Tommy broke the tragic news to a shell-shocked Agnes who collapsed at Tommy's feet, crying out, hands clenched above her head, sobbing and lamenting, indeed even rebuking the Lord. "Why me, why me? ... my family, my husband ... why, why?" Tommy's heart went out to her, for he understood what was to lie ahead for her and six young children now that the breadwinner of the house was gone. News spread across the community like a gale force wind, delivering an echoing heartfelt concern for Agnes and her family.

The McGinley cottage was packed for the next two nights as people from neighbouring towns and from far and wide came to pay their respects. Frank was loved in the community and would be badly missed by all the local farmers who were in shock at this horrific tragedy. What now for

Agnes and her family? Surely she couldn't raise six children on her own? With no more help from her husband to feed her offspring then some changes had to take place and soon - very soon.

Cissie, the eldest, was the first target for help. Agnes sat Cissie down one night beside the peat burning fire and confided sadly in her. Holding back tears and with her throat parched she said "Cissie, we need help to survive." The frail little Cissie, fearing the worst, answered in a whisper, "What is it, Mammy?" Agnes said, "I need you to be strong because what I'm about to tell you will come as a shock." Trembling on her seat with fear and anticipation, Cissie asked with a lump in her throat, "What is it, Mammy?" "I'm afraid I have to tell you that you must go to Scotland and work." There was a heavy silence filling the room before a brave Cissie murmured, "Alright, Mammy, if this is what is needed I'll go." Agnes, wiping away the tears from her eyes, took the soon-to-be thirteen year old in her arms and both cried bitterly.

The next morning the family gathered for breakfast in the cramped little kitchen as Agnes informed them that Cissie was heading away to Scotland to find work. On a spring morning in March little Cissie set off on her journey to Scotland - her destination Clydebank. She arrived at the port of Stranraer later that night. By the time she arrived in Clydebank it was almost midnight. She was met by Nellie McIntyre, the owner of a youth hostel which bore her name - *Nellie's*. Poor little Cissie, petrified, jaded and hungry, was shown to her room where she was to spend what could possibly be a long time. Cissie unpacked her little homemade handsewn bag and bedded down for the night.

The next morning she came downstairs for an early breakfast and set off to look for work in the town of Clydebank. which had been almost obliterated by bombs. So horrific was the sight, it shook her to the core, and she remembered hearing about how Clydebank had been almost obliterated by bombs. She didn't know where to begin searching for work. Then just by chance a man shouted to her, "Hey, you there, wee lassie." Cissie, not knowing it was her he was addressing, turned her head and looked in the other direction, and then suddenly realised it was directed towards her. She quickly shouted back to him, "What is it, Sir?" He asked her, "Are you lost?" "No, no", said Cissie, "I'm just here looking for work." The man, Andy Connolly, asked her what her name was. "I'm Cissie ... from Ireland. "Ah ... Ireland, a wee Paddy", he chuckled. "Well, Hen, what is it you're looking for exactly?" She said, "I dunno, really ... anything at all." "Well what can you do?" "I can make tea and clean." "Make tea, you say... hmm", the man murmured. "Well, make tea it is, but you'll have to make dinners too - and clean." Cissie exclaimed, "I can do that, Sir." "Andy - the name is Andy", said Mr Connolly. "When can I start, Sir - oops - Andy?" she blurted out. "You can start today." He took her to meet the workers in the kitchen - well if you could call it a kitchen - a wooden prefab thrown up quickly to help out with the feeding of the workers who were frantically trying to rebuild the bomb-wrecked town. Andy introduced Cissie to the women inside. Most of them were in their thirties or forties, but there was one other young girl the same age as Cissie. Her name was Annie.

The women, most of them mothers themselves, quickly took a shine to little Cissie. Cissie struck up a good relationship with Annie, and they discovered that they shared the same birthday - April 20th. On her first day at work Cissie was washing dishes and helping with all the clean-up work alongside Annie. The women prepared dinner and tea for the workers. There were block layers, roofers, plumbers, etc - all working every second of daylight that God provided. At 9:15pm the workers called it a day, and Cissie made her way back to the hostel to get some sleep after a hard day's work. She didn't know what she would be paid until the end of the week, but she was looking forward to being able to send some money back to her mother as quickly as possible. The little girl knelt down at her new bedside and said the prayers that she was accustomed to back home in Ireland, a practice she had learned from her mother Agnes, a devout woman through and through. The words of Agnes echoed through her head nightly as she repeated her prayers. "No matter what you lose do not lose your faith", she always exclaimed. Armoured with this wisdom Cissie intended on keeping her mother's counsel. The weeks went by and Cissie was now earning £6 per week, of which she would send her mother £10 every fortnight. She ate her meals at work and saved the little money she had.

Annie McCoy and Cissie were approaching their teens daily and the women were planning a surprise party for both the girls. Saturday night was barn-dancing night for the women of Clydebank and the topic on a Monday morning was always the same: who danced with the most men, who drank what and who went home with whom - but the upcoming Saturday was to be of a different theme. The girls both celebrated their thirteenth birthdays on that Saturday. That evening the women had a party set up for the girls at work. There was cake, and sandwiches, and a present each. The women, knowing too well what Cissie was like, gave her a little prayer book. This delighted the little one so much she wept because it evoked memories of her mother, Agnes, back home. Cissie now had new prayers to learn and this would pass the odd hour for her at night while she prayed happily She treasured that book like gold dust. Annie got an atlas as the women were accustomed to hearing her chatting every day about where she was going to travel to when she turned eighteen. She would tell Cissie, "When I get older I'm going to travel to the USA and I want you to come with me." She said, "I'm going to be a doctor one day and have a big house with horses and stables and you can come visit me and stay whenever you want to, Cissie." Cissie admired her ambitions and believed strongly that one day she would achieve her dreams because, like herself, Annie was a hardworking girl. The girls grew closer every day and told each other everything. Annie informed Cissie that her parents were separated since she was seven and she was helping her mum out as much as possible. So both girls were without a father although Annie's father was alive, but he was an alcoholic and never visited her and didn't even send a card for her thirteenth birthday or indeed any birthday. This however didn't faze Annie one little bit; in fact it made her all the more determined to succeed, and one day she would. As the years rolled on and the girls got older and the town of Clydebank was almost back to normal things were going well for both girls. Annie kept bringing home the money to her mum, and Cissie sending money to her mum back home.

Just over five years had now passed, and the girls were nearing adulthood. Cissie said she would return home when she was eighteen, which was only two months away. She was looking forward so much to seeing her mother again it was all she could think about. The weeks went on and the day came when the girls became women. It was a foggy morning in Clydebank, April 20th 1947, when the two girls showed up for work to the sound of applause from their colleagues, congratulating them and welcoming them to the world of adulthood. The girls blushed simultaneously with a subtle hint of innocence. Tina McPherson, a livewire by nature, shouted out, "You know, ladies, I do believe we are going to have two extra faces on Saturday night for the barn dance." The girls giggled but they couldn't deny that they were both thinking just the same thing. The girls said, "We think we will give it a few weeks yet" - actually Cissie said it; Annie had no intention of waiting. It wasn't easy for the girls juggling work with school. They'd be at work for 7am, then at 9 o'clock they went to school, back for an hour at dinner time to help out again before three more hours at college and then spent the rest of the evening working, not to mention homework later on each night. It was tough on them and was starting to take its toll. Nevertheless the girls carried on in this way for years.

Saturday night was nearing and Annie was getting all set for the barn dance. It took her from Monday to Friday to persuade Cissie to go to the barn dance and it finally worked. Cissie gave in and said "Ok, I'll go." The girls got off work around 2 o'clock on Saturdays as was the routine of the builders and labourers every week. This gave them plenty of time to do a spot of shopping, and they did just that. The girls went to lots of shops that day and ended up buying a new dress each. They complimented each other on what they had bought. Cissie was to wear her floral dress on the night ahead and Annie would wear a striped dress for the occasion. The girls made arrangements to meet up later with the other women at the workplace before heading to the dance. Tina McPherson brought along a few bottles of beer she had blagged from her brother who worked in a local bar. Cissie was reluctant to drink at first, but with non-stop "go on, go on" from Tina she finally succumbed. They had a party beforehand in the kitchen, and they shared jokes and laughter and thoughts about the future. It was now coming up on 9 o'clock so they all decided it was time to make a move to the dance as the band that was performing there stopped playing right on the stroke of midnight. So off they went. Cissie and Annie were both nervous as it was to be both the girls' first ever dance and they didn't know what to expect.

They arrived at the dance just after half past nine. Tina McPherson had brought a bag with her which had in it a few bottles of the hard stuff. She got everyone seated and shared it around. The banter that arose from the women was electric. It was now almost 11pm and the girls were all tipsy and wanted to dance. Cissie was apprehensive, but with non-stop encouragement from Tina she finally got up and tried her dance moves on the old barn floor. The band mixed up the music, first playing fast tempo songs, and then they slowed things down. From the start of the night a man named George Ferguson had his eye on Annie McCoy who looked amazing in her brand new dress. The slow set of songs had just begun so he made his way over to ask Annie out to dance. George was a tall, dark and handsome man and was dressed in fine attire. When he approached Annie to dance she immediately said "Yes" and out they went. George had a friend Johnny Byrnes who was not easy on the eye, and when he saw his friend out dancing with the fine looking Annie he thought he would make his move on Cissie, but when he asked Cissie out to dance she kindly said "No." This didn't go down well with Johnny and he took it to heart. He asked her again, and this is when Tina intervened and told him to sling his hook. Cissie tried to explain to the rest of the women - who were beside themselves with laughter - that she wasn't attracted to him, but they all said "Hold your tongue, you don't have explain anything to us!" He was not the kind of man any of them would dance with. As the girls laughed it off Johnny stormed out of the dance and left. Meanwhile George wasn't wasting any time with Annie as both of them were sharing a passionate kiss on the dance floor. Johnny actually got a glimpse of them before he left the building, just adding more salt to his wounds.

The women were all singing outside while walking home. They walked together for the best part of a mile before separating and going their own ways. It was to be another quarter mile or so for Cissie to make it home to the hostel. It was pitch dark and Cissie kept humming to herself during her journey home, which seemed like forever because she was frightened to death. Any sound whatsoever made her startle. Johnny Ferguson followed close behind her, keeping his distance so as not to be seen. Just as he was nearing her from behind, Nellie McIntyre came along in her car and stopped to give Cissie a lift home. Cissie nearly leaped out of her shoes with relief, but Johnny, hearing the car approaching, hid in the woods, thumping the ground in anger. He had plans in his head for Cissie. It was divine intervention that night for Cissie as she, unbeknownst to herself, escaped the terrible fate that Johnny had planned for her. Nellie stuck on the kettle when they got inside the hostel and made Cissie and herself some coffee. They both talked into the small hours about the night they had both spent. Nellie had been to a landlords' meeting which was held in the town hall two miles further south of where Cissie had spent her evening. The young girl didn't know just how fortunate she had been when Nellie pulled up to give her that lift home. Nellie asked her, "Well, had you any luck with the boys tonight?" Cissie answered, "No, I hadn't, but Annie had. She met some lad called George." "George!" said Nellie. "Not George Ferguson by any chance?" "I don't know", said Cissie. "Well, what did he look like?" asked Nellie "He was tall, dark and handsome and was dressed really nice", said Cissie. "Hmm", said Nellie. "Yes, that sounds like George Ferguson alright. He is a wealthy businessman's son. His father is the head engineer here in Clydebank - William Ferguson. Don't worry, Cissie, your knight in shining armour might be there next Saturday night."

The women said goodnight and went to their rooms to retire for the night but, just as Nellie was making her way upstairs, Cissie asked her, "Do you know a man with rough features, curly hair and a shaggy beard that was with George?" Nellie said, "Yes, I know him. He is called Johnny Byrnes, a waster from up the road. Why? What about him?" "Aw, it's nothing' really. He asked me to dance but I said 'no'. I think he accepted my decision at the start, but when the women started laughing at him I really became concerned because he looked very angry." "Don't worry about him, Cissie. You don't have to dance with someone if you don't wish to. Now get some sleep and I'll give you a shout for church in the morning." "Okay, Mrs McIntyre, night-night." Cissie found it very hard to sleep that night. She was still disturbed about the event that had taken place earlier at the dance. She tossed and turned but she eventually nodded off.

Nellie kept her promise in the morning and shouted on Cissie to come down for breakfast before Mass. So Cissie came downstairs and ate her breakfast with Mrs McIntyre. Nellie drove them both to the church where the congregation was assembling outside in their dozens. Among them was this very handsome young man who caught Cissie's eye. He looked really attractive. Nellie had noticed her looking at him and said, "Now, now, Cissie, remember where you are going." Both chuckled and went into the church. Part of the gospel that day was "Watch out for wolves in sheep's clothing" (Matthew 7:15). Cissie had never missed Mass one Sunday in the five years she had been away from her home back in Ireland. That same day she was having flashbacks of her mother,

Agnes, who would be at their local church back home. On the way out of the church she again noticed the young man who this time simultaneously was looking at her. They both blushed and went into their cars. The young man was along with his mother, Frances, whom Nellie recognised as Frances McNally. She couldn't recall the young man's name, but she thought it was Hugh. In fact although she couldn't remember the lad's name it turned out she was spot on because just before getting into the car his mother shouted to him, "Hugh, go back in and fetch my umbrella. I left it under the pew." Nellie and Cissie looked at each other and Nellie smiled and said, "Mystery solved."

Later on that day Cissie went for a walk to visit spots which had been bombed by the Luftwaffe bombers. She visited the Dalnottar Oil Depot and prayed outside while walking back and forth at a leisurely pace, and then she went on to pay her respects outside the Singer factory and repeated her actions. She remembered hearing that 528 civilians lost their lives during the bombings and a further 617 were seriously injured. Cissie found visiting here very satisfying and rewarding. She felt even in a strange sort of way that it was her duty. On her way back to the hostel she met Hugh McNally who just happened to be out for a Sunday walk. The two shared a glance and a friendly "hello". Cissie walked on a bit before she felt a nudge on her shoulder. This startled the young girl and Hugh apologised for frightening her. He said, "I'm sorry to bother you, but I've noticed you now for the last couple of weeks at Mass and I just wondered what your name is. My name is Hugh. I live a mile or so outside the town with my mother." The girl stuck out her hand and announced "My name is Cissie." "That's a nice name" said Hugh. "Do you spell that with an S or a C?" "I spell it with a C" she answered. "Are you out for a walk?" he asked her. "Yes, I was. But I'm heading back now to the hostel as Mrs McIntyre will have dinner prepared for all of us - not that there are many of us left now because most of the people have either gone back to their homes, or they are about to very soon in the next few weeks because work here is starting to slacken now. I was thinking on going back to Ireland myself", said Cissie. "Oh!" said Hugh, "I'm sorry to hear that. Maybe I can buy you dinner someday, or a cup of coffee?" "That would be nice", said Cissie. "Okay then", said Hugh, "I'll see you around." They both departed after their mini meeting and went their ways.

Cissie made her way back to the hostel and came inside, humming and smiling. Nellie looked at her and said, "I see someone is happy." "Yes", said the young lass. "I am indeed." "Anything you'd like to share with me?" asked Nellie. "Later on after dinner I'll fill you in with the gossip", she giggled. "Make sure you do", said Nellie. After dinner the young people helped Nellie clear up the dishes, and when Cissie and Nellie had time to themselves they got talking. "Right, you promised me a bit of gossip", said Nellie. "Okay", Cissie said. "Guess who I bumped into today?" "I don't know", said Nellie. Just then, though, she paused and said, "You didn't meet that young lad by any chance?" "Yes I did", said Cissie, smiling from ear to ear. "I went down to visit the spots where the unfortunate people lost their lives, said some prayers like I do every Sunday, and on my way back here I met him." "Well, did you talk to him?" "Not at first", she said. "We just met and we both said hello and walked on." "That's not much gossip!" said Nellie. "Hold on" said Cissie. "While I was walking away I felt somebody tap me on my shoulder." "Never!" said Nellie. "Yes", said Cissie. "He came back behind me and apologised for scaring me. We got talking for a bit and he asked me my name ... and he wants to buy me dinner one day, or a coffee." "Well, what did you say?" "I said that would be nice and then I made my way back here." "You're a dark horse", said Nellie. "So when are you going to meet up for this dinner then?" "I dunno. Hopefully I'll bump into him again next Sunday. I know he goes to Mass because he said he saw me there a few times. Maybe he will come over and talk to me." "Alright", said Nellie. "We will just have to wait and see."

After their chat, Cissie went up to her room and started to write her fortnightly letter to her mother. She was now able to send home £15 as she was earning a bit extra. Over six years had passed now since Cissie left Ireland. She had finished school two years earlier, herself and Annie. Now the girls were working fulltime along with the rest of the women. Cissie couldn't wait to see Annie on Monday morning as she had at least a hundred questions for her as to what happened on Saturday night with her tall, dark and handsome man.

On Monday morning the girls met as usual outside the work hut. But bad news struck them at ten o'clock in the morning when the foreman walked in and announced that they would have their work completed in less than two months. The women were upset, but they were kind of expecting it at the same time. Clydebank was now almost back to its old self again. At the tea break Cissie started grilling Annie about her new man. "We are meeting up again this Saturday night", Annie said. "He is a very nice man. Oh, by the way why didn't you dance with his mate, Johnny?" "I couldn't", Cissie said. "I just wasn't attracted to him. I hope he wasn't angry?" "Well, he said to George, 'I'll teach that wee snob a thing or two when I see her again', so just be careful Cissie." "I will indeed" said Cissie. "So you didn't dance with anybody then, Cissie?" asked Annie. "No, but I met a man yesterday after Mass." "What?" said Annie. "How did you manage that?" "Well, I was at Mass with Nellie, and outside afterwards, I saw this really good looking man staring in my direction. Nellie knew his mum but didn't know the fella. Just then his mum asked him to go back in and collect her umbrella that she'd left behind her. That's when I caught his name - it's Hugh." "So did he talk to you there?" "No, we went home to the hostel after Mass, and an hour or so later I went for a walk and on my way back home I bumped into him. He wants to meet me for a coffee or dinner someday." "He isn't Hugh McNally by any chance?" said Annie. "Yes, that's his name" said Cissie. "Do you know him?" "Yes, I do! He lives four doors down from my brother's house. In fact my brother and Hugh play football on Saturday evenings every week. If you like, I can get him to come along to the barn dance this Saturday night." "Now, how do you propose to arrange that?" asked Cissie. "Well, I'll ask my brother Manus to get him to go." "Ooh, Annie, will you? That would be brilliant." "Hmm, you must really like him" said Annie. "Yes, I do."

The week at work had come and gone and the women were arranging another Saturday night out. Annie kept her promise to Cissie and had asked her brother Manus to persuade Hugh McNally to go to the barn dance. He said to Hugh, "There is a young girl going that you just might be interested in." Hugh said, "Who might that be?" "Well, you'll have to attend to find out." Later on in the evening the ladies met up at the kitchen where they worked, and went through their usual routine - a few drinks together and loads of banter. Annie was a little late in arriving as she'd waited for her brother Manus to come back home from football. She wanted to be informed with news about Hugh and whether he would be coming to the barn dance. Manus told her that Hugh was going but might be late getting there because his mother Frances was going to the bingo in the town hall and would be taking the car. Manus went back to Hugh's house for tea after the football, and when the boys said that they were going dancing later Frances said, "I'll drive you there after the bingo." Anyway, Annie informed Cissie that Hugh would be attending, and the women began to emit "woo-hoos" towards Cissie who was blushing but excited. The girls joked and laughed until after ten that night before they all made their way to the dance. Annie was to meet her man George in there.

It was nearly eleven o'clock now and Cissie was getting anxious that Hugh hadn't yet turned up, but her anxiety was short-lived when Hugh walked through the door. Cissie whispered to the women, "There he is." Tina McPherson, hearing the whisper, made a dash towards the young Hugh and dragged him over to where they were seated. The women made Hugh feel at ease by introducing themselves all to him, and shared some of their drink with him. Quicksteps came and went with the band and finally the tempo slowed down and Hugh asked Cissie out to dance, and the girl willingly agreed. While they danced Johnny Byrnes, unnoticed, watched from the side of the floor. Still smarting from the week before, he was enraged that the girl who refused to dance with him was embraced on the dance floor talking nose to nose with another man. He knocked back four or five shots of whiskey and left with a look of raging anger on his face. The music ended as it always did at midnight. The girls talked for a while outside and then departed. Hugh offered to walk Cissie home to which she willingly replied "Yes." So off they went strolling along the road home.

Lurking close behind was Johnny Byrnes watching every move they made. He sneaked up from the back of them and struck Hugh over the head with an empty whiskey bottle, knocking the young man to the ground, unconscious. Before Cissie had time to react Byrnes grabbed her from behind. She managed to look up and recognised his face even though he had it covered with a scarf. When Hugh regained consciousness several minutes later there was no sign of Cissie. He called her name repeatedly. Then he heard loud cries. He realised the cries were coming from the old shed beside a derelict house along the road. Holding his injured head he made it as quickly as he could towards the sound of crying. Inside he saw Cissie's half naked body. He quickly ran over to the girl and covering her with his jacket took her in his arms and went onto the road to seek help. Miraculously Nellie was driving home at the time. Cissie recognised her car approaching and asked Hugh to flag her down, which he did. Nellie almost glued the car to the road and hopped out shouting, "What in heaven's name happened?" Hugh said, "Somebody attacked us from behind. I was knocked out, but when I came round Cissie was gone." Cissie was still crying in his arms and kept repeating the words, "It was horrible, it was horrible." Nellie asked Hugh, "Where did you find her?" and he said, "In the shed just back up the road a bit." "Oh my God" said Nellie, "we must get her to the hospital, and you too Hugh - you might need stitches." "Don't worry about me. I'm more concerned about Cissie", he said. "Well, let's get a move on." Nellie sped her way to the hospital as fast as she could.

Inside, the doctors asked the young girl what had happened but she just cowered in her chair, trembling and sobbing. Hugh was taken into a separate room where his head which required several stitches was treated. The doctor asked Nellie, "Do you know the girl?" to which she replied, "Yes, she is staying with me at the hostel." "Well I must inform you that I think she has been sexually assaulted, but we won't know fully until we do tests." Nellie waited in anticipation as the doctors performed their tests. Fearing the worst, Nellie couldn't sit still, and at last at 1:45am the doctor came out and told her, "We must contact the police." Nellie almost collapsed with shock at the news, for her worst fears for the girl had become a reality. The doctor said she had been raped.

The police arrived about ten minutes later and started asking Hugh some questions as to what had happened because he was their first suspect. Unfortunately for him, Cissie had cried herself to sleep. It was to be an hour or more later before Cissie awoke from her sleepy ordeal. The police asked her about Hugh - was it him? "No, of course not!" the girl cried out. "Then who was it? "I didn't see his face completely because he had a scarf tied around it, but I think it was a friend of my best friend's boyfriend. "And who is this boyfriend of your friend?" "His name is George Ferguson and his friend Johnny Byrnes asked me to dance last Saturday night, but when I refused he got very angry." "Now, why do you think it's him?" "Well, my friend Annie told me to watch out for him as he'd called me a snob for not dancing with him. He said when he met me again he would teach me a lesson."

On hearing this the police made their way to the Byrnes household, but when they knocked on the door there was no reply, so they rapped on the door again, and this time they saw a dim light go on upstairs. The owner of the house was shouting, "I'm coming, I'm coming. Hold your horses." When Alex Byrnes came to answer the door he was convinced it was his son Johnny who had forgotten his key, but on opening the door he was shocked to find the police outside his home. "Is your son Johnny home?" one of the policemen asked. "I thought it was him knocking on my door because he sometimes forgets to bring his key", Alex said. "Well, can you check?" "Of course", and Alex went to Johnny's room, but it was empty. He came back to inform the police, and asked them, "Is there something wrong?" "We are not sure yet, but we need to ask your son some questions as to his whereabouts tonight. Do you know where he could be?" "The last time I saw him was teatime after he came in from work. He got dressed up and said he was going for a few beers. I thought he would be home by now. He might have stayed at the Fergusons' house." "Alright. Thanks for your cooperation", said the officer. Old Alex shut the door gently and went inside and hung his head down towards his hands - for he knew something bad had happened.

Meanwhile the police made their way over to the Ferguson household. They knocked on the door and could hear laughter and talking inside. Young George Ferguson answered the door and his girlfriend, Annie, was shouting out, "Who is it?" She was concerned when George called back, "It's the police." Annie listened to the police from the sitting room. One of them asked George, "Did you see Johnny Byrnes tonight?" He answered, "No, I can't say I have. Why? Is there anything wrong?" "Yes, a young girl has been raped tonight and we think he might be the culprit." On hearing this, Annie came storming out to the front door "Oh no, oh no ... who was it?" The police tried to calm her down, but she was really upset. "Is it Cissie?" she cried out. "Yes, it is", they replied. On hearing all the commotion at her door Julia Ferguson came down from her room to see what was going on. She came to the front door fearing the worst - that something had happened to her son, George, but the police quickly set her mind at ease and told her, "No, there is nothing to be concerned about regarding your son. We are looking for a Mr Johnny Byrnes." "I'm not surprised" said Julia." "What do you mean?" said the officer. "Oh, anything bad happening around these parts I'd suspect he wouldn't be far away from it." "Do you know him, Ma'am?" they asked. "Yes, he is a bad egg", she answered. The officers thanked them for their help and announced they were heading back to the hospital to ask a few more routine questions. On hearing them say this Annie asked them if she could cadge a lift with them as she wanted to see her friend, Cissie. The officer agreed and said

"Of course", but on hearing there was something wrong with Cissie, Mrs Ferguson intervened and said, "I'll take my car, Annie." Annie followed the officer to the police car and said, "It's okay now, Officer. Mrs Ferguson is going to take us there." "That's fine", said the officer. So Annie went with George and his mother Julia Ferguson to the hospital to see Cissie.

Inside, the young girl was still sobbing her heart out. On seeing her in this state Annie ran over to her and embraced her and both cried together. The police were already there. They asked a few more routine questions before calling it a night. The doctors had decided to keep both Cissie and Hugh in the hospital for the night. Annie was talking with Cissie and had a few questions of her own for her. She suspected that Johnny Byrnes had something to do with what happened to Cissie. "I warned you about him, Cissie" she said, but just then the doctor came over and said, "Alright, folks, I must ask everybody to leave now because I want these young people to get some rest." Then he said to Annie, "You can call back later on in the morning to see her." So Mrs Ferguson drove back to her house, dropping Annie off at her home on their way. The lights were on at Annie's house so just to explain things Mrs Ferguson walked Annie to her door where Teresa McCoy was beside herself with worry. Julia explained to her what had happened, and after gasping on hearing the news about Cissie, Teresa said "Poor little thing", and she took her daughter inside and offered Mrs Ferguson a cup of tea. "No, it's getting late now, Mrs McCoy. I'll just push on home." "That's fine, Mrs Ferguson", said Teresa, and she said goodnight to Mrs Ferguson and George.

The next morning the police came knocking once again at the home of Alex Byrnes. Alex answered the door. The officer on duty asked him if his son had returned home yet. "No", said Alex. "I haven't heard from him." The absence of Johnny Byrnes left the police all the more suspicious, and they wanted to track him down now all the more. They went back to the police station to figure out their next plan of action. Firstly, they went to the hospital to visit Cissie and Hugh and to ask some more questions. They asked Cissie did she remember any other clothing that the perpetrator might have worn apart from the scarf that covered his face. Cissie said, "I remember vaguely that he had a purplish coat on, but that's all I can recall." So they asked Hugh the same question, but Hugh said, "I didn't see what he was wearing because he struck me from behind." The officers left then and went in pursuit of their suspect. Nellie arrived ten minutes later at the hospital to see how Cissie and Hugh were doing. The doctor spoke with Nellie and said, "She can be discharged now if you wish to take her home." "That's good news", said Nellie. "I will indeed, Doctor." A few moments later Frances McNally arrived at the hospital in a state of hysteria having heard the news of her son Hugh. "My goodness, look at your head!" she said. "It's all stitched up. What happened?" Hugh told her the story. "I was asleep and didn't know all this had taken place" she said. "I'll be okay, Mother", said Hugh. "What about the young girl?" Frances asked. "Will she be alright?" Nellie said, "I'm taking her home now. The doctors have done all they can for now." "What about Hugh?" said Frances to the doctor. "He can go home too, Ma'am. Just keep an eye on him, and if there is any problem with the stitches or if he gets any pain in his head then bring him back here as quickly as you can." "That's fine", said Mrs McNally, and she walked her son Hugh to the car.

Back home at the McNallys, Frances told Hugh, "You're too young to get into a relationship. You have your whole life ahead of you, and there is college to consider." "What do you mean, Mother?" said Hugh. "I can still see Cissie at the weekends, and besides, I'm not going to break it off with her now, especially after what has happened to her." "Well, I hope you know what you're getting yourself into", she mumbled, and shook her head, continuing, "Now, let me take a look at your head before I go to Mass. You stay here today. I don't want the people at church thinking you were in a fight last night. Have you any pain now?" "No, Mum, just a little ache." "Right, lie down for a bit, and when I get back I'll fix us some dinner." Then Mrs McNally set off for church.

Over at Nellie's hostel, Cissie was in her room holding a prayer book in her hands and sobbing. Nellie came in to check on her before setting off for Mass. She, too, told Cissie not to go to church today - "I'm sure Our Lord will understand." At the church the police were parked outside waiting to interview people after Mass to see if anybody knew Johnny Byrnes and if they knew about his whereabouts or where they might find him. They talked with several people outside but nobody seemed to know where he might be. People all kept asking the same questions of the police: "What is it you want him for? Is he in some sort of trouble." "We don't know yet", the officer said, "but we do need to talk to him." One man had seen him on the night in question, and that was Manus, Annie's brother. Manus had left the barn dance early to go home because he said it was no good and he was bored. One of the policemen overheard him say this to somebody and came over towards him. The officer said to him, "I believe you might have some information for us." "Yes, I do", said Manus. "Well, did you see Johnny Byrnes last night?" "Yes, I met him on my way back from the dance. He looked very drunk and upset. I spoke with him briefly, but I really couldn't make out what he was saying, except he kept repeating these words ... 'She thinks I'm ugly, eh! She thinks I'm ugly'. I just said goodnight to him and walked on." "Well, do you remember what he was wearing?" "Yes, I remember clearly. He was wearing a purple jacket. I recall it well because I was looking at a jacket that looked the same in a shop on Wednesday and thought about buying it, but it was too dear and I didn't bother." "Thanks", said the officers. "That is fine. You can go on your way now, young man."

The police set about looking for Johnny Byrnes. Outside the church they picked up on different characteristics of the suspect - his height, build, etc. They knew he was wearing a purple jacket at the time of the attack, and since he hadn't been home yet, it was highly likely he was still wearing it. They set up a full-scale manhunt for the fugitive. First, they doubled back to Alex Byrnes' house just to check if he had come home, but he hadn't.

Mass was now over but that wasn't what was on people's minds. The gossip at Sunday dinner throughout the area was about Johnny Byrnes. Over at Nellie's, Cissie was refusing to leave her room to come down for dinner. Nellie was understanding, and brought her up some food, but she could only manage a few nibbles as she was still upset and crying. She wouldn't be spending Sunday afternoon in her usual manner, visiting the bombed areas and reciting her prayers. Instead she just stayed in her room, contemplating going back to her mother Agnes in Ireland. She was having flashbacks of her mother during prayers in her room. The police searched high and low for Johnny Byrnes all day and into the late night hours, but to no avail. It looked like the culprit had fled the town. They called off their search for the day and said they would resume first thing next morning.

Monday morning arrived, and the workers over at the prefab were wondering why Cissie and Annie hadn't turned up for work. None of them had been to church so they didn't realise what had taken place on the Saturday night. Then Annie turned up late and filled them in on the happenings. The atmosphere was a mixture of anger and concern. The questions came at Annie from all angles from the women. At breakfast time when the builders and labourers came in to eat they could sense something was up. They all noticed Cissie was missing. When they asked where she was one of the women just replied that she was off sick. The men believed this because Cissie hadn't missed a single workday in six years, so it seemed credible enough. One of the workers, however, had been at Mass the previous day and was mentioning that something had taken place on Saturday night. He said, "The police were outside the church yesterday asking questions as to the whereabouts of Johnny Byrnes. One of the officers asked me some questions about him, but I was no help to him because I wasn't outside the door on Saturday night except to bring in coal from the shed." "Why, what has that maggot got up to now?" asked one of the men. Annie slipped down to the back of the kitchen out of harm's way to avoid any awkward questions about her best friend, Cissie.

Meanwhile, over at the shop where Johnny Byrnes reputedly worked the police were asking the owner some questions about his employee Johnny Byrnes. He told them he hadn't turned up for work that day for some reason. "When did you last see him?" they asked. "I last saw him on Saturday evening when I paid him his wages. I assumed he was ill today when he didn't turn up for work." "Well, if you hear from him contact us immediately at the station." The man, getting worried now, said he would indeed. The police now went about putting up flyers on windows of local shops and other places of business. Days passed, and the week passed by. Cissie didn't go in to work the entire week. She certainly wouldn't be going dancing on the Saturday night ahead. Instead of going to play football on Saturday evening Hugh went to see how Cissie was coping, and he tried to cheer her up. They talked for a bit and Cissie decided it would be best for them both just to stay friends for the time being. Hugh agreed, and after staying for the tea that Nellie offered him he gently kissed Cissie on the cheek and went on home to his mother. He explained to his mother that he and Cissie had decided to stay just friends. His mother was relieved to hear this. She wanted her son to go to college and further his education with no distractions.

On the Wednesday morning a week and a half after Cissie's ordeal she decided it was time to return to work. The women were delighted to see her again, and so too were the builders and labourers. Everybody knew now what had happened to Cissie but nobody mentioned it or even attempted to bring the topic up. All the workers continued with their day as if nothing had ever taken place. The women decided to let Cissie go home early after dinner, but she wanted to see the day's work to a finish - not that there were many days left because the foreman predicted that Saturday fortnight would see them through with the work. The women were already worrying about where they would get employment next. At evening tea break the foreman brought some good news. The council had approached him with a proposition. They had asked him would he and his builders be willing to build a block of flats just out of town. He had accepted straight away. At the tea break he broke the news to the women. They all jumped with excitement, and Tina McPherson chuckled. "It looks like I'm stuck with you gang forever", she joked. The women worked the rest of the day pressure-free and full of delight.

With the days passing by it looked like the trail on Johnny Byrnes was turning colder than an Alaskan blizzard - that was, until he was recognised on a train by someone who thought he looked like the man on the flyer in a shop window he'd seen the day before. When the man got off the train at Dumbarton station, just about six miles from Clydebank, he went as quickly as he could to the police station to inform the police there of what he had seen. He told them that the man was still on the train. The police set about capturing him.

They alerted all the stations that the train was bound for. The next stop the train made was in the town of Balloch; it was here the police apprehended Johnny Byrnes. They took him to the station for questioning. Inside the station, while being interrogated by detectives Johnny Byrnes denied everything. The police knew they had their man though, and after several hours of interrogation he finally confessed to his crimes. He would face a judge on the Thursday morning of the following week. The news reached Clydebank just as the women were ready to quit work for the day. On hearing the news Cissie was relieved. A sense of fear lifted from her, like a dark, heavy burden of worry vanishing into thin air. Annie gave her a big hug, and the women followed suit. The Thursday came and Cissie was called to testify in court. However, since the client pleaded guilty she didn't need to, and her lawyer represented her. On the first count he got one year for assault on Hugh McNally which caused him to have six stitches to his head; the judge gave him two months for each stitch. For the rape on Cissie McGinley he received a further nine years, bringing the total up to ten years behind bars for his transgressions. The people who attended the hearing applauded and cheered as most of them either knew Cissie or worked with her.

The news was great and the women took Cissie to a nearby pub to celebrate. They only stayed for two drinks, though, because most of them had to return to prepare the evening tea for the builders. Annie took the rest of that Thursday off along with Cissie, and the two girls did a little shopping together. On the way home to the hostel Annie said to Cissie, "You need to get out and about again now, Cissie." "I know", said Cissie, "but I just want to leave it for a few weeks yet until I'm fully over it." "That's okay", said Annie. "Just let me know when you are ready and I'll come over to the hostel and we can both go out together." Cissie asked her, "Are you going out this Saturday night?" "Yes, I'm going out with George to the cinema. By the way, George was devastated for you. He can't believe his friend Johnny was such a gruesome animal. He will never visit him in prison or talk to him ever again, and if he does I'll break it off with him."

Hugh and Cissie went for a walk together on the following Sunday down to the bombed areas. Hugh was pleasantly impressed by Cissie as he watched, and admired her reciting prayers at the site, at which point he joined her in prayer. Many a day during the war years they had thought that something like that might happen again at any time, but the war was well over now, and just the aftermath was showing its ugly memories. The day came when the builders had finished up on their project in Clydebank town, and were nearing their next mission. They were to start the council houses the following week. The women were looking forward to a well earned couple of days off work before starting on their next site. It would take a few days to move the prefab to its new location two miles outside of town.

The weeks passed by, and the women were working again in perfect harmony. It was six weeks since Cissie's assault had happened and it was now stale news. This all changed however. One Friday morning Cissie visited the toilet on three separate occasions to throw her guts up. At first she thought it was something she had eaten the night before, or maybe it was something she ate for breakfast. It got really bad and Tina recommended that she go home and rest up. Saturday morning was the exact same for Cissie and she didn't even bother turning up for work. She decided to leave work until the Monday morning to see if she would improve. By Sunday morning Cissie felt a little queasy, but not as bad as the two previous days. She went back to work on the Monday morning again but one hour into her shift she made a quick dash to the toilet to evacuate the contents of her stomach. When she came back out Tina said to her, "You're still not better, are you?" "Yes, I'm okay, really I am", said Cissie. "I think it's just a relapse from the food poisoning. I'll be fine." She came back into the kitchen and completed her day's work.

On the Tuesday morning, after another bout of vomiting from Cissie, one of the elderly women, a mother of four, Mrs Susan Henderson, started to believe Cissie was showing signs of pregnancy; however, Tina rejected this notion. Susan had said to Tina, "I'm telling you, I have had four children, remember." "Right, if she is no better by Friday I'll take a half day off and take her to the hospital, but I'm telling you it's nothing" said Tina, "just a stomach bug." "Okay, I hope you are right", said Susan. Wednesday and Thursday were no better for Cissie, and because of her lack of knowledge on conception it was then that Susan said to Tina, "Listen, I wouldn't even wait until tomorrow. Take that young girl to see the doctor." Tina persuaded Cissie to go and see the doctor with her. They both arrived at the surgery which was two minutes walk from the bus stop. Inside after seeing the receptionist, they sat down and waited to be called. Eventually the doctor called out the name Cissie McGinley. Tina said to her, "Right, that's you, my dear. I'll come in along with you if you like." "Of course", said Cissie. The doctor asked her what her symptoms were. With a few glances going back and forth towards Cissie, the doctor finally realised he recognised the young girl. He had been the doctor on duty the night Cissie and Hugh were taken to the emergency room after their assaults. On remembering her, he asked her, "When did you start vomiting?" Cissie said, "It's been a week or so now. "Hmm", he murmured. "Right, Cissie, I'll be blunt with you - I've been in this profession for the best part of 25 years now, and unfortunately I have to inform you ... you might be pregnant. In fact I'm pretty darn sure." The doctor performed some tests on the girl, and confirmed his own suspicions.

Cissie left the hospital devastated. She ran out the door crying. The doctor asked Tina to bring Cissie back in to see him on the next morning, but Tina had to explain they might not get more time off work. The doctor said, "That's okay, but I need to talk to her privately soon", as Cissie had run out and didn't wait to talk anymore with the doctor just when he was about to suggest something to her. "We just work until dinner time on Saturdays", said Tina. The doctor said that would be fine as he would be working at the weekend. "Bring her to see me on Saturday about 2pm", he said. Tina said, "I won't be able to bring her, but I know Annie, her friend, will come along with her." "That's perfect", he said. "Tell Annie to bring her to see me." He shook Tina's hand and said, "Make sure she turns up." "I will", said Tina, and off she went in quick pursuit of Cissie. When she finally caught up with Cissie just shy of the bus stop she didn't even know what to say. Tina was in shock too. She hugged her and said, "Listen, Cissie, everything will be fine." Wiping the tears from her eyes, Cissie suggested they head back to work and say nothing. She said to Tina, "Promise me you'll say nothing to the rest of the women." Not knowing how to respond to this, Tina could just say reluctantly, "Right ... alright, if that's what you want." "Yes, that is what I want", said Cissie, and both returned to work.

At work Susan asked Tina, "Well? What's the news?" Tina lowered her eyebrows in her direction and whispered to her, "I'll tell you later on the way home." Susan winked to her and said,

"That's okay", swiftly changed the subject, and all the women went about their work. On the way home that evening Susan asked Tina once again about Cissie. "What did the doctor say about Cissie? What does he think it is?" "Alright, but you must promise not to mention one word to anybody", said Tina. "Alright, I promise" said Susan. "It appears you were right", said Tina. "The doctor told her she was pregnant." "I told you so", said Susan. "Yes, you told me so." "Goodness, poor little thing", said Susan. "The thought of her having a baby to that monster must be sickening." "Yes", said Tina, "but how can you be sure it's him and not her boyfriend?" Susan said, "Cissie doesn't have a boyfriend." "How do you know?" asked Tina. "I'm friends with Frances McNally and her son Hugh", said Susan. "I went over to see Hugh just last night. Turns out he is going to university in November. I know this because I asked him how he and Cissie were getting on, and Francis quickly intervened, saying, 'there is no him and Cissie, they are just friends, and that's all they ever were, or ever will be'." Tina then said, "Well, that's her words and not Hugh's." "Well, Hugh agreed and said that he and Cissie were just friends", said Susan. "He told me face to face that all he and Cissie ever did was kiss on the dance floor during the barn dance on the night of their horrible ordeal." "Do you believe him then?" asked Tina, "Yes, I do", said Susan. Tina said, "Gosh! If that pig left Cissie pregnant I don't know how she will cope." "Me either", said Susan.

Cissie couldn't face work the next day. The women who did turn up, though, started grilling Tina about the visit to the doctor. Tina had promised Cissie that she wouldn't mention a word to anyone, but with enquiries coming from all directions she finally succumbed. The women were stunned. On hearing the news Annie rushed out of the workplace and went as quickly as her feet would carry her to see Cissie. She turned up at the hostel with a look of despair on her face. Nellie opened the door and when she saw Annie looking so pale and anxious she knew something was up. "Hello, Annie", she said, "Is anything the matter?" "No, no", said the girl, trying to hold back tears. "I just want to see how Cissie is." Then Nellie took her to Cissie's room. Annie knocked gently on her door. "Who is it?" said Cissie. "It's me - Annie." Cissie opened her door and when she saw Annie's face she realised right then that everybody at work was aware of her pregnancy." "Who told you?" asked Cissie. "We were all concerned", said Annie. "We just asked Tina what was wrong with you, but when she wouldn't tell any of us, we all feared the worst." "Well, you all know now", said Cissie. "I might as well tell Nellie now, too." Then Cissie burst into tears and said, "I don't know how I'm going to tell my mother. It will destroy her emotionally." "I'm sure she will understand, Cissie" said Annie. "It's not your fault what that pig has done to you. Why don't you come back to work in the afternoon and maybe we can cheer you up." "No, I don't think I can face anyone today", said Cissie. "Sitting in here will only make you feel worse", said Annie.

After much persuasion, Cissie agreed. Before Cissie left with Annie she told Nellie that she had to talk with her later. Nellie said, "Tell me now - what is it?" "No, I'll tell you later", she said, and both girls went to work. At work the women stayed tight-lipped. They all carried on with their chores without trying to upset Cissie. On their break Tina asked Annie would she be kind enough to take Cissie to the doctor on Saturday. Annie asked, "What does he want to see her about?" "I don't know", said Tina, "but he wants to see her tomorrow at 2 o'clock. The thing is I haven't told her yet." "Oh", said Annie. "I'll see if I can get her to go." "That would be great, Annie" said Tina. "I have a christening tomorrow, otherwise I would take her myself." "No problem", said Annie. "I'll take her." Annie told Cissie that the doctor wanted to see her and that it was important. "Why?" asked Cissie, "and when?" "Tomorrow", said Annie. "I wonder what he wants", said Cissie. "Well, we will know tomorrow, Cissie. That's all I can tell you", said Annie. When Cissie came home from work that evening, Nellie reminded her that she had something to talk to her about. "Yes, I might as well tell you, seeing that everybody else knows." "Knows what?" said Nellie. "I've been sick all week at work", said Cissie. "I didn't know that", said Nellie. "Well, it was only when I was at work it happened," said Cissie. "Is there anything wrong with you now? Are you still sick?" "It's worse than that", said Cissie. "I'm pregnant." "Oh my God", said Nellie, "you are not, are you?" "Yes", said Cissie, and broke down. Nellie took her in her arms and consoled her. "You don't have to keep the child, you know, Cissie", she said. "You can get rid of it if you want." "I'm confused", said Cissie. "I don't know where my head is. I can't even think straight for a moment. The doctor wants to see me tomorrow for some reason." "I hope you are going to keep that appointment", said Nellie. "I can't see the point", said Cissie, "but I suppose he can't give me any worse news." "Yeah, I suppose you're right there, my dear" said Nellie, "but you'd better go anyway to see him." "I will", said Cissie, and she excused herself and decided to have an early night.

After their half-day at work on Saturday, Annie and Cissie went to the doctor. At the surgery they were told to wait a short while until the doctor came back from his lunch break. Three minutes later the doctor arrived. The receptionist called out Cissie's name. Cissie asked Annie to come in along with her. "Okay", said Annie, and they entered the room. "Cissie, take a seat", said the doctor. "Now do you want me to ask you some personal questions in private, or do you want your friend present?" "I would prefer if Annie stays, if that's alright with you, Doctor." "That's fine by me, but if you change your mind then please tell me", said the doctor. "Now, Cissie, I must ask you about your sex life. Now, don't take any offence to my enquiries please. I must know if you have had sex with your boyfriend." "No, I never had sex with anyone before in my life", said Cissie, "except for when that brute raped me. Why do you ask?" "Well, it's like this", said the doctor. "You don't need to keep this child." "What do you mean? I don't have any choice." Cissie was unaware of abortions; she'd never heard of them before. The doctor told her, "I have a friend in London who performs terminations. "What the heck is that?" said Cissie. "You mean you never heard of an abortion before?" "No, I never", said Cissie. "What is it?" "Well it's a termination, in other words if you don't want to rear this child, then my surgeon friend can help you." "I am ignorant, Doctor. I'm afraid you still haven't told me what it is." "Right, I'll explain to you. At a certain stage in a pregnancy, one can make a choice to keep the child or not, depending on the circumstances. The surgeon can operate on you and terminate the pregnancy." "What? Do you mean kill the baby?" "Well, that's another way to put it", said the doctor. "I'm only thinking of you - not many girls want to keep a child fathered by a rapist." Annie put her arm around Cissie and said to her, "You know, what he is telling you makes sense, Cissie. Do you want to keep it, Cissie?" "I really don't know if I can go through with such a decision, Annie." The doctor intervened, saying, "Well, the longer you put it off, Cissie, the more difficult it will become. I must inform my friend as soon as possible. Tell you what, go outside and talk it over with your friend. I need to know today." Annie said to Cissie, "Cissie, what is there to even think about? You don't want to keep a child fathered by a vicious thug, do you? Look, tell the doctor right here and now that you'll do it." "Okay, I suppose you're right."

Cissie told the doctor, "Right, I'll do it, Doctor. I'll get rid of it." "Good girl", said the doctor. "I'll contact my friend straight away and arrange your appointment." The doctor gently put his hand on her head and assured her that everything would be fine. "Don't be afraid", he said. "My friend Ben is the very best in the profession." Cissie attempted a smile, and she and Annie left the hospital.

On the way home Cissie said to Annie, "How the hell am I going to get to London?" "Look, I'll come along with you if you want - we can take the train down. I'll stay by your side the whole time", said Annie. Then Cissie thanked her, and the girls got on the bus and headed home. When Cissie went inside the hostel she was met by Nellie. "Well, how did your appointment go?" she asked. "The doctor wants me to get rid of the child He suggested an abortion. I never heard of an abortion before in my life. Did you ever hear of this?" she asked Nellie. "I have", Nellie said. "I was going to tell you before you left that I suspected this is what the doctor wanted to discuss with you, but I figured I'd leave it up to him to explain." "I must be stupid", said Cissie. "I never heard of such a thing. I don't know, Nellie, if I can go and have such an evil thing done to a child." "Don't think like that", said Nellie. "It's not a grown child, it's only a foetus - it would fit in the palm of your hand." "Would it not still have feelings though?" asked Cissie. Not really knowing what to say, Nellie just answered, "Of course not. Now why don't you freshen up and help me prepare dinner." After dinner Cissie went to the church and prayed for guidance. She was thinking of how many children her own mother had. There was no one in the church except herself, but just then a priest came in and saw her on her knees praying. He smiled and acknowledged her. The priest recognised her face from the newspaper as the assault had been reported in the local papers. The priest lingered around for a while. When Cissie got up to leave he approached her and said, "Hello, how are you?" Cissie answered, "I'm fine, Father." "Nice to talk to the man above now and again", he said. "Yes, you are right, Father", she said, "just a pity he can't talk back to us direct." "He does", said the priest. "You just have to dig deep in your heart to find his answers. Is there anything you'd like to ask me?" "Well, actually, there is but I'm quite afraid to mention it". "Don't be afraid", he said. "You can ask me anything. There isn't very much I haven't heard before, believe me." "It's a very serious thing, Father ... I am pregnant." "Oh, I see", said the priest. "Well, I take it you are not happy? Is it because you are young and don't want to get married, or do you not love your boyfriend? Surely it can't be all that bad?" Although the priest was asking these questions, in his own mind he had an inkling as to who was responsible for Cissie's predicament. "Well, Father", Cissie said, ... gosh, I don't know how to tell you this, but...." Just then the priest stopped her. "I believe your name is Cissie", he said. "Yes, that is correct", she answered. "You know, Cissie, I think I might hazard a guess as to who the father of your child may be." "Oh", said Cissie. "What do you mean, Father?" "Well, Cissie, I do read the papers, and I keep in touch with the goings-on in my community. So tell me what's really bothering you." Cissie broke into tears and she said to the priest, "The doctor wants me to get rid of the child." "I see", said the priest. "I'm gathering by your reaction that you don't want to get rid of it", he said. "I don't know what to do", she said. "I don't want to have a child to a monster, but there is something tugging at my heart telling me different. I can see Mum in my mind all the time I think about it. I think it's murder, Father, don't you?" "Of course it is, Cissie." "The little child didn't do anything bad, Father. That's what I keep thinking", she said. "Well, Cissie, maybe that tugging, as you put it, is your own mind telling you to do the right thing. As Christians, we all try to do the right thing. I can tell you now ... if you act on the way that you are thinking now, then you are being a very good Christian." The priest blessed the girl and said "I'll pray that you do the right thing". She said, "Thank you, Father", and left.

Cissie was feeling restless on Saturday evening, so she decided to join the women over at the prefab for a bit of company. She set off on foot and walked the two miles there, despite the fact that it was pouring rain. When she reached the prefab, the women were already tipsy. Inside, Tina brought her over a drink, but she said, "No, I'd better not." She overheard one of the women over in a corner saying, "What's she worried about? It's not as if she's keeping that baby." Cissie pretended she hadn't heard her. She just had a soda, but the women were knocking back drink like it was going out of fashion. The whispering got louder and louder about Cissie's impending abortion. It got to the stage that one of the women said, "Let's propose a toast!" "To what?" asked one of them. "To Cissie getting rid of the little monster." In an amplified response they all agreed. Then they held up their glasses and shouted, "Good riddance to the little monster." Cissie realised then that they all were in favour of a termination, even her best friend Annie. She wished them all a good night ahead of the barn dance and left. Outside the rain was still pouring down, but refusing to take the bus, she just walked, and did some serious thinking. Her thoughts were to go to London on her own without Annie or anybody else. It was to be in London that she was going to make a decision that would change her life for good.

Coming inside, drenched from head to toe, she was met by Nellie who asked, "Where have you been Cissie? You are soaked." "I went over to have a bit of banter with the girls before they go dancing." "Why didn't you go along with them?" Nellie asked. "I need my money for the train fare, Nellie", she answered. "So, when are you going to London?" asked Nellie. "I'm not quite sure, to be honest. The doctor said he was going to contact his surgeon friend called Ben. I am sure he will let me know then somehow." "Well, I can go and talk with him on Wednesday, if you like", said Nellie, "as I know you have to work, so it's up to you." "That would be great, Nellie. Thank you very much." Monday gave way to Tuesday, and on Tuesday evening the doctor was notified by his friend Ben in London that he was able to fit Cissie McGinley in for an appointment the approaching Friday at 8:00am if she was prepared to come up and see him. When Nellie went over to the surgery on Wednesday, as she'd promised, the receptionist greeted her, "Are you okay, Madam?" "Yes, my name is Nellie McIntyre, and I'm here on behalf of a girl called Cissie McGinley, who resides at my hostel. I am just enquiring about an upcoming appointment she might have with a surgeon in London." The receptionist didn't know what she was on about, but then Nellie explained to her that the doctor who'd seen her on Saturday might know ... "because I think he and the surgeon are friends." "I'll just check", she said. When the receptionist asked the doctor did he know anything about a Miss Cissie McGinley, he answered, "Yes! Yes indeed. Is she here? I need to see that girl." "No, she isn't, but the woman she lives with is here." "Send her in", he said. Nellie came in. The doctor told her, "I just got word from my friend Ben yesterday. I was going to contact Cissie. It appears he can fit her in this coming Friday morning at 8:00am." "Golly, that quick!" said Nellie. "Well, I gather you know about the situation", said the doctor. "I do", said Nellie. "Well, tell her everything will be fine", said the doctor, "Ben is the most reliable surgeon you'll ever come across." "I will", said Nellie, and after thanking the doctor, she left and made her way to Cissie's workplace.

Nellie arrived just as the girls were on their break. She waved Cissie over towards her and Cissie approached her. "Cissie, I have news for you", she said. "What is it, Nellie?" "I went to the hospital, and I talked with the doctor there. He asked me to tell you that the surgeon in London can fit you in on Friday morning early." "Gosh, I didn't expect that it would be this week!" said Cissie. "Yes, it's this Friday, Cissie, and he said it would be 8:00am ... now, seeing that you'll have to go all the way to London, then you would need to leave tomorrow. "My goodness, you are right!" said Cissie. Then Nellie left. "What was that all about?" asked the women. "Oh, it's nothing ... Nellie said that she will be heading out tonight, and she just wanted to let me know." Cissie had told them this white lie as she didn't want Annie to find out. On her way home from work, she paid a visit to the train station, and purchased a ticket for London. That night she packed everything she possessed into a bag.

Next morning she got up early and sat down for breakfast with Nellie. She seemed very nervous. Nellie said to her, "You'll be fine, Cissie." Cissie said, "I hope so." When Nellie noticed her bag she couldn't help but wonder - and commented, "Gosh, how long are you planning to stay away for, Cissie?" Cissie gave her a sort of a half smile and said, "Ah, you never know what might go wrong ... they might have to keep me all weekend." "Well, let's hope not", said Nellie, "but ... I suppose you could be right." Little did Nellie know, but Cissie had plans of her own - and the bag, packed to capacity, was part of them. Cissie aroused a little suspicion in Nellie as they talked at the table during breakfast. She was talking in a way that seemed like past tense to Nellie. Nellie couldn't exactly put her finger on it but she had a feeling that she might not see the girl again. Cissie would talk about each individual woman she worked with; she was quoting things that they used to say, and reminiscing about the antics they'd got up to at work. One minute she was laughing, and the next her face was filled with sadness. Nellie said to her, "You know, Cissie, you will be back here before Monday. You are not leaving the country." "Oh, I know," said Cissie, "but you never know what could go wrong." "Ah, you'll be fine", Nellie said. Cissie finished her breakfast, and it was now time to go. Nellie offered to drive her to the station. "I'll just get the car out of the garage" she said. With lighting reactions, Cissie ran upstairs, and left a note she had written to Nellie the night before on her pillow. At the station she hugged Nellie tight and gave her a gentle kiss on the side of her cheek. The next train bound for London was just moments from departure. Cissie boarded the train with a look of despair on her face one moment, and then the next moment that look was replaced by one of pure relief. In her mind she would never return to Clydebank.

CHAPTER TWO

CISSIE SETTLED INTO HER SEAT and prepared for the long journey ahead. She had a sensation of pins and needles as the train started up. As the train pulled out of the station she caught a glimpse of Nellie who was waving to her from the platform. The girl smiled and waved back. There were quite a lot of stops to be made on the route to London. Cissie kept falling in and out of sleep. The train would stop - drop people off, and pick people up. At one stop just outside of Manchester, a young girl boarded the train. She sat down opposite Cissie who at this time was asleep. Ten minutes later Cissie awoke. She saw a new face sitting across from her. The girl said "Hello" and introduced herself. "My name is Kathleen", she said. Cissie said, "Nice to meet you. My name is Cissie." "So where are you headed?" asked Kathleen. "I'm going to London", said Cissie. "Are you going down to work there?" "No, I'm going there for a short break." Just then Cissie arose from her seat and made an urgent visit to the toilet. When she came back she excused herself. "Sorry about that", she said. "You look very pale", said Kathleen. "Are you not feeling well?" "I'm just a little sick from travelling", she said. "It has been a long journey so far." "Where are you coming from?" asked Kathleen. "I'm from Clydebank." "Oh, that's a long way away", said Kathleen. "I thought you had a strange accent, but it doesn't seem Scottish." "No, I'm from Ireland", said Cissie. "I guessed that", said Kathleen. "My parents are from Ireland, but I was born in London. My dad came over here over twenty five years ago for work. He met my mum at his work. I am named after his granny." "Small world", chuckled Cissie. "I have an aunt called Kathleen but everyone just calls her Kate." "Oh, I get called Kate too" said Kathleen. "All my friends call me Kate. So how long are you planning to stay in London?" "Oh, I dunno", said Cissie, "maybe just for the weekend." "Are you going to stay with family members, or friends?" asked Kathleen. "No, I don't have any family in London." "So you are going to stay with friends then?" Now feeling a little bit cornered Cissie said in a soft voice, "I don't have any friends in London either. I'm hoping to find a hotel down there at a reasonable price." "Gosh, Cissie, you will be lucky to find anywhere cheap in London. Do you know of any hotels in London then?" asked Kathleen. "I will just look around when I get there", answered Cissie. "Well, we will be there in an hour or so", said Kathleen. "If you like, I can help you look for one at a decent price. I know the city well - after all I've lived there all my life." "That would be fantastic", said Cissie. "That's really considerate of you, Kathleen." "I'll be glad to help. Besides, it'll pass the time before I get my bus home. I live down south", said Kathleen.

Nearing London, Cissie got very nervous, and felt guilty that she had been lying to Kathleen. The train stopped one more time. Kathleen announced to Cissie, "The next stop is the terminus." "Oh, my gosh, is it?" said Cissie. "Yes, it is. Are you ready to paint the town red?" asked Kathleen. Then Cissie put her hands over her face, rested her elbows on her lap and began to cry. "What is it? What's wrong?" asked Kathleen. "I'm not going to London on holidays at all", sobbed Cissie. "I have to be in hospital in the morning for 8 o'clock. I have to meet some surgeon called Ben. I don't even know what hospital I'm supposed to go to. I am very sorry I lied to you." In a state of bemusement, Kathleen said to her, "You know, if you don't know what hospital you are meant to go to, then you are in bother, my dear. This place is massive, and there is quite a number of hospitals. Are you sure you don't know? Maybe you will remember." "No, I'm positive I don't know", said Cissie. "The reason I don't know is because I will not be going." "You know, Cissie, if there is something seriously wrong with you, then you will need to find out the name of the hospital somehow, and make sure you make it there in time." Cissie couldn't hold back any longer. She broke down and blurted out, "I'm keeping the baby! I'm keeping the baby."

Kathleen twigged it immediately, and asked, "Were you meant to do what I think you were about to do?" Cissie was still sobbing, but she managed to ease out a faint "yes." Kathleen said, "You know that there is nothing to be ashamed of. I don't know the reason why you were about to go through with the ... can I guess ... abortion? But, for whatever reason, it's none of my business. All I can say is that I'm proud of you for deciding to keep it." "Really?" said Cissie. This brightened Cissie up so much. All the friends she had back in Clydebank had been pressing her to have an abortion (then again they all knew who the father was) and here was a girl she had just met and she was being supportive. Cissie then wondered if she told her the circumstances, would it be a different story? She thought about telling Kathleen before she got off the train, just to see her reaction, but decided against it, knowing she was about to be helped by Kathleen to look up cheap hotels, and didn't want her disappearing, leaving her on her own and isolated.

The train stopped at Euston, and the two girls got off. Cissie looked bewildered; she didn't even know what she was doing there. "Are you hungry?" asked Kathleen. "Yes, I am starving", said Cissie. "Right, I know a cafe just about a ten minute walk from here, we can go there and have lunch if you want, and then we can search for a hotel for you." "That will be great", said Cissie. "I'm so glad I met you." "Well, I'm glad I met you too." The two girls made their way to the cafe, and after a short wait at the table, they ordered some food. While eating her dinner Cissie thought to herself, "I wonder will I tell Kathleen the real reason about the abortion?" She said to Kathleen, "I have something to ask you." "What is it? asked Kathleen. "Apart from someone you loved, would you have someone else's child?" "I am not really sure I know what you mean", said Kathleen. "If you had an affair, I suppose it would be the same, provided he was willing to be a father." "What if I didn't even have a boyfriend, or I never had an affair, ever?" said Cissie. "Now you're confusing me", said Kathleen. Cissie went silent, and after a long pause said, "I was raped!" Kathleen took both her hands in hers and said, "Listen, I still think you are brave keeping the child, and for what it's worth, even though I would be horrified if I were pregnant to a rapist, I would still keep it too. I am so sorry you were raped, Cissie. I am so, so sorry. What is the real reason you are down in London? If you are not going through with the abortion, then you must be planning on staying. If you are planning on staying, then I can tell you this ... your money won't last long staying in hotels." "I know ... you are right", said Cissie. Kathleen said, "Listen, why don't you come back with me to my flat, and you can stay for a few days until you get your head around what it is you want to do." "You have your own flat?" said Cissie. "Yes, I do." "That's amazing", said Cissie, "I would love to have my own place. If it's okay with you, Kathleen, then I would love to. Thank you ever so much." Then they went and did a bit of window shopping to pass some time until the bus came.

The bus arrived, and the two girls boarded and set off to their destination which was Sutton, where Kathleen lived. On the way down Cissie couldn't help but notice all the advertising for the upcoming Olympic Games, which were to be held the following year in London. She was commenting on them to Kathleen. "This place is going to be so alive next year", she said to Kathleen. Kathleen just laughed and said, "This place is always the same, Cissie. I can say one thing though, there is lots of work here at the moment. If you are planning on staying here, you might want to look for a job." "Do you think I might get a job?" asked Cissie. "It all depends on what sort of work you do. What sort of work would you do?" asked Kathleen. "Well, I did kitchen work up in Clydebank, I think that's all I could do really", said Cissie. "Well, did you serve the food, too?" asked Kathleen. "Yes, I did" said Cissie. "Then I know of a place that's looking for waitresses", said Kathleen. "If you are up to it tomorrow, we can go there." "Do you know the place well?" asked Cissie. "Yes, I work there", said Kathleen. "Really?" said Cissie. "Then I will be ready first thing in the morning." "That will be great", said Kathleen. "You can come along with me in the morning when I'm going in to work. You never know, you might even get to start straight away. My boss is beginning to get really fed up with people ringing in sick. He said there is a couple of girls in particular that are doing it too often."

The girls arrived at the flat in Sutton. Kathleen showed Cissie to her room. "I still can't believe how lucky I am to have met you", said Cissie. "If I hadn't met you, I don't know where I would be staying tonight." "It's nothing", said Kathleen with a smile. "Anyone from Ireland is welcome." "I don't know about you, Kathleen, but I am shattered" said Cissie. "Yeah, you must be", said Kathleen. "You must have been on that train for hours." "I think it was over seven hours", said Cissie. "If it wasn't for all them stops, it probably would have been less - then again I met you thanks to the stops", she said. "Yes, that is true", said Kathleen. "Right, I showed you the room. You might as well get some sleep. I'll give you a shout in the morning and you can come along with me to work." So the girls bade each other goodnight and went to bed.

The next morning Cissie set off with Kathleen to her work place. Kathleen introduced Cissie to her boss. "This is Cissie from Ireland", she told him. "She is looking for some work, if you have any spare shifts." "Well, normally I wouldn't have", he said, "but Alice has rung in sick again for the second time this week. I have had enough of her. She rang in last week too, and the week before. Enough is enough." "Well, what do you say?" asked Kathleen. "She can start today, if she wants", answered the boss. Kathleen turned around to ask Cissie, who was already saying, "Yes! Yes, I'd love to." "Then, welcome to *Jean's Restaurant*", said the boss. "You can keep an eye on her until she settles in, Kathleen." "I will indeed", said Kathleen. It was a busy first day, but Cissie took to the work like a duck to water. The boss was very impressed; he told her to come in on Saturday as well. "I will make out a time sheet for you tomorrow", he said. "I would do one for you today, but my wife

Jean is off for a hospital appointment." The two girls gave each other a knowing look. Cissie was remembering her original reason for coming to London "My wife Jean does all the time sheets", he said. "I will see you girls in the morning." Cissie skipped happily out of the restaurant. "Oh Kathleen, I can't believe I'm getting a job in London", she said. "I couldn't be more excited. When I get my first pay packet I'll look for a place to stay. I don't want to be imposing on you, Kathleen." "Listen", said Kathleen, "if you like you can live with me. You can stay in the spare room if you want to. You do like the room, don't you?" "Of course I do", said Cissie. "I would love to, Kathleen. I will pay you rent." "We'll sort that out next week", said Kathleen. After the shift on Saturday, the boss handed Cissie £10. She nearly fainted; she couldn't believe the wages for two days - this was way better than the rate she'd been paid in Clydebank.

Up in Clydebank, Nellie had read the letter Cissie had left for her. In it she thanked Nellie for her hospitality. She said that she wouldn't be back in Clydebank, and she asked Nellie if she would tell the women some day. "I will be forever grateful if you could", she wrote. Cissie asked Kathleen if the boss had made a mistake with her wages. "No", said Kathleen. "That is the rate of pay." "My gosh, this is great. Now I can send Mum a bit extra next week." Cissie suddenly became withdrawn and pensive. "What is it?" asked Kathleen. "When I send Mum over my next letter with her money she is going to see the London postmark", said Cissie. "What should I do? She thinks I'm still in Clydebank." "Listen, why don't you write her a note, stating that the work dried up in Clydebank, and you and some of the other girls were offered work in London?" "Do you think she won't suspect anything?" asked Cissie. "Of course not. Besides, you are still working away from home. I can't see the difference." "I suppose you are right", said Cissie. "I don't know what I am going to do this Christmas. There is no way I am going back to Ireland pregnant, and if the date is anything to go by, I might even have the baby by then." "We will think of something before then", said Kathleen. "It's still seven months away after all." "I go home every Christmas", said Cissie. "If Mum knew I was pregnant she would have a fit." "You will have to tell her sometime", said Kathleen. "Oh my goodness!" said Cissie. "What is it now?" asked Kathleen. "My rape trial was in the newspaper up there." "So what are you saying?" "What if someone saw it that knows Mum? Oh my goodness it would devastate her." "No one is going to see it, apart from the locals", said Kathleen. "I hope you are right", said Cissie. "Come on, Cissie, let's get home", said Kathleen, "I am dying for a cup of tea." "Yes, me too", said Cissie. "That's the spirit" said Kathleen, "and stop panicking. Everything will be fine. Who on earth would see it who is related to you? You don't have family in Clydebank, do you?" "No I don't", said Cissie. "I went there alone when I was twelve." "Twelve! You are kidding me", said Kathleen. "No", said Cissie. "My word, I can't even begin to imagine how frightening that must have been for you. I don't think I could have done that. In fact I never would have." "Well, I didn't have a choice in the matter. My dad died in a freak accident, and Mum was left with six children." "You must be the oldest then", said Kathleen. "I am the oldest of the McGinley clan", Cissie said. "McGinley?" said Kathleen. "So that's your surname. I never even asked you your surname. Come to think of it, I never told you mine - it's Murphy. So your dad is dead as a result of an accident. Your poor mum must have been heartbroken." "Yes, she was. I don't think she will ever get over it, to tell you the truth." The girls talked over tea for an hour or more, getting to know each other better. Cissie checked the time. She was thinking about the women, and what they would be doing at this moment. She said to Kathleen, "The women up in Clydebank would be in the kitchen now, getting boozed up before going to the barn dance." "Whose kitchen?" Kathleen asked. "The place where they work." "Does the boss allow them?" "Yeah, he doesn't mind, as long as they clear up after them." "What are you like!" said Kathleen, and laughed her head off. "Tell you what, I am going out for a drink tonight with Rob, my boyfriend. If you want to join us, you are more than welcome." "No, not tonight", said Cissie, "maybe next Saturday, if that's okay." "No problem", said Kathleen. "You can listen to the radio and relax. I'm going to get washed and ready." "I might have an early night" said Cissie, "I want to go to Mass in the morning. I noticed a chapel on our way home." "I have to take my hat off to you, Cissie", said Kathleen. "I didn't think you were a holy Mary, but there are worse places you could go." "I have been going ever since I can remember. No point in changing now", Cissie laughed. "Yeah, I suppose you are right. Okay, make yourself at home. I'm off to wash." Twenty minutes passed by, and Kathleen was all set to go out. "If I am not back by twelve, then I will stay over at Rob's house. If I am back by then, though, I'll do my best not to wake you", she said. "That's fine by me", said Cissie. "Right, I'm off", said Kathleen. "Have a great night", said Cissie.

It was well after midnight, and there was no sign of Kathleen. Cissie was still up, and she was feeling lonely - talking to herself - so much for an early night. She was worrying about her pregnancy, and was contemplating telling her new boss, sooner rather than later. He would notice in due time. Sunday morning came, and Cissie went to Mass. When she came back again, Kathleen had just arrived home. "Oh hello", said Kathleen, "how was Mass?" "It was nice", said Cissie. "I take it you had a good night then." "Yes, it was good. We went for a drink and then we went back to Rob's house", said Kathleen. "Did you sleep okay?" "I was still wide awake until well after midnight" said Cissie. "I was wondering should I tell the boss about the pregnancy tomorrow at work?" "What!" said Kathleen. "Are you mad? Give yourself a few weeks at least." "I don't know", said Cissie. "What if he notices?" "He won't notice you", said Kathleen. "Besides, if he does he will get jealous." "Why? What do you mean?" asked Cissie. "He and his wife, Jean, have been trying for children for years, but to no avail." "Aw, that's sad" said Cissie. "Well, it's not for the want of trying, I'd say", laughed Kathleen." "That's not fair", said Cissie, but she had to laugh. "I'm only joking", said Kathleen. "I think Jean had her womb removed at a young age, but that's probably just gossip - then again most of the people who know them best say this - so there is no smoke without fire, as my dad would say. You never know, they might try to steal your baby, Cissie." "Well, they are welcome to it. If I wasn't reared a Catholic then I wouldn't be here working. Remember?" "I guess you are right", said Kathleen. "So what if you weren't a Catholic, Cissie?" "I don't know", said Cissie, "I don't want to get rid of it, but at the same time I don't want to keep it, if that makes any sense." "I wish I could answer you, Cissie, but I can't. I sort of know what you mean, and I really admire that you decided to go through with the pregnancy. Only time will tell, Honey."

The week at work was going well for Cissie. Jean had made out the time sheet for her. She had one day off per week, in addition to every Sunday; her day off was to be a Wednesday. She decided this would be her chosen day, once a fortnight, to post her mother over some money. The following Wednesday Cissie did just that. Along with the money, she wrote her mother a note telling her that the work had ended in Clydebank. She felt a bit guilty writing this, but a little white lie won't hurt anybody, she thought.

A few weeks into her work, Cissie thought it was time to tell the boss about her pregnancy. She waited until she got her wages on the Saturday. When Michael Smith, her boss, handed her the wages she said to him, "Michael, can I talk to you a moment? I have something to tell you." "Sure, what is it? said Michael. "I know I should have told you from day one, but I was afraid to … you see the thing is … I am pregnant." "Oh dear", said Michael. "Now that is a revelation! So you were afraid to tell me? Cissie, there is a bond of trust required between workers, you know." "I know", said Cissie. "I am so sorry. You will probably need to find someone else now, I suppose. I wish I had told you at the start." "Not to worry, my dear. If you think I am going to sack you for being pregnant, then you are crazy", said Michael. "How long have you been pregnant, if you don't mind me asking?" "I think it's about eight or nine weeks now, Sir, but if I am anything like my mother, I'll be able to work right up to two weeks before I am due, if that's okay with you." "Eight or nine weeks? Well, if my maths are anything to go by then I will not be expecting to have you during the party season. We get very busy during the weeks of December with staff parties. Then again, if that's when you are due, there is nothing much we can do about it." "I will do my best to make it up to you, Sir, I promise", said Cissie. "Never mind that", said Michael. "If all my staff worked as hard as you do, Cissie, then I'd have nothing to worry about. By the way, thanks for letting me know. Now go home and enjoy your weekend." Cissie was so relieved and happy. "I will, Sir, and thanks for being so understanding." "It's nothing. Now run along, and I'll see you on Monday." "You certainly will, and thanks again."

When Kathleen saw the big grin on Cissie's face, she had to ask her, "What are you all smiles about?" "You'll never guess what I'm after telling the boss." "I hate guesses, Cissie. Just tell me", said Kathleen. "I told him about the baby." "Did you? What did he say?" "At first, I thought I was going to get fired, but he was so understanding, I could hardly believe it. He did mention trust between the workers, though, and I can't say he is wrong. I just wish I had told him earlier." "Well, the thing is you told him now and you didn't get sacked, so happy days! So will you come and celebrate with me tonight then?" asked Kathleen. "What are we celebrating?" asked Cissie. "You still having a job, you clown", laughed Kathleen. "Yes", said Cissie, "I never thought on that … Right, you're on, I'll go out along with you." "Good, now let's get home." The two girls put their arms around each other, and off they went, joking and laughing. The girls went down to a tavern in Sutton that Kathleen knew well. There was a band playing in the background. Some of the songs they were singing brought back memories to Cissie. She recalled them from the barn dances up in Clydebank. Kathleen noticed a change in Cissie's mood. "What are you all sad about?" she asked her. "It's nothing … I just remembered the girls out dancing to some of them songs. Tina was really hyper!" she said. "It's nice to have memories, Cissie, but you are down here now, and hopefully you can have good memories from here one day", said Kathleen. "Yes, you are right, Kathleen. I think we will drink to that, so raise your glass, and let's declare a new beginning." The girls raised their glasses and said, "To a new beginning." They stayed until closing time and then went home. Cissie asked Kathleen to set the alarm for her so she could get up for Mass in the morning. "Why don't you have a lie-in tomorrow?" said Kathleen. "You have been up early all week, and you've been drinking all evening. I think God will forgive you for missing one Sunday." "Yeah, I suppose you're right", said Cissie. The girls made some tea and toast and then went to bed.

Next morning, even though Cissie didn't have an alarm in her room, she still woke in time to attend Mass. She quietly got up so as not to wake Kathleen, and made her way to the church. When she came back Kathleen was still asleep. Cissie slipped back into bed, and Kathleen was none the wiser. The girls got up at dinner time. Kathleen was trying to wind Cissie up by saying, "You sinner - missing church on a Sunday, tut tut." "That's what you think", said Cissie. "I was up at nine this morning while you were still asleep." "No, you weren't", said Kathleen. "Yes I was, and when I came home I went back to bed. The gospel was from Mark 12:3, and I can quote it: 'And they took him, and beat him, and sent him away empty handed' - that's just the part I remember." "I know by your face you are telling me the truth. My word, Cissie, I wish I had your faith! You should become a nun." "To tell you the truth, I've thought about it a few times", said Cissie. "I don't think I would qualify now, somehow. A pregnant nun wouldn't go down too well with the Catholic Church." "I am sure many a woman who had a baby became a nun, Cissie", said Kathleen. "I am not so sure about that", said Cissie. "There must be someone who is a nun who once had a baby", said Kathleen. "Well, I wouldn't feel good about it now, anyway", said Cissie, "so I won't even think about it anymore. It would be interesting to find out though ... I am sure there are women who had children who went on to become saints, though, that I've heard of." "Saint Cissie! That's a good title for you", laughed Kathleen. "So what will we do today then?" "I don't know. What do you have in mind?" Cissie asked. Kathleen said, "I was going to visit my parents today. If we go there now they might make us dinner. I can't be bothered cooking today. I would like you to meet them. They will be interested to know who I am renting the room to." "That's fine with me", said Cissie. "Right", said Kathleen, "that's what we'll do then. I am just going to have a cup of tea first, and we can be on our way then. Do you want a cup?" "Yeah, why not, if you are making one."

The girls had their tea, and then set off on the bus to Kathleen's parents' house, which was two miles away. Kathleen introduced Cissie to them. "This is Cissie from Ireland. I am renting out the spare room to her." "Nice to meet you", said Mr Murphy. "So you are from Ireland. What part are you from?" "I am from a small village in County Donegal called Mulldish." "I can't say I've heard of the village", said Patrick Murphy, "but I have been to Donegal many a time. It is lovely up there. I am from Cork myself - we couldn't be further apart", he laughed. "Yes, you are well down. I have never been to any other county", said Cissie, "except just passing through." "You don't know what you've missed. Cork is the nicest place on earth", joked Patrick. "Are you ladies hungry?" asked Mrs Murphy. Kathleen gave Cissie a little smile and she said, "Yes, Mum, we are starving." "Well, you are in luck today", said Sally Murphy. "I was held back this morning at the church. I had to sing in the choir at a funeral, and I am only getting around to making the Sunday lunch now." "Cissie should be your daughter", said Kathleen. "Why is that?" asked Sally. "She never misses Mass. She goes every week without fail." "Good for you, Cissie", said Sally. "You should take a leaf out of her book, Kathleen." "I sometimes go, though", said Kathleen. "I know you do, but not near enough", said Sally. "Do you need any help with dinner?" asked Cissie. "No, you are fine, Dear. Sit yourself down and I'll do it", said Sally. "So how do you like London, Cissie?" asked Patrick. "It is massive", she said. "I think it would take me ten years to get to know this place." "You would be surprised", said Patrick. "You will soon get to know it." "Next year should be great here, with the Olympic Games taking place", said Cissie. "Yes, it will be some occasion, indeed", said Patrick. "Do you like sports, Cissie?" "Yes, I love all sports", she answered. "I am hoping I can save enough money to go to some of the events." "Where are you working? asked Patrick. "I am working in *Jean's Restaurant* along with Kathleen." "That's great", he said. "Well, if you both save up then you never know." One hour later Sally called the girls into the kitchen for the dinner - roast beef, carrots, potatoes and gravy. "Something smells good", said Kathleen, and they sat down and ate their fill. "When Cissie got an opportunity, she whispered to Kathleen not to mention her pregnancy. "Don't worry, your secret is safe with me", she answered. After spending most of the day with the Murphys, the girls decided it was time to make their way back to the flat. "It was nice meeting you" said Sally and Pat to Cissie. "You, too" said Cissie, "and thanks for dinner. It was delicious." "We hope to see you again", they said. "Yes, that would be nice", said Cissie.

The girls followed their usual routines over the months that came and went. They worked all week and they went out sometimes together on a Saturday night, but Kathleen went out with her boyfriend every other Saturday and Cissie just stayed in. "It is hard to believe, Cissie, but you will be down here six months next week", said Kathleen. "Are you sure?" said Cissie. "Yes. You came here on the eighth of May. Today is November the first." "Gosh, where does time go?" said Cissie. "I know", said Kathleen. "It will be no time until you will be having your baby." "Don't remind me", said Cissie. "I am dreading it." In at work one day during the week the girls saw Jean crying. Kathleen, being the most upfront of the two girls, asked her what was wrong. "I went for another hospital appointment today", said Jean, "and the doctor confirmed to me that I would never have children." Jean then turned and looked towards Cissie and said, "You are so lucky, Cissie. I wish I was as lucky as you." For the first time in her life Cissie lost control. She said to Jean, "What do you mean lucky? You know nothing about me and my life! I am only eighteen years old, and I don't want to be lumbered with a baby." Then she started crying too. Jean, seeing that she'd struck a nerve, apologised to her. "I am so sorry", she said. "I didn't mean to upset you." "I am the one who should be apologising" said Cissie. "Forgive my ignorance. I am really sorry that you are not able to have children. I really am." Kathleen suggested to Jean, "What about adoption? Have you ever thought about that?" "Yes, I have, but I never wanted to believe that I couldn't have my own, and now that I know for sure then I think I might have to." "Why don't you talk about it with your husband?" said Kathleen. "Maybe you are right, Kathleen", said Jean. "I think I might just do that. Tell you what, girls, there are only two customers left - why don't you both head on home and I'll see you in the morning. I will clear up the dishes." "Are you sure you will be alright?" asked Cissie. "Yes, I will be okay. Now run along." "We will see you in the morning" said the girls, "and goodnight."

On the way home Kathleen asked Cissie, "What was that all about?" Cissie said, "I just flipped. The very thought of having this child is getting to me. I can't understand how life can be so cruel. Here I am, ready to have a baby that I don't want, and there is Jean not able to have children. I am feeling so guilty now." "Cissie! Jean doesn't know you were raped. She probably thinks you have a partner. If she knew that you were having a baby as a result of rape then it would be her feeling guilty", said Kathleen. "I guess you are right", said Cissie.

Michael arrived at the restaurant later that night with supplies of vegetables and meat for the restaurant. When he came inside all the customers had gone. Seeing a light still on in the kitchen, he went in and found his wife sitting sobbing. He went over to her straight away, "What is it, Jean? What is wrong?" When Jean looked up at him her face said it all. Michael said, "So you were at the hospital then?" Jean just managed to nod her head. Michael put his arms around her and said, "I promise you, we will have a child someday." Jean wasn't so certain though. "How, Michael?" she asked. "How?" "I don't know yet, Jean, but we will." "Well, I can't see how we will, unless we adopt", she said.

Michael said, "If we both want children then that is what we will have to do. But there is no point in trying now until after Christmas." Jean suggested applying for adoption before Christmas, to which Michael responded, "Yes, okay. If that's what you want, then that is what we will do." Jean put her arms around him and cried with relief; the thought of having a baby - even through adoption - would make her life feel complete. When they arrived home and had settled in for the evening, Jean told Michael that the girls had caught her crying. "I wouldn't worry about that", said Michael. "No, that's not what bothered me. It is something that I said to Cissie that is bugging me." "What was that?" asked Michael. "I happened to make a remark to Cissie about her being lucky enough to be having a baby." "So!" said Michael, "There is nothing wrong with that. She is lucky to be having a baby." "You should have seen her, though" said Jean. "She nearly went berserk. I couldn't believe it ... she said, 'What do you know about me and my life?' and she said that she didn't have a boyfriend." "And what did you do then?" asked Michael. "I apologised and she did too. I don't know, Michael, but I get the feeling that she doesn't want the baby." "Maybe it's just her hormones", said Michael. "My friend Anthony's wife was like a woman ready to hang him when she was expecting." "Maybe you're right", said Jean. "Do you think?..." "Think what?" asked Michael. "Ah, it's nothing", said Jean, "I am off to bed." "I will be up later", said Michael. "I just want to sort out these order sheets, and I'll be up soon. If you're asleep I won't bother you."

Jean had crazy thoughts rolling around in her head. These thoughts were about Cissie's baby. "What if Cissie didn't want this baby? What if she was prepared to let me and Michael adopt it?" This went through her head repeatedly. Michael came up the stairs an hour or so later. "You are still awake", he said. "Yes, I can't sleep." "Is it because of the hospital today?" "Yes", she answered. Jean asked Michael a question that he really didn't know how to answer. "Do you know if Cissie drinks?" she asked. "I don't know", said Michael. "Why do you ask?" "It's none of my business, I suppose, but wouldn't it be bad for the baby?" asked Jean. "I suppose it would", said Michael, "but I don't think she drinks too much." "How do you know?" asked Jean. "To be honest with you, Jean, I really don't know. I am just assuming. Where is this all leading?" he asked. "Ah, it's nothing ... she is young, and she might not be aware of the dangers", said Jean. "Look, Dear, my mother drank when she was expecting me, and I turned out alright, didn't I? Well I hope I did, anyway", he laughed. "Now why don't you get some sleep. We both have to get up early."

"I was going to ask you something earlier, then I stopped", said Jean. "Do you think Cissie wants the baby?" "Jean! What sort of question is that? Of course she will want her baby." "When did she come to London?" asked Jean. "She started with us sometime in May", answered Michael. "Didn't she say that the baby is due sometime around Christmas?" asked Jean. "Yes, I think she did mention that alright. Why are you asking?" "Well it's just ...she said she didn't have a boyfriend, and if she is expecting sometime in December, then that means she must have been two months pregnant when she came to London." "And what's wrong with that?" asked Michael. "Maybe it's just my mind telling me things it shouldn't, but what if she is running away from somebody?" "Listen", said Michael, "she obviously had a boyfriend in Scotland. Maybe he was cheating on her, and she wanted to get away from him, or maybe when she found out she was pregnant, she realised she was too young to settle down and get married ... it could be any number of things." "Yeah, who knows? I guess you could be right", said Jean. "Okay, I am going to try and get some sleep." "That's more like it", said Michael, and kissed his wife on the forehead. "I'll set the alarm. I don't want to be stuck in traffic in the morning - you know what it's like after nine."

When morning came Jean told her husband to go ahead in to work without her. "Are you still feeling upset?" he asked. "Yes, a little", said Jean, "I don't know if I could contain my emotions today. Seeing Cissie and her bump might just trigger me off." "It's no problem, Darling", said Michael. "You take it easy today. You had a horrible day yesterday. Are you sure you will be alright?" "I'll be fine", Jean answered. "I'll see you later", said Michael, and off he went to work.

It was a good few weeks later, and Cissie was now almost eight months pregnant. Michael had a proposition from Jean. She told him that it wouldn't be good for Cissie to be in the kitchen too much now that she was so far gone, "I think I'll let her help me with the bookings for our upcoming parties - at least then I can keep an eye on her." "Yes, that will be a good idea", said Michael. Jean put an advertisement in the restaurant window, seeking a waitress to work for a few months just to fill in for Cissie. Jean approached Cissie and asked her to help her with the bookings. Cissie said, "Yes, of course." The advertisement received a lot of attention. Michael spent a few hours interviewing the girls who turned up, and chose one of them, a girl with previous restaurant experience. Her name was Susan Ward. Kathleen showed her around the kitchen. Jean now was all set for her plans with Cissie. She asked Cissie, "Are you going home for Christmas?" "No, I don't want to travel when I am like this. I am too afraid something might happen to me on the boat." "Wouldn't your mother be upset, missing out on seeing her grandchild being born? I am sure she would love to be there for you." Cissie said, "She doesn't know she is becoming a grandmother." "What do you mean?" asked Jean. "Surely you must have told her by now? You only have about six weeks or so left." "I will surprise her in the summer of next year", said Cissie. "Does any of your family know?" asked Jean. "No, none of them knows."

Jean's suspicions about Cissie not wanting the baby were becoming more apparent. "Are you going out for a drink this weekend?" she asked. "I don't know", said Cissie. "I think Kathleen is meeting her boyfriend this weekend. I go out with her every other week." "Would you drink much when you are out?" asked Jean. "It depends", said Cissie. "Some nights I just want to get drunk and forget about everything, and other nights I only drink a few." "You shouldn't be drinking now when you are pregnant", said Jean. "It is not good for your baby." "What is it with you and this baby?" said Cissie. "Could we just change the subject?" "I am sorry", said Jean, "I thought you were looking forward to having a baby." "Well I am not", said Cissie. Jean was inwardly delighted; she had more questions in store for Cissie over the coming weeks, but she didn't want to push her too far that day. "Right, Cissie," she said, "I'll leave you to it for an hour or so. I am going down to the butchers to collect some meat for tonight's menu. I'll see you when I get back. You know where everything is." "That's fine", said Cissie. Michael came into the office to see how the women were getting along, and noticing that Jean wasn't there he asked Cissie where she was. "She is away to the butchers", answered Cissie. "She said she was getting meat for tonight's menu." Michael didn't want to mention to Cissie that he had already collected the meat from the butchers. He realised that something odd was happening, and his wife Jean must have some motive for her disappearance. When Jean came back about two hours later he asked her where she had been. Jean said, "I was right." "Right about what?" asked Michael. "Cissie told me point blank: she does not want the baby. I had to get out - I told her I was going to the butchers. I was just so excited." "Excited about what?" asked Michael. "Can't you see? This is a perfect opportunity for us." "I can't say I'm with you", said Michael. "Look, if Cissie doesn't want the baby, then why don't you and I adopt it? We can make her an offer. What do you think?" "I don't know Jean ... what will her mother say? I am sure she is looking forward to becoming a granny." "No, her mother doesn't know!" said Jean. "What? Her mother doesn't know?" said Michael. "No. She said that she was going to surprise her mother next summer. Oh Michael ... what if her mother never was to know? Do you think that we could adopt this child without anybody knowing?" "Jean, I think you shouldn't be doing this to yourself - and what about Kathleen?" "I'll think of something to say to Kathleen", said Jean. "Just leave that to me."

"Look Jean, do not let this get any further. When the time comes for Cissie to have her baby then she will most probably change her mind. You can imagine how she will respond when she sees a little child in her arms for the first time. What if she agreed to letting you adopt her child, and then, after the child is born, she turned around and decided to keep it? You would be heartbroken with grief", said Michael. "You are not being very supportive to me", said Jean. "Jean, if you want to pursue this, if you are serious about this, then I will go along with it, but I can't see any good coming out of it. I am only being realistic with you - that's all. I do not want to see you getting hurt all over again, my darling." Jean was so excited about the potential outcome she could barely stand still. "Michael, do you think we should move Cissie in with us in mid December just to keep an eye on her?" "Why, what is wrong with Kathleen's flat?" asked Michael. "Nothing", said Jean, "but I think Kathleen's parents are going back to Ireland again this year like they did last year to the grandparents' home. If they are, then it means Cissie will be left all alone in the flat with nobody to watch out for her. If something happened to her - like if she started to go into labour - it could be disastrous." "What makes you think that Kathleen's parents are actually going to Ireland for Christmas?" asked Michael. "I suppose I am only assuming, really", answered Jean. "I know they went last year and the year before." "This year could be different though", said Michael. "I will ask Kathleen tomorrow about her plans for Christmas", said Jean. "If they are going to Ireland then I will offer Cissie free accommodation with us for a fortnight or so, just to be on the safe side. I can't see how she would refuse, Michael." "What if Kathleen decides to stay behind this year with Cissie?" said Michael. "Now that she has a good friend in Cissie then she might want to stay in London, especially with her friend's baby due at that time." "I know what you are saying", said Jean. "Only time will tell, I suppose."

In at work the next day, with Cissie working in the office and Kathleen working in the kitchen, Jean wanted to ask Kathleen about her plans for Christmas. "Hello, girls" she said, and then asked

Susan, "How are you settling in?" "I am loving it", said Susan, "and Kathleen has been great. She is keeping me informed on what to do. "That's brilliant", said Jean. Jean called Kathleen over to one side. "Can I ask you, Kathleen, what your plans are for Christmas?" "Sure you can. It will be the same as last year", said Kathleen. "So will you be heading across to Ireland with your family?" "Yes", said Kathleen. "We are hoping to go over on the 23rd if all goes to plan. I don't really want to leave Cissie on her own." "Don't worry about that", said Jean. "We were thinking of asking her to stay with us for a couple of weeks - that is, if she will accept." "Jean, that is so considerate of you and Michael! I must tell her the great news. I was worrying about her staying in the flat on her own", said Kathleen. "No, don't mention anything just yet, Kathleen. I want to ask her myself, now that I know you won't be there." "No problem", said Kathleen. "Thank you so much for thinking of her."

Jean went back into the office. "Cissie, I was talking with Kathleen just then. She told me that she and her family are going over to Ireland for the Christmas holidays, and I want to ask you what your plans are? I know you are not going home." "I haven't given it any thought", said Cissie. "I suppose I'll just have to spend it alone - nothing much else I can do really." "Not unless you stay with us", said Jean. "No, I don't want to impose", said Cissie. "You won't be imposing", said Jean. "What about your family? You will need all the space you have for them", said Cissie. "Cissie, my dear, I don't have a family, remember. Well, I have brothers and sisters but they are all abroad, in America and Australia, so it will be just Michael and myself." "Jean, that is very thoughtful of you. Can I sleep on it tonight?" asked Cissie. "Of course, but can you let me know tomorrow?" said Jean. "I will, indeed", said Cissie.

Later that night Cissie and Kathleen got talking. "Do you know what Jean suggested to me today?" said Cissie. "No, but I can guess", said Kathleen. "She asked me what my plans are for Christmas, and she invited me to stay with her and Michael", said Cissie. "So what did you tell her?" "I told her I would sleep on it." "I think you should consider it, Cissie", said Kathleen. "It is a kind gesture, I know", said Cissie, "but I don't know if I could handle all the lecturing about the baby." "Why? What does she say to you about the baby?" asked Kathleen. "No, not so much about the baby. It's the fact she mentions drinking to me, and how it will damage the baby ... stuff like that." "Maybe she is trying to protect it for herself ... she might want to keep it", joked Kathleen. "You are joking but that's what I am beginning to think", said Cissie.

Kathleen said, "Cissie, can I ask you a serious question?" "Yeah, sure!" "Do you really want to have a baby so young? Now, don't get mad. It's just you will not be able to work, and rearing a baby without support won't be easy." "Don't worry, I am not going to get mad", said Cissie. "I have already given it a lot of thought. I never said I would keep the baby, but I always knew I would be having it." "What if Jean and Michael make you an offer?" "What do you mean?" asked Cissie. "Well", said Kathleen, "they are well off financially. The only thing missing in their life is a child of their own. You know, Cissie, they are great people, and if you wanted the child to have a great home, then who better can you think of?" "I think in my heart that they are going to ask me, Kathleen, about this - to tell you the truth. Jean is very protective of me. Right, I am going to bed. I'll give Jean her answer tomorrow about my decision as to where I'll stay for Christmas." Kathleen said, "Cissie, if I were you I wouldn't even think about it. You would be safer, believe me. Now have a good sleep and I'll see you in the morning." "Night, night, Kathleen - and I'll sleep on it."

It didn't take too long the following day before Jean asked Cissie about her decision. "So, Cissie, did you sleep on your decision?" she asked. "Yes, I have, and I would love to stay for Christmas with you and Michael." "That's great news, Cissie. I will let Michael know. He has to prepare the spare room." "I can bring over my blankets if you like", said Cissie. "No, not at all", said Jean. "We have plenty of spare blankets." Later that evening, Jean told Michael the news about Cissie's decision to stay for Christmas. "You will need to fix up the spare room, Michael. I think we will be so happy this Christmas, Michael - imagine … a little child will be present … my heart is beating fast already. Feel my heart, it's beating at a hundred miles per hour." Michael said, "Jean, remember the child will only be around for a short stay. Cissie will want to take it back to the flat after the holidays." "I know", said Jean, "but let's make the best of it. What do you say?" "To be honest, Jean, my heart is beating fast too." "This is going to be the best Christmas ever", said Jean.

The restaurant was getting a bit chaotic now with the early Christmas parties. People from all the surrounding working environments were celebrating the upcoming Christmas - which was now only two weeks away - like maniacs.

Jean thought it was time for Cissie to move into their home. She asked Cissie, "Do you mind moving in with us this weekend? "I thought I was to move in next week", said Cissie. "I think it would be better to move in this weekend. You never know, Cissie, what could happen", said Jean. "What about work? It is so busy now with the parties", said Cissie. "Kathleen and Susan will be fine. Besides, you and I have taken all the bookings. We know the dates for all the parties. And you can't be waitressing in your state so I want you to take your leave. Don't worry, we will still pay you what you would have been earning at work." "If that's your choice, then it's fine by me" said Cissie. "That's that, then", said Jean. "You can finish your shift today, and Michael and I will pick you up tonight from the flat." "Tonight? Oh, I promised Kathleen that she and I would go Christmas shopping tonight. What about tomorrow night?" asked Cissie. "Tomorrow night will be soon enough", said Jean. Cissie said, "It's just that I need to get all my things together." "It's no problem, Cissie. Michael will have the room ready for you, so I will see you tomorrow night." "Why? Won't you be at work tomorrow?" asked Cissie. "Yes, I will, but you are on leave, remember." "That's right", said Cissie, "I forgot. I will see you tomorrow night then."

Kathleen and Cissie went out on a shopping spree. "Do you think the dress suits me?" asked Kathleen. Cissie paused for a moment and said, "Yes, it does." "Whatever is the matter?" asked Kathleen. "Old memories came flowing back to me just then. I remember buying my first dress with Annie back in Clydebank. I wore it the night I met my boyfriend. What happened afterwards I don't think I'll ever forget." "Why? Was that the night of your attack?" asked Kathleen. "Yes! And I thought it was going to be a really special night." "Just goes to show you - you never know what to expect when you leave your home", said Kathleen. "That's for sure", said Cissie. "Anyway, try and forget that for today, Cissie. Let's make this a good day's fun - we probably won't get a chance to shop much more now, with the restaurant being so busy." "Oh ! I forgot to mention", said Cissie, "Jean is giving me leave." "When?" asked Kathleen. "I am actually on leave now at the moment. She told me she would still pay me my normal wages." "That's brilliant, Cissie. No other employer would do that. My friend, Sarah, didn't get a penny from her workplace when she had her baby two years ago. Only thing is - she met a doctor three months later and is now married to him." "Is he the father of her baby?" asked Cissie. "No! That was some loser from Newcastle. She met him at a wedding, and both of them had a one night stand so you can read between the lines what took place. I don't think he ever knew that he became a father, to be honest. Poor Sarah was sickened at the time but she loves the baby, and so does her husband." "Did she have a boy or a girl? Do you know?" asked Cissie. "A girl - little Emma is two now in January. It's nice that she met someone who loves not only her but the baby too. You never know, Cissie. You might meet a doctor or a big, rich businessman one day." "Yeah, but I don't think he would be very much attracted to me looking like this. I look like Mount Everest." Both girls starting laughing at that remark. "Kathleen," said Cissie, "I never told you yet - Jean wants me to move in with her and Michael tomorrow night." "When were you going to tell me?" asked Kathleen. "It slipped my mind. I'm sorry. She wanted me to move in tonight but I told her I had plans with you", said Cissie. "Not to worry", said Kathleen, "let's make the best of tonight. We will be going over to Ireland next week anyway, so I will only be on my own for a few nights." "I am still going to pay you this week's rent", said Cissie. "Never worry about that", said Kathleen. "Of course I will. Fair is fair", said Cissie, "you will need the money for Christmas so you will get my share and I am not taking no for an answer." The girls shopped around for a few hours and bought their Christmas presents. Cissie didn't buy her mother a present though; she decided she would send extra money instead, along with a Christmas card.

Back at the flat Cissie wrote out some Christmas cards. She posted one to her friend Annie up in Clydebank, and included a little note apologising for not saying goodbye to her, and added "no hard feelings." Nellie was to get one also, and there was one for the girls in the kitchen up in Clydebank. Kathleen said, "I see you have your Christmas cards all prepared to go." "Yes! I just need to post them tomorrow." "Is that how you spell your name?" asked Kathleen. "Yes, it is. Why?" "You must be the only one with that name that I ever knew who spells it like that", said Kathleen. "They all - well both of them - spelt it S-i-s-s-y." "My mum likes being awkward", laughed Cissie. "To Mum, love Cissie", joked Kathleen, "which should be Sissy ... ah well, at least it sounds the same." "There you go, then," said Cissie. "No problem." "You know Cissie, I am going to miss you so much tomorrow night when you move out of the flat" said Kathleen. "It will only be for a few weeks", Cissie assured her. "Besides, you will be in Ireland soon, and by the time you get back, I'll be moving back at almost the same time." "Never thought about it like that", said Kathleen. "Right, do you want me to give you a hand with anything before you leave tomorrow night?" "No, it's fine", said Cissie. "I was going to bring my blankets, but Jean said not to bother because she has plenty of blankets." "If you ask me, Jean has plenty of everything. She is loaded."

The following night Jean came over to collect Cissie. Kathleen was feeling lonely watching her leave. Cissie gave Kathleen a big hug and said, "I'll come over at the weekend to visit." "Why don't you call into the restaurant tomorrow during my break for a coffee?" said Kathleen. "That's a good idea. I'll see you tomorrow then." Jean showed Cissie her room. It was a big double room and had a double bed. Cissie was very impressed with it. "Right, Cissie", said Jean, "I'll show you around the house. If you need anything just let me know. I am going over to the restaurant for a while - I'll see you later."

Michael was in the restaurant. Jean came in and got to talking with him. "Do you think it would be a good idea to ask Cissie straight out now about the offer, Michael?" she asked. "No, I don't think that would be a good idea, my dear", said Michael. "I think we should wait until after the birth. I know how girls can change their minds. We only have a few more weeks to wait - better to be sure than sorry. Let's just wait until then, Darling." "Okay, Michael, if you think it's for the best then we will wait." "Jean, don't ask Cissie too many questions about the baby, please," said Michael. "We don't want to go scaring her off now, do we?" "Sure, Honey. I won't mention a word, I promise," said Jean.

Michael and Jean were treating Cissie with kindness at their home, and this made her feel very welcome. "How do you like it here?" asked Jean. "I love it", said Cissie, "but I miss my nights in with Kathleen." "That's understandable", said Jean. With Michael gone, Jean thought she would ask Cissie a few questions about the baby, even though she had promised not to. "So, Cissie, have you thought about any names yet for the baby?" "No, I haven't given it any thought at all", said Cissie. Jean said, "I think if I had a little girl I'd call her Anne and if it was a boy I'd call him Matthew." "Nice names", said Cissie. Jean said, "Come on! You must have some idea." "It's better to wait until it is born", answered Cissie. "You know, you are probably right. Let's go down town, Cissie, and buy some baby clothes. What do you think?" asked Jean. "What sex are you going to buy for?" asked Cissie, "I mean if it's a boy, then you would only be wasting money if you buy girl stuff, and vice versa." "What difference does it make?" said Jean. "A lot of difference. Let's just wait and see, Jean, until it's born, then you can buy stuff if you want to", said Cissie who was now getting upset. "I am just so excited, my dear. I didn't mean to upset you", said Jean. "I wish I could share your excitement", said Cissie. "Do you not feel a little excited?" asked Jean. "No! The quicker it's all over the better", said Cissie. "I just want to see my family again for Christmas, that's all." "We will do our best to make sure you have a great Christmas here with us, Cissie", said Jean. "That's very kind of you, Jean, but I don't know the first thing about children", said Cissie. "My mother wouldn't have a problem, though. She had plenty." Jean asked Cissie, "What age were you when you left your home?" "I came to Clydebank when I was twelve." "What? Twelve! My Lord, that was very young - you must have been frightened, my dear." "Yes, I was, but there wasn't any choice in the matter. My dad died young, and there was no money coming in, so Mum had no choice but to send me away to earn some money as she couldn't work herself. So I did, and have been doing so ever since." "Poor thing! I'm so sorry", said Jean. "What am I going to do now?" asked Cissie. "How am I going to send my mother money now with a child on the way? Prams, cots, clothing and God knows what else." "Well, you can always leave it with me", joked Jean. "Don't tempt me", said Cissie, and continued, "Jean, I think I'll go to bed now. I feel tired." "Sure, Pet, do you want a cup of hot chocolate or anything before you settle in?" "No, I'm fine, Jean", said Cissie, and went to bed even though it was only half past eight.

Jean went to the shops by herself and did a bit of browsing in the baby department. While shopping, Jean couldn't stop thinking about what Cissie had said. The words "don't tempt me" kept echoing inside her head. Jean could only wonder, "Whatever happened to turn Cissie against this child?" She thought maybe Michael was right; she had fled either because she didn't want to get married or tied down at a young age. It just didn't make any sense to her. Nonetheless, Jean was feeling happy at the same time. She was confident she could be a mother to this child. The only thing was: she would have to convince her friends that she had adopted it legally - if, of course, she could talk Cissie into that. When Jean arrived home all smiles, Michael was curious to know why. "Where have you been?" he asked. "I've been shopping" answered Jean, although she was clearly empty handed. "Did you forget your purse?" he asked. "Just a bit of window shopping, my dear", said Jean. "Let me guess! You went to the baby shop, didn't you?" "Guilty!" said Jean.

Jean didn't tell Michael that she'd been questioning Cissie about the baby but Michael already had his suspicions. "Where is Cissie?" he asked. "She went to bed after eight", said Jean. "She was feeling tired." "I'm tired myself", said Michael. "I think I'll go to bed too." "Don't go just yet", said Jean. "I want to talk to you about something." "Can't it do until breakfast? I am very tired", said Michael. "It'll not take long, my dear", said Jean. "Alright then, what is it?" "Right! You probably already know ... but the thing is ... I was talking with Cissie earlier." "I thought so", said Michael, "well, carry on." "Yes, and I'm sorry. Thing is, when I asked Cissie did she want to come baby shopping with me, she was not one bit interested." "So what's wrong with that?" asked Michael. "The girl doesn't know what she is having yet." "No! I didn't mind that so much, but when I joked with her about leaving the child with me ... you know what she remarked?" "I've no idea. What?" "She said, 'don't tempt me'." "Did she really?" asked Michael. "It would appear that it wouldn't take much persuasion, don't you think, Michael?" "Probably not, my dear. Goodness! I wonder what happened to that poor girl", Michael said.

The days passed, and on December 23rd the restaurant was closed up for seven days. It would open again on New Year's Eve. Cissie asked Jean if they could drive around to the flat to see Kathleen so she could say her goodbyes, as Kathleen and her family were heading over to Ireland for the holidays. The tears flowed for a bit as the two girls met. "When I get back you will be a mum", said Kathleen. "Yeah! Imagine", said Cissie. "Unless you hang on until I get back", said Kathleen. "I'll be back in a week." "Yes, make sure you do. You have to work on New Year's Eve, remember", said Jean. "How can I forget?" said Kathleen. "It's the busiest night of the year." Then Kathleen's parents arrived. "Are you ready?" Sally asked. "Ready as I'll ever be", said Kathleen. "Right, let's go", said Patrick. Cissie was feeling sad; knowing that they were going over to Ireland, it almost broke her heart. They departed, and Cissie fell into Jean's arms. "We will look after you, my dear", Jean said. "Don't be sad - the week will fly in. Before you know it, they will be back. Come on, let's get you home. Do you fancy fish and chips on they way home? It might cheer you up." "Go on then", said Cissie. "I am very hungry." "Attagirl. We can bring it home, or we can sit in the cafe." "Let's bring it home" said Cissie. "I don't like people staring at my belly."

On Christmas Eve morning Cissie came down from her room clutching her stomach. "Are you okay?" asked Jean. "I have a little pain", answered Cissie. "Well, you just take it easy today, my dear", said Jean. Michael came into the kitchen. "Did you put the turkey into the oven yet, my dear?" he asked. "Not yet", said Jean. "I'll wait until this evening when I'll have more time. I have to do a bit of last minute shopping first." "Do you want me to come with you?" asked Michael. "No, I want you to stay here with Cissie. She is having bouts of pain - you'd better keep an eye on her ... unless you want to go and do the shopping for me" said Jean. "Whatever you want", said Michael. "You'd be better here rather than me. I'd be no use if anything went wrong. I wouldn't know the signs." "Alright", said Jean, "I'll make you out a list. You will have to take a bus though." "Why?" asked Michael. "We will need the car here, just in case Cissie goes into labour." "Never thought of that", said Michael. So Jean wrote Michael a list for the shopping, and off he went to catch a bus. Later on that evening, Cissie was feeling much better, and Jean asked her, "Do you feel strong enough to go over to the square to hear the choir singers?" "That would be lovely", answered Cissie. "Nice one", said Jean. "I'll just put the turkey into the oven first and we will make our way over." Then she shouted to her husband who was in the bathroom, "Michael, we are going over to hear the choir. Keep an eye on the turkey." "How long will you be away?" asked Michael. "Not long. I don't want Cissie to be out in the cold for long. I'll be back in an hour or so." "That's fine, Dear", he shouted from the bathroom. "You'd better take the car. You never know what could happen with Cissie." "Yes, I will. But if we get a parking space it'll be a miracle." "Stay at the back", said Michael, "in case you need to get away quickly." "It will be alright" said Jean. "There were paramedics present last year, as far as I can remember." "Better to be safe than sorry, though, my dear. It might not be the same this year", said Michael. "We are off now, Dear", said Jean. "Catch you later."

When Jean and Cissie finally found a parking space, they couldn't believe the crowd that was already gathered at the square. They made their way over but they stayed near the back just in case of an emergency. The choir singers were in fine voice. Jean and Cissie joined in on the chorus to all the carols. Jean knew them all. Cissie only knew some but when they started singing *Silent Night* her eyes lit up. "It's my favourite" she said with a cheery smile. The two women were singing full heartily, until Cissie spotted someone in the crowd that caused her to pause - actually almost freeze still - on the spot. Jean looked at her and noticed the expression on her face. "What's the matter, Darling?" she asked. "What is it?" With quick thinking, Cissie said, "Oh it's nothing. I was just thinking on my mother, that's all." "I see, Dear. Try not to be sad - you will see her in the New Year, I am sure" said Jean. The person Cissie had spotted in the crowd was none other than Hugh McNally, the man who had been persuaded by his mother to break it off with Cissie. He had come to university in London, and he was singing in full harmony with the carol singers. Wrapped around his arm was a pretty looking brunette. Cissie tried her best to keep singing, but when Hugh turned around to kiss his girlfriend on the lips, his eyes unintentionally looked in Cissie's direction. He recognised her immediately. When he tried to wade his way through the crowd to get over to talk to her, Cissie's heart beat faster. Cissie saw him drawing nearer and, turning to Jean, said, "Can we please go home? I am not feeling well." "Sure, my dear, if you want." Cissie couldn't walk fast enough, and Hugh was nearing with every step - with his girlfriend close by his side. Before Jean and Cissie could make it to the car Hugh and his girlfriend - who was wondering what the hell was going on - caught up with them. "Hello, stranger!" shouted Hugh. Cissie pretended not to hear him but Jean turned around to see who was shouting. When she looked at Hugh, she saw he was shouting towards Cissie. "Can I help you, young man?" Jean asked him. "Cissie McGinley!" exclaimed Hugh. Cissie reluctantly turned around. "Do you two know each other?" asked Jean. "That's what I'd like to know", said Hugh's girlfriend. Cissie said to Jean, "This is an old friend of mine from Clydebank. His name is Hugh." "Nice to meet you, young man", said Jean, with a curious look on her face. Jean wondered, "Could this be the father of the baby that Cissie is carrying?" "So how do you two know each other?" she asked. Cissie said, "We were friends at work." Hugh went along with it and said, "Yes, I used to work with Cissie in the kitchen in Clydebank," and asked Cissie, "So how are you keeping?" "I am fine", answered Cissie. "Are you not going home for

Christmas?" Hugh answered, "Yes, I am getting the last train up to Scotland." "You are leaving it late, aren't you?" said Cissie. "It'll be the small hours before you get there." "I know", said Hugh. "I am going now in the next ten minutes. Well, it's nice to see you again." Jean overheard the girl whispering to Hugh. "Isn't that the girl who got raped in the spring of this year." Hugh gave her a nudge but it was too late. Jean had heard clearly what she said, and Hugh realised it. He tried to tell his girlfriend, "No! It's another girl. You must be mixed up." "No, I am not", she said. "I recognise her face from the paper you have in your room." Hugh was shocked; he had taken a copy of the newspaper which had the rape story in it with him to London. "Were you snooping in my room?" Hugh asked her. "I was cleaning your room one day, and I just came across it." Cissie could now hear everything that was being said, and in her agitation her waters broke. She was in pain, and when she started moaning loudly, Jean sprang into action. She helped Cissie into the car as quickly as she could. Hugh asked Jean, "Is there anything I can do?" "Yes!" Jean asked Hugh to rush over to the police officer who was on duty nearby and ask him to clear a way for them so they could get away quickly as possible. Hugh ran to the officer and explained to him, "Officer, the girl in that car has to get to hospital straight away. She is pregnant and her waters have broken." The officer got into his patrol car and escorted Jean to the nearest hospital. When Hugh went to follow them his girlfriend pulled him away. She said to Hugh, "You two were more than just friends, weren't you?" Hugh said, "No, we were just friends." "Don't lie to me. I can tell you are lying." Hugh said, "We might have kissed once, but that's about it." "I knew it", said the girl.

Over at the hospital, Cissie was rushed to the maternity ward, with Jean close by her side holding her hand. Hugh was in two minds whether to stay behind or to go home for Christmas. He thought for a while, and decided to go home; after all, his mother had wanted him and Cissie to break it off in the first place. It would take some explaining to his mother that he missed Christmas because of Cissie, so he boarded the next train leaving for Scotland. In the hospital, Jean was looking for a phone so she could ring Michael. When she finally got a chance, she rang home, and Michael answered. "Turn the oven off", said Jean. "Why? What's up?" asked Michael. "Cissie is in the hospital. Don't worry, everything is fine. Her waters broke, but the contractions haven't started yet." "I am on my way", said Michael. Cissie was in a ward on her own. Jean came in and sat down at the bed beside her. The nurse said, "Come to the desk and let me know if the contractions get stronger." Jean responded, "Certainly, Nurse. I'll keep a close eye on her." "Thank you", said the nurse. "I'll be coming in and out every so often to check." Twenty minutes later Michael arrived. "How did you get here so fast?" asked Jean. "I got Damian to give me a lift over here. He was just getting out of his car and I shouted to him." "That was nice of him", said Jean. "So! How is she?" asked Michael. "She is fine now, but I have to keep a close watch. If the contractions start I have to inform them at the desk immediately." "Do you want a cup of coffee or tea?" asked Michael. "That would be great, Michael. I'm dying for a coffee actually." "Right, I'll be back in five minutes. Oh, will I get Cissie anything?" "No she will be fine. We don't want her to get sick." Cissie nodded off to sleep, and when Michael came back with the coffee, Jean asked him, "Was there anyone coming behind you up the corridor." "No. Why?" said Michael. "I'll just double check", said Jean. She whispered to Michael, "Cissie was raped." "What!" said Michael. "How do you know?" "Some lad named Hugh recognised her in the crowd earlier, and he came over to say hello. There was a girl with him who seemed to know Cissie's face from some newspaper article. She was talking about it to Hugh and he tried to hush her up but I heard everything clearly. I think Cissie heard her too. I think that's what upset her and caused her waters to break." "Do you mean to say the rape case was in some newspaper?" said Michael. "Apparently so." "My goodness!" Michael said, "I can see now why she isn't interested in keeping the baby". "That's what I was thinking", said Jean. "So what do you think?" she asked. "Think about what?" asked Michael. "If she doesn't want to keep it, then would you be prepared to adopt a child, even if it was the result of a rape?" asked Jean. "I suppose so. I mean, it will still be a little child, won't it", Michael answered. "My thoughts exactly", said Jean. Michael said, "We will talk about it again. Let's just see what happens first." "Yes, you are right", said Jean.

The hours started to fade away, and Cissie eventually woke with excruciating pain. She started crying out. Jean made a dash to the desk and informed the nurse on duty. The doctor was quick on the scene. Cissie's contractions were coming fast. Michael left the ward. Jean stayed in with her, holding her hand and rubbing her brow. Michael was pacing up and down the corridor, just like a husband awaiting news about his own child. He could hear all the moans. At 1:47am on Christmas morning Cissie gave birth to a little girl. Jean cried with happiness. Cissie was exhausted after giving birth but she was also very relieved. The nurses and the doctor congratulated her. Soon afterwards, they took the baby away to weigh her, check her heart rate, and carry out the standard procedures. After all the tests were done, Nurse Corinne came into the ward and handed the child to Cissie. "There you go", said the nurse, "a healthy little girl." "What weight is she?" asked Jean. Her birth weight is 7lb 4oz", answered the nurse. "Fantastic! A healthy little thing", said Jean as she wiped the tears of happiness from her face. "Have you thought of any names yet?" asked the nurse. "No, not yet", answered Cissie. "I have a few in mind, but I haven't decided yet. "If you do decide before I finish my shift, could you let me know?" asked Nurse Corinne. "Certainly I will", said Cissie. The nurse told Michael who was still outside the ward, "You can go in now, Sir, if you like." "Thank you", said Michael. When Michael came into the ward he saw the joy emanating from his wife's face. Michael came over and gave her a big kiss. He gave Cissie a kiss, too, on her forehead. The nurse came back into the ward. "Cissie! I think it's time you had a little rest now. I'll just take the baby into the baby room, and I'll bring her back to you after you've had your breakfast in the morning." "Just let me hold her one more time before you take her away?" asked Jean. "Why not?" said the nurse, and after a loving embrace from Jean, the newborn girl was brought by the nurse into another room so that Cissie could get some rest. Jean told Cissie, "I'll see you in a few hours, my dear. Michael and I had better make our way home. Happy Christmas, Darling. I will bring over your present in the morning." "I have yours in my room" said Cissie, "I'll give it to you when I get out." "Don't worry about that, Honey, I think you've already given me the best Christmas present possible, watching the birth of a little child", said Jean. "Right, Michael, we'd best make our way home", and Jean and Michael left the hospital.

On the way home, Jean and Michael couldn't stop thinking about Cissie and what had happened to her in Clydebank. "What did that poor girl go through, Michael? Do you think she came here out of pure fear?" asked Jean. "Either that or she might have come for another reason", said Michael. "Like what?" "Well," said Michael, "where do most young girls go if they don't want to keep a child?" "Do you mean to say that she might have come here initially for an abortion?" asked Jean. "You never know. I mean, we both know she isn't interested in the child", said Michael. "Well, if she did then I am glad she changed her mind", said Jean. "Let's forget the reasons for now", said Michael. "It's Christmas." "Yes, you are right, Darling. Happy Christmas."

Michael and Jean arrived home just before three in the morning. Jean said, "You know what, Michael? I think I'll just stay up now and finish cooking the turkey." "Whatever you wish, Honey", said Michael. "I'm off to bed. Will you give me a knock at eight, Honey? I think I'll go over and check on the restaurant after breakfast." "I'll go with you", said Jean, "and we can call and see Cissie then. I want to bring the present we bought for her. Might as well kill two birds with one stone." Jean had the turkey ready just before eight. Michael and Jean called in to see Cissie after breakfast via the restaurant. Cissie was just finishing her breakfast when the nurse brought in the newborn baby girl. "Well, I am finishing my shift now", said Nurse Corinne. "Have you thought of a name yet?" "Not yet", said Cissie, "maybe after dinner time. I can't decide on one just now." "Well, if you are still here on Boxing Day maybe you will have thought of a name by then", said the nurse. "I am off until tomorrow night. Happy Christmas, folks." "Happy Christmas to you, too, Nurse", said all three. "How are you feeling, Cissie?" asked Jean. "I am still a little stiff but I feel much better." "That's good, Honey. Look, I brought you your present." Jean handed Cissie over her present - tickets for the upcoming Olympic Games, to be held in the summer of the following year. Cissie's eyes almost popped out of her head, "Oh, my heavens, this is the best present of my entire life! Thank you so much - I can't believe it." "We didn't know what you liked", said Jean, "but I did overhear you and Kathleen one day talking about the Olympics taking place next year, so I got a nice deal through some of our suppliers. As you can see, they are all double tickets. They are for both you and Kathleen." Cissie gasped, "These are amazing, Jean. I can't wait to show Kathleen." "Well, I am glad you like them, Darling. So is it true that you haven't thought of a name yet for the little princess?" asked Jean. "I have a few in mind but I am not sure if I want to choose them because of the circumstances." "What circumstances?" asked Jean. Cissie answered, "My great grandmother died after giving birth to Granny so I wanted to call the baby after her, but I am not sure if I will because of the father, and I think it would be unlucky." "The father?" said Jean. "What do you mean?" "Let's not pretend", said Cissie. "I know you heard everything that the girl said - the girl who was with Hugh. It's fine, honestly. I wanted to tell you myself but I just didn't know how to." Jean started sobbing, "My poor dear, it wasn't your fault. I am so sorry about what you went through." "It's over now and he was put away for a long time", said Cissie. "Proper order too", said Michael. "Well, forgive me for saying so, but I think this little thing is beautiful", said Jean as she held the baby in her arms. "Just as a matter of interest", she asked, "what was the name of your great grandmother?" "She was called Cassie", said Cissie. "My mother sort of half named me after her but she changed the spelling a little." "I see", said Jean. "I always wondered about your name and how you spell it." "Don't go there", laughed Cissie. "I've heard it hundreds of times." "What does it matter how you spell your name!" said Michael. "So if it's not going to be Cassie then what will you call her now?" asked Jean.

"When I was very small, my daddy bought me a doll for my fourth birthday. It got burned by accident and it broke my heart something terrible. I cried for days. So I said if I ever had children I'd call one of my babies after my great grandmother, and one after my doll. Well I don't want my great grandmother to be honoured in this way now, given the fact that I was raped, so I am naming her after my doll." "What was the name of you doll?" asked Jean. Cissie said, "Molly!"

Michael and Jean looked at each other kind of inquisitively. "That's my first time to ever hear that name", said Jean. "What about you, Michael? Have you ever heard that name before?" "Once before, years ago, but I can't remember where I heard it ... I think it might have been the name of a customer." "Well, I think it's a lovely name", said Jean. "Me, too", said Michael. The baby started crying and Jean asked Cissie if she could feed her. "Be my guest", said Cissie. After Jean had fed the baby, Michael said, "We'd better make our way back home, Darling, just in case we get visitors." "Very well then", said Jean. "We will call and see you later, Cissie, after dinner. I hope the dinner in here will be nice for you." "It'll be fine", answered Cissie. After dinner they called back, and then the following morning and afternoon too. Nurse Corinne came on duty on the night of Boxing Day. She called in to see Cissie. "How are you feeling now?" she asked her. "I am feeling much better now", answered Cissie. "I never would have thought that one year on from last Christmas I'd be in hospital holding a baby." "There you go", said the nurse. "So have you decided on a name?" "Yes, I am calling her Molly." "Molly. What a nice name! I love it", said the nurse. "I must get back to the ward now. I am on duty in casualty tonight - I just popped in to see how you were." "Thank you, Nurse." "Right, Cissie, you will probably get out tomorrow so if I don't see you before you go then all the best." "Thank you for everything, Nurse, and I hope your shift isn't busy." "Can't see that happening, Cissie. Boxing Night is the busiest night of the year in casualty." "Okay, look after yourself, and God bless", said Cissie. "You too! Bye bye."

Later on that night, the doctor called in to inform Cissie that she could go home the next day. "Great news!" said Cissie. "Thank you." Then she asked the doctor, "Were there any other children born on Christmas Day, Doctor?" "Yes, sure! Five in total, but yours was the only girl." Michael and Jean arrived at the hospital for their last visit of the day. "How are my two girls doing now?" asked Jean. "The doctor said I can get out tomorrow." "Very good!" said Jean. "Do you know what time?" "He didn't say", said Cissie. "Michael, why don't you go down to the desk and ask what time Cissie is being discharged tomorrow so we can come and collect her in the car." Michael went down to reception and asked the nurse on duty. "I'll just check for you, Sir", she said. "Ah ... she is being discharged at 10:00am, Sir." "That's fine, Nurse. Thank you." Michael brought the news to Cissie and Jean. "We will prepare the room for you, Cissie, and we will see you in the morning", said Jean, "and now try and get some rest, the both of you." "Molly is already resting", joked Michael - as the baby was fast asleep. "Little darling ... I'll see you tomorrow", Jean whispered to Molly. "Very well then, Michael, we will make our way home. Night, night."

Back at the house, Jean brought a cot out of the spare room. Michael never knew she had it. "Where did you get that?" he asked. "I bought it off an old friend", answered Jean. "Really! What did she say to you when you asked to buy it?" asked Michael. "She was curious, but I said it was for my niece and she is none the wiser. Anyway, she only wants the cash for booze - she won't give a monkey's." "Probably not. It wasn't Elizabeth by any chance?" asked Michael. "Yes! How do you know?" answered Jean. "She is the only one of your friends I can think of that loves the booze." Jean smiled, "Yes, poor Liz, she would sell the cat for booze."

The following morning, Michael and Jean arrived at the hospital to pick up Cissie and the baby. Back at the house, when Cissie saw the cot, she was speechless. It had finally sunk in that she was now a mother. "Do you like it?" asked Jean. Cissie, in a state of confusion, stuttered, "Yes ... yes, I like it. Where did you get it from?" Jean fibbed, "Oh, it was given to me years ago by a family member. She guessed we would need it one day - little did she know that I wouldn't become a mother myself." "Maybe you will yet", said Cissie, and thought to herself, "probably quicker than you think." "Don't see that happening, Cissie, but I hope you are right."

Three days later, Kathleen and her family arrived back from Ireland. Kathleen made her way over to the Smiths to see Cissie. Michael answered the knock on the door. "Look who it is!" he shouted to Cissie, who sprang up from her seat and came to greet her. "Did you have the baby?" asked Kathleen excitedly. "Yes! She was born on Christmas Day." "Amazing! What did you have?" asked Kathleen. "A little girl" said Cissie. "Come on in and see her. Jean is feeding her just now." Kathleen came in. "She is beautiful! Look at all the size of her", she said. "Isn't she beautiful", said Jean. "Yes", Kathleen agreed, "she is so gorgeous." "You'd better get used to her crying during the night", joked Michael, to which Jean responded with a piercing look. Knowing that Jean was annoyed, he swiftly changed his tune and said, "She can stay here with us if you can't stand the crying." Jean smiled, "Now that's not a bad idea. Is it, girls?" "Be careful what you wish for", said Cissie, laughing, but meaning it at the same time. "Listen to you lot", said Kathleen. "All babies cry. She won't cry all the time, you know." "Of course not", said Jean. "We are only teasing you." "So how long will you be staying here, Cissie?" asked Kathleen. "I don't know", answered Cissie as she looked at Jean. "We were hoping you could stay until after New Year's Day", said Jean. "That's only two days away", said Kathleen. "Well, tomorrow night I'll be late getting home from work, so it's for the best as I'd probably only end up waking her up. I'll look forward to this little thing coming over then after New Year's Day." Jean felt sad at that remark; she was already bonding with the little baby. "Are you okay to go for a walk, Kathleen?" asked Cissie. "Sure!" "You don't mind looking after Molly for a bit", Cissie asked Jean. "Are you kidding? Certainly!" said Jean. "It will make my day." "Molly ... nice name", said Kathleen, and then, addressing all three of them said, "I'll give you your presents now." "Talk about presents! Look what Jean and Michael bought us for Christmas", said Cissie, as she produced Olympic tickets from her pocket. "What!" said Kathleen. "Michael and Jean, you didn't ... I can't believe it. Thank you a million times over. Gosh, what a great present! This is awesome - I feel guilty now handing over mine", said Kathleen. "Don't be silly" said Michael. "We can afford it, and we hope you enjoy them." "Enjoy them? Are you off your head?" said Kathleen. "We will for sure. Thank you both from the bottom of my heart."

Kathleen and Jean went for their walk. "I am so excited", said Kathleen, "Imagine, you and I will be going to the Olympics during the summer, YIPPEE!" "Only six months to go", said Cissie, "I can't wait." "How do you feel about being a mother, Cissie?" asked Kathleen, "Do you really want to know?" "Yes!" said Kathleen. Cissie said, "Well, it's like this ... I feel as if I did my bit for the child, and now I just want to give her away." "Don't say that. Give yourself time. Who knows? You might end up loving her", said Kathleen. "No way! When she was born, I could barely look at her", said Cissie. "Remember, I know who the father is, and I don't want a constant reminder as I watch her grow up." "Just give it time" said Kathleen, "that's all I'm saying. Now, come and give me a hand to unpack my stuff back at the flat." "Sure", said Cissie, "I want to go there anyway to collect the Christmas presents that I made for Michael and Jean."

After helping Kathleen to unpack, Cissie said, "I'd better get back over to the house. Jean will be worrying - I've been gone for nearly four hours." Kathleen gave Cissie a huge hug. "I am so happy to see you again, and I look forward to January 2nd so we can get back to normal again", she said. "Back to normal? You are forgetting something - there will be a third party now", said Cissie. "Never mind. It will be fun", said Kathleen. "We will see. Anyway I'd better go. I'll see you soon" said Cissie, and off she went.

Cissie made her way back to the Smiths' house. "How was she?" she asked Jean. "I am sorry for being late. We were just catching up." "That's fine, Dear - not a bother - she is fast asleep now." "Did she cry much?" asked Cissie. "No, not at all. She was like a little mouse. I fed her and she has been sleeping ever since." "Shall I check her to see if she needs her nappy changed?" asked Cissie. "You can, but I changed her a little while ago." Cissie went in to check on Molly who was still asleep and dry as powder. "Here! I have your presents", said Cissie. "You shouldn't have bothered, Darling", said Jean. "For you, Michael", as Cissie handed him a hand-knitted jumper. "This is for you Jean, it's a hand-knitted cardigan." "They are beautiful!" said Jean. "Where did you learn to knit like that? They are very well knitted. I am impressed." "My mum taught me when I was very young." Michael tried on his jumper, "A perfect fit, I must say." Jean put hers on too. "It fits like a glove! Thank you, my dear", she said. Cissie said, "I kinda guessed your sizes. Thank God I got it right." "You sure did, Cissie", said Michael, "great judging."

New Year's Eve! The restaurant was reopened for business. Kathleen and Susan arrived early for the first of their split shifts. Jean and Michael were separated from Molly for the first time in almost a week. Cissie was now all alone with her for the first time. Molly started to cry. Cissie, not wanting to even hold her, still managed to pick her up and feed her. As soon as Jean got a chance, she made her way back to the house to check on her. "How is she?" she asked Molly. "She is a bit restless", said Cissie. "Let me hold her", said Jean. "Come here, my little princess. I missed you so much." Cissie admired how Jean was with Molly; the look of love in her eyes was beyond belief. Jean gave Molly a loving kiss. "I'll see you later, Gorgeous. I must get back to the restaurant - it's hectic. I can't imagine what tonight will be like. If you need any help with anything, just call me at the restaurant", she said to Cissie. "Right, I must dash. I'll see you two later." "Hey, you don't want to swap roles, by any chance?" asked Cissie. "No, my dear, you are not strong enough yet, especially on a night like this. It's seriously busy. We will get through it somehow. Michael doesn't know I'm gone yet so I really must hurry. Take care, you girls. We will see you sometime tonight." It was nearly two in the morning when Michael and Jean came home from the restaurant. Cissie and Molly were fast asleep. "Look Michael, the little princess looks so cute. I don't know what I'm going to do after tomorrow night when they spend their last night here. My heart is starting to break already." "We can call and see her as often as you want", said Michael. "It won't be the same", Jean sighed.

New Year's Day 1948, and it was the last night for Cissie and Molly to stay over at the Smiths. Jean asked Cissie, "Won't you consider staying for another week?" "You have already done enough for us, Jean", said Cissie. "I don't want to put you out anymore." "Don't be silly! One more week won't hurt", said Jean. "If you don't mind, then I suppose I could stay for another week", said Cissie, "but I promised Kathleen I would go out with her tonight. You don't mind looking after her, Jean?" "Now let me think about it for one second. Of course not! I don't think I could spend the first night of the year with anybody more precious than this little darling", said Jean. "If we are going to be really late then I'll probably stay with Kathleen and I'll come over as soon as I can tomorrow. I don't want to be waking the whole house up", said Cissie. "Not a problem, my dear. You'll be time enough after dinner. Tell you what ... why don't you and Kathleen come over here for dinner tomorrow?" "Are you sure?" Cissie asked. "I mean, you are already doing me a huge favour." "The favour is all mine, Darling. I love spending time with this little angel." Kathleen and Cissie headed out to the pub, and they started catching up on everything. "You'll never guess who was there on Christmas Eve at the square when Jean and I went to listen to the carol singers", said Cissie. "Who?" Kathleen asked. "Hugh McNally", said Cissie. "You mean, the Hugh that you told me about?" asked Kathleen. "Yes, and he was with some girl." "Did he see you?" "Yes", Cissie said. "He came over to say hello, and I freaked out. The girl with him knew all about my history. I was embarrassed in front of Jean." "How did she know?" asked Kathleen. "Apparently", said Cissie, "she saw my story in the paper. Hugh had brought a copy with him and must have kept it in his room and she came across it and read it." "Bitch! Did she reveal this in front of you and Jean?" Cissie answered, "She started whispering to Hugh about me, and Jean heard everything. That's what started me on my way to having the baby - I was so upset that my waters broke." "For heaven's sake, ignorant cow!" "Well", said Cissie, "it's out in the open now. Even Michael knows. If you ask me, Jean couldn't care who the father is. She really loves Molly. You should see her with the baby, Kathleen - she absolutely adores her." "What about you, Cissie? Are you starting to bond with her yet?" Kathleen asked. "No! And I don't think I ever will." "Shouldn't you try?" said Kathleen. "I mean, if you are going to be moving her into the flat, you'd better make an effort." "Jean wants me to stay with them one more week", said Cissie. "I told her I would." It sounds like Jean is starting to feel lonely already", said Kathleen. "Anyway, I told her I was staying at the flat tonight", said Cissie. "Did you indeed? Right, in that case let's get hammered", said Kathleen. Cissie said, "We can't drink too much though. Jean asked us over for dinner tomorrow." "What did you say?" asked Kathleen. "I said yes." "Shucks, I wanted to lie in until well after dinnertime tomorrow", said Kathleen. "We were so busy last night I wanted to dive into a hole. Well, I suppose we could have a free dinner ... yeah, why not - it's only dinner time." "Exactly! Plenty of sleeping time", said Cissie.

Back at the Smiths' house, Jean wanted to run something past Michael. "Can I ask you something, Honey?" "Sure. What is it?" enquired Michael. "I was thinking ... wouldn't it be a good idea to let Cissie go back to work?" "Who would take care of Molly?" asked Michael. "That's what I want to discuss with you ... I think I should take care of her. After all, she knows me already, and Cissie could earn some money again." "Are you sure you want to do this?" asked Michael. "Yes! It will be perfect for everybody. Cissie will be able to keep sending money back to her mother, and I will be able to spend time with the little angel." "Did you discuss this with Cissie?" Michael asked. "Not yet, but Kathleen and Cissie are coming here tomorrow for dinner. We can put it to her then." "Very well ... if you want, but you should take things a bit slower - you never know how Cissie might feel about Molly within the next month or so. We can talk about it tomorrow with her", said Michael.

Next day, Kathleen and Cissie arrived for dinner at the Smiths. Jean let a couple of hours pass before she popped the question. "How would you feel about returning to work next week, Cissie?" Cissie answered, "I'd love to but what about the baby?" "If it's okay with you, I would love to look after her", said Jean. "But you need to be at work, too", said Cissie. "January is very quiet", said Jean. "Besides, I can take all the bookings from here. All I have to do is change the number on the advertisement board to our home number." "I don't know what to say, Jean, except - thank you very much!" "So. It's sorted", said Jean. "You can return to work next week." "Where will the baby stay at night?" asked Kathleen. "She can stay here", answered Jean. "You two will need your sleep for work in the morning. You can both call over every day and see Molly whenever you wish." "Sounds good to me", said Cissie. A week and a half later, Cissie and Kathleen were back working together in the restaurant. Susan was kept on as well, as Michael said she was a great worker.

CHAPTER THREE

Summertime London 1948

CISSIE AND KATHLEEN WERE WORKING double shifts on their chosen days at the restaurant so that they could attend some of the events taking place at the Olympics. The city was extra busy. There were people from all over the world present. Both the girls were beside themselves with excitement. Every day at work, all they could talk about were the events. Over at the Smiths' house, Jean was preparing a party for the first six months of Molly's time on earth. The contrast of love for Molly between Cissie and Jean was striking. Cissie just wanted nothing to do with her and Jean loved her to bits.

Kathleen and Cissie couldn't wait until their next big event which was to be rowing, and the coxless pairs. Ran Laurie and Jack Wilson were representing Great Britain. The support they received from the British public was powerful. Among the supporters shouting them on were Cissie and Kathleen. The event got really intense, and it was a close finish but the two British men took gold, and the crowd erupted with joy and pride. The British did well on the water events, with David Bond and Stewart Morris taking gold for sailing. Dickie Burnell and Bert Bushnell triumphed also, taking gold for the sculls doubles in rowing. The games were now entering into the final week, and business everywhere around the city was thriving. *Jean's Restaurant* was no exception with a healthy boost in profits. The build-up to the Olympics had been the same, with the restaurant packed day and night. Jean said to Michael, "We need to talk tonight after you come back from work." "You sound serious, my dear. Can we talk about it now?" "No. Later, when Molly is asleep, and Kathleen and Cissie have gone home for the night. Actually I need to talk to Cissie, too. In fact, we both need to talk to her." "Whatever about?" asked Michael. "Look! Just finish up over at the restaurant, and I'll prepare a candle-light dinner, and we can discuss it then. Don't be nibbling too much at the restaurant - I am preparing roast pheasant with all the trimmings." "You are making me hungry and curious at the same time." Michael kissed Jean on the lips, and said, "I'll see you later then, my dear." "Don't be late" said Jean. "Until later - be safe."

After Michael finished his shift at the restaurant, he came back to the house. There was a lovely aroma coming from the kitchen. Jean came out of the kitchen wearing a sleek black dress, with her hair beautifully styled - she looked like a movie star. "Who? Oh ! You look stunning, my darling. What's the occasion?" "Just making an effort for the man I love, that's all. I hardly set eyes on you these past three weeks." "Sorry about that, Darling. The restaurant's been chaotic for the last few months", said Michael. "I know, Darling", said Jean, "I was going to throw a party for Molly's six-month birthday, but it's a bit late now and might look stupid - it's closer to seven months anyway so I'll give it a miss." "Not really", said Michael. "It's only two weeks past six months." "Sit down, Honey, I'll bring out our dinner", said Jean. "Do you need a hand?" "No. You sit and relax. You've had a hard enough day serving everyone else at the restaurant. It's your turn now to get served." "If you insist, Dear, I won't argue with you", Michael said. Jean brought in the dinner. First there was soup with rolls, then the roast pheasant with fried onions, mushrooms, potatoes, cauliflower and gravy. "This looks delicious", said Michael, as he dug in. "It tastes delicious too, yummy." After they ate their dinner, Jean was ready to ask Michael a question. "Michael, have you noticed how Cissie is around Molly?" "Yes, I have noticed. What are you saying?" "Well, she only came round once to see her these past ten days. I thought she might have called round tonight - but then again I think that every night." "They were really late each and every night, though, with the events and were probably wrecked tired", answered Michael. "It's no excuse, Michael. I think it's inappropriate." "Why are you complaining, though? I thought that you wanted her all to yourself." "I do", said Jean. "Then what's the problem?" asked Michael. "No problem yet, but people are starting to wonder why I always have a child at home. You know yourself that there is gossip going on behind our backs." "From who?" asked Michael. "Joanne, Angela, Tara, to name a few." "Did they say anything to you, or ask any questions?" asked Michael. "Not yet", said Jean, "but it's only a matter of time. Anyway, the important proposal I have for you is this ... what if we sell the restaurant, and head away to start a new life together somewhere else?" "When you say start a new life together does this include Molly, by any chance?" "Of course. I couldn't live without her." "My! That is a proposal", said Michael. "Does Cissie know anything about this?" "Not yet. I was hoping we could both talk to her on Sunday after Mass. My plan is to take her to church, then take her back here for dinner, and then ask her upfront." "Darling, this sounds more like a revelation, not a question", said Michael. "What do you mean?" asked Jean. "Exactly what is it that you are going to ask Cissie? I mean, you are going to reveal to her that we are going to sell the restaurant? And then what? - oh, by the way we are taking the money, and heading away to another place with Molly?" said Michael. "No! It won't be like that ... I am going to tell her about us selling the restaurant, but I am going to ask her can we take Molly with us." "She might say no, and what will we do then?" said Michael. "You see how she is though. Why would she say no?" asked Jean. "The way things are at present", said Michael, "is suiting Cissie just fine. She is able to work, earn money, and has no bother rearing a child but that could all change when she realises that Molly will be leaving." "How do you mean?" asked Jean. "What if she doesn't know yet that she really does love Molly?" said Michael. "We will find out on Sunday", said Jean.

At the restaurant, the crowds were still coming in their dozens in between Olympic events. Michael asked Cissie, "Would you like us to take you to church on Sunday, and then come back to our house for dinner?" "Sure!", said Cissie, "I would love that. It's not like you two to be going to church." "We go most weeks", said Michael. "Some weeks is not how it works", joked Cissie. "You are right", said Michael. "Anyway, I'll let Jean know - she will be glad to see you again." "I should have called round more", said Cissie, "but what with work and the Olympics, I just didn't find the time. Can you explain that to Jean please? I feel guilty now." "No need to. She understands", said Michael. "Gosh, I hope so", said Cissie. On Sunday morning Jean drove round to the flat. Cissie was dressed for church. "Good morning, Cissie", said Jean. "Are you all set for some prayers?" "Yes! I could be doing with them", said Cissie. "Where is Michael?" "He can't make it. Something came up, but he will be joining us for dinner. What about Kathleen? Does she want to come with us?" asked Jean, while hoping she wouldn't. "Kathleen is fast asleep" said Cissie. "You know how she likes to lie in late on a Sunday. We will have dinner eaten by the time she rises." "Okay then, let's go." After Mass, Jean and Cissie joined Michael for dinner. Things were going smoothly, and while they were seated drinking tea, Jean asked Cissie straight up, "Do you love Molly?" Michael was shocked, "What sort of question is that to ask the girl?" Cissie said, "That's okay, Michael. It's a fair enough question, and to be honest, I don't." "You can't mean that", said Michael. "I am afraid I do, and I don't think I ever will." Jean said, "Cissie, we have something to tell you. Michael and I have decided to sell the restaurant." "Why?" asked Cissie, "It's doing really well. What would make you want to sell it? And what about Kathleen and myself? Where would we work?" Jean answered, "You two girls are fine workers. There are lots of restaurant owners who would be glad to hire you. Isn't that right, Michael?" "I'll second that, my dear", said Michael. "I know two owners who would hire you girls in the morning - and Susan too." "Look, I won't beat about the bush", said Jean. "We want to start a new life together - Michael, myself and ... Molly." "You are planning to take Molly?" said Cissie. "Not planning, we are hoping you will give us permission", said Michael. Cissie said, "Right now, I'm ... well, I don't know what I am supposed to say. Can I think this over?" "Of course you can, Pet. It's not like we will sell the restaurant overnight", said Jean. "Could you take me over to the flat now?" asked Cissie. "Sure, Darling. Let me just grab my coat."

When Cissie came into the flat Kathleen was just getting up. "Where have you been, Cissie?" asked Kathleen. "I was at Mass with Jean." "Did you walk there?" "Jean called round for me", said Cissie, "and then took me back to their house for dinner. I didn't want to disturb you - I know how you like your lie-in on a Sunday." "You are right there", said Kathleen. "I could have slept for England today I was so tired." "You might get plenty of time for sleeping very soon", said Cissie, "if Michael and Jean's plan comes to pass." "Why? What are you talking about?" asked Kathleen. "They are planning on selling the restaurant and moving away to some other neck of the woods." "Whatever prompted this?" asked Kathleen. "It has something to do with Molly", said Cissie. "Molly! Why? What's it to do with Molly?" asked Kathleen. "Well, apparently they want to take Molly with them when they go", said Cissie. "Did they discuss this with you first?" "Yes! Today after dinner. I wondered why they asked me if I wanted to go to church with them. I smelt a rat right away." "Maybe you might miss Molly", said Kathleen. "That's the thought that came into my head today when they asked me", said Cissie. Kathleen said, "What if you really love Molly, Cissie? But you don't realise it yet?" "It's possible, but I never really think about her in a loving way", said Cissie. "But you are going to give it some thought though?" asked Kathleen. "Of course I am", said Cissie. "After all, I am her mother although I don't show it much. I mean, Jean is her real mother - I am just her biological mother really. We didn't call round to see Molly once these past two weeks. What kind of parent am I?" "Don't be hard on yourself, Cissie", said Kathleen. "You carried that child for nine months, remember, and you didn't get rid of it. Not many girls in your shoes would have done the same." Cissie said, "My culture would never get rid of a child. The travellers are very religious and superstitious." "You are from the travelling community, Cissie?" asked Kathleen. "Yeah! What's the matter with that?" "Nothing, Honey. You never mentioned it before, that's all", said Kathleen. "The reason I didn't mention it is because I don't know how people down here in London would treat me", Cissie said. "Not many people down here are like that, Cissie." Cissie answered, "Wish I could say the same about my own country, Kathleen. They look upon you as an alien - that's why it's best to say nothing about it. As far as anybody knows, I am Irish and that's it."

Sixteenth day of the Olympics, and it was the day of the closing ceremony. The girls had their last tickets to use. They went along to Wembley Stadium on August 14th 1948. The stadium was full of people from many nations. The atmosphere was electric. Cissie and Kathleen made their way up to the front, hoping they would be caught on camera by some random photographer working for a newspaper. By luck they had their wish fulfilled, as a man from the press snapped a photo of the athletes right smack in front of them. "Did you see that?" said Kathleen. "Yes! I did. Oh Kathleen, do you think that he got us?" "He was bound to. We are right in front of him." "Thing is, though, what paper is he working for?" asked Cissie. "I haven't a clue", said Kathleen. "Tell you what, we can search them all, starting tomorrow", suggested Cissie. "Imagine appearing in the papers, Kathleen! Wouldn't it be great?" "Wouldn't it just! We could brag about it in years to come. A little bit of history ... I can see us talking about our time at the Olympics, wearing bedroom slippers and sipping tea, at a old people's function", joked Kathleen. "Not too sure I want to grow old now", said Cissie.

Kathleen and Cissie made their way over to a pub for a few drinks after the closing ceremony. "Where did those sixteen days go, Kathleen? They just flew in." "True what they say, Cissie. Time flies when you are enjoying yourself." The pub was jammed and the atmosphere was buzzing. Kathleen made her way up to the bar to get another round of drinks in. While she was waiting to get served a young man in his mid twenties was already standing at the bar. Kathleen glanced at him and thought she'd seen his face before somewhere. Then she looked at him again, and the second time she looked at him, she recognised him. Kathleen spoke to him, "Don't I know you from somewhere?" she asked. "Maybe you do", said the young man, "but I can't say I know you." Just then it came to her, "Aren't you the man who was taking the photographs at Wembley?" "Yes, I certainly was. How do you know?" asked the man. "We were there, my friend and I." "You were?" "Yes, and we were standing right in front of you while you were snapping the athletes", said Kathleen. "Do you think by any chance that we might come out in the photos?" asked Kathleen. "There is a good chance you will" answered the young man. "My camera has a wide scope. It can capture a lot." "Who do you work for?" asked Kathleen. "I am not being nosey but if we know what paper you work for then we can buy it tomorrow." "I work for the *Observer*", said the young man. "The photos won't be published until next weekend, though, as it would be too late tonight to get them in on time because printing has already begun." "That's great! Thank you very much", said Kathleen. "What's your name?" asked the young man. "My name is Kathleen." "The only reason I am asking you is if you do come out in the photos then I might write a little article." "You'll what? Are you serious?" asked a very excited Kathleen. "Sure I am", he said. "Come on over and meet Cissie, my friend - you might want to observe her face too." The young man giggled, "Observe!" "What are you laughing at?" asked Kathleen. "Nothing much. It's just you said 'come over and observe'." "And?"

"You know I work for the *Observer*? Aw, never mind, I'm just being silly", said the young man. "Oh! I get you now. That is sort of funny", chuckled Kathleen. The man made his way over to the table with Kathleen to where Cissie was seated. "Do you know who this is?" Kathleen asked Cissie. "No ... can't say I do." This is none other than the photographer who took photos today of the athletes at Wembley." "You are joking me", said Cissie. "No I am not. He works for the *Observer*. "And his name is...?" enquired Cissie. "Silly me. I didn't ask you your name", said Kathleen to the young man. "My name is Duncan." "So, Duncan, will we be in the photographs?" asked Cissie. "You never know. I am presuming so. You will find out next Sunday - printing has ended for tonight." "Why is that?" asked Kathleen. "Well, it's Saturday and most of tomorrow's sport news will be about medal counts and winners, etc." "Who won the most medals?" asked Cissie. "The USA won the most", said Duncan. After spending a few hours with the girls, Duncan left to go home. "Nice meeting you", said the girls. "The pleasure was all mine. I might see you around some other night." "We are here most Saturday nights", said Kathleen.

After waiting impatiently all week, the girls got up early on Sunday morning to go and buy the *Observer*. They flicked through the pages until they got to the sport columns. Low and behold! There they were. Both girls were gobsmacked. "Look! It's us", said Kathleen, "I can't believe it." "Me either. Let's buy a copy each", said Cissie. "We should buy two copies each", said Kathleen, "just in case we lose one, or one gets destroyed." "Let's do that then", said Cissie, and they bought two copies each.

Later that day the girls brought the newspaper into the restaurant. "Can you spot anybody in here, on the sport pages?" Kathleen asked Michael. "Let me have a look ... well, what do you know ... it's none other than my trusty workers themselves. How did you two worm your way into this?" Cissie and Kathleen with big smiles on their faces said, "Read what it says below the photo." Michael started to read, "A large crowd attended Wembley Stadium for the closing ceremony of the Olympics. Among the crowd were Cissie McGinley and Kathleen Murphy ... Oh, my God, you two are legends!" "We can't help it", joked Cissie. "We are just famous - what can we say?" "I agree", laughed Kathleen. "You must get one of the photos framed", suggested Michael. "That's not a bad idea", said the girls. "There is a place that does great framing work not far from here", said Michael. "You must give us the address", said Kathleen. "I don't know the name of the shop offhand but I'll drive you over there on our way home. I do know the street that it's on. We had our official opening night photo framed in there", said Michael. "Good! Let's do that", said Kathleen. "Tell you what ... I'll get one enlarged, and I'll frame it and hang it up on the wall in the restaurant", said Michael. "Wouldn't that be just great", said Cissie. Kathleen murmured, "Hmm ... whoever the new buyer is going to be ... might not want to keep us hanging around - so to speak - if you know what I'm saying." "You know about the restaurant going up for sale then?" said Michael. "Yes. Cissie informed me." "Sorry! I was meant to tell you", said Michael. "So when are you going to sell up?" asked Kathleen. "We are getting the auctioneer to put up a sign next week." "That soon?" said Kathleen. "That's a bit of short notice, don't you reckon?" "I suppose you are right but we've been planning it for some time now."

After he had had finished his paperwork, Michael drove the girls around to the framing shop. In the shop Michael asked the assistant to frame three photos, "I want one of them enlarged to twelve by eight inches." "Certainly", said the man, "but I won't have them ready until tomorrow, if that's any use." "Tomorrow will be fine", said Michael. On the way back to the restaurant, Michael said to the girls, "Would you like to call over to our place later for evening tea?" "Why not?" said Kathleen. "Save us cooking at home for a change." "Fine", said Michael, "I'll let Jean know."

The girls arrived at the Smiths for their evening tea. When they had finished the tea, Michael produced the *Observer* and told Jean, "Take a look at page 14 of the sports pages." "Why? Is there something in here I should see." "Not something, more like someone, or better still - some two." "Let me see." Jean looked at the picture, "Heavens! It's you two. How did you wind up in here?" "What can we say? You are either popular or unpopular", laughed Kathleen. "Very good", said a giggling Jean. "We should get one of these enlarged, Michael, and hang it up." "One step ahead of you, Darling. We are already on to it", said Michael." "Nice thinking", said Jean. "Did you visit the same shop where we got our last photo enlarged?" "We sure did. They will have them ready by tomorrow evening", said Michael. "Brilliant! We can put one up in the dining area", said Jean. "If you get a buyer for the restaurant, though, then Cissie and I want the photo", said Kathleen. "Fair enough", said Jean. They could hear crying from the sitting room; Molly was hungry. Jean brought her into the dining room. "What's wrong with my little honey? Are you hungry?" Cissie was feeling a little uneasy; the situation made her feel awkward. "Look who's here to visit you", said Jean. Kathleen asked, "Can I feed her?" "Why, sure you can", said Jean, and then asked Cissie, "Can you give me a hand with the washing up, Cissie?" Michael said, "Let me help you. Cissie can relax - she is our guest." Jean gave him a negative nod and said, "No, you only get in my way" and pretended to laugh. "Whatever you wish", said Michael. While washing up, Jean asked Cissie, "So? Have you thought about what I said?" "Yes I have, and I see how great you are with Molly, and I know you love her, but I think a lot of people know that you can't have children. You can't take her out in public without onlookers noticing. What will you tell them?" "Tara and Angela already know I am taking care of her. I told them I am thinking of fostering her. They don't know who the mother is yet", said Jean. "What will they say if they find out I am her mother?" asked Cissie. Jean answered, "They won't find out. That's why we want to sell up and get out of here as fast as we can before they do." "In that case, I will give her to you," said Cissie, "but at a price." "At a price?" asked Jean. "What sort of price?" "I'll talk to you at the weekend about it", said Cissie. "What's wrong with now?" "No, not now. I want to visit the church first and pray for guidance.

"Letting your conscience take over might not change the fact that you don't love Molly", said Jean. "Most probably not, but it will make me feel better about myself, though." Just then Kathleen walked into the kitchen, "I think we should get back now, Cissie. I have some ironing to do." "I'll be there in a minute - just drying off these dishes." "Okey-doke", Kathleen said, "Michael said he will drop us home. I'll be in the sitting room." "Before you go, Cissie", said Jean, "I want to give you tomorrow off work. I'll tell Michael now. Susan can work your shift. I'm sure she will be glad of the extra shift, and she needs the money." "Why, though?" "I want you to go and do whatever you have to do at the church tomorrow, and we can have dinner here at the house. I will come and collect you over at the church - then we can discuss this once and for all." "If you like, I'll give you my decision tomorrow one way or another", said Cissie. "Right, I must go now. Kathleen is waiting." Michael dropped the girls home. Back at the flat, when Kathleen had finished the ironing she sat down beside Cissie on the sofa. "What were you two talking about in the kitchen?" she asked Cissie. "Wouldn't you know! She was on to me again about Molly. She is even giving me tomorrow off work so we can discuss her again." "She doesn't give up, does she?" said Kathleen. "And why is she giving you tomorrow off work?" "I told her I want to visit the church. I thought she would wait until Sunday but I was wrong. I told her that Molly would come at a price, too." "What sort of price?" asked Kathleen. "You know I carried that child for nine months. I feel I should get compensated, don't you?" "Yeah! Too darn right. What have you in mind?" Kathleen asked. "Dunno yet", said Cissie, "but if they manage to sell the restaurant then they will have plenty of money, and they can afford to give me some. I want to put a deposit on a flat." "Don't you like where you live now?" asked Kathleen. "Yes, but what if we have to find work somewhere else when they sell the restaurant? I am fed up taking the bus everywhere", said Cissie. "Why don't you take driving lessons and you can buy a car?" "Not such a bad idea", said Cissie.

The next day, while Kathleen got ready for work, Cissie made her way over to the church. She prayed, "Please forgive me for what I am about to do ... I do love children but I can't love this little girl. You know, Lord, what I went through, and I feel I've kept up my part of the bargain by giving birth to her, so if you find it in your heart to forgive me then I will be forever grateful. Amen." When Cissie came outside the church Jean was sitting in her car waiting to pick her up. Cissie didn't notice the car at first but when Jean beeped the horn she turned around and saw Jean waving to her. Cissie got into the car and Jean drove back to her house. "So, Jean, what do you want to discuss?" Cissie asked. "I thought you said you would let me know today, one way or another, about your decision on Molly", said Jean. Cissie said, "When I was in the church I prayed for forgiveness, not so much about giving her away but..." Just then Jean interrupted, "What? You're giving her up? Oh Cissie, this is unbelievable!" Cissie continued, "As I was about to say ... but I am going to sell her to you." "Sell her to me?" "Yes! I think I deserve it", said Cissie. "Hold on a minute. I am rearing that little girl since Christmas - that's nearly seven months now", said Jean. Cissie said, "Tell you what, Jean, why don't I put her up for adoption? There are a lot of people out there that would jump at the chance to adopt a child." "Slow down, don't be like that", said Jean. "How much do you have in mind?" "Jean, I want my own house and a car, so I calculated it out, and my price is £9,000." "We don't have that kind of money. I mean we do, but not in ready cash." "Well", said Cissie, "that's my offer, Jean. Take it or leave it. I won't stay for dinner ... you have until Sunday to give me your answer. This time you make a decision for a change. See you on Sunday."

Cissie then left the house and went back to the flat. The postman had dropped in a few letters. Among them was one from her mother. "What the...?" She opened it up while panicking at the same time. She kept thinking to herself, "Why is Mum sending me a letter? Please let there be nothing wrong." The letter read, "Dear Cissie, you are probably wondering why I am writing to you?" "Too right I am!" thought Cissie. "Don't be alarmed, I just want to let you know that your brother Matthew is getting married in October, and he wants you to come over to the wedding. If you can make it then he will be delighted. Love, Mum." Cissie was thinking, "Matthew is getting married? He can't be! He is only seventeen - is he off his head?" At the bottom of the letter, it read ... "P.S. missing you." "Flipping heck", she thought, "I can't believe this!" Later that day, when Kathleen came in from work, Cissie had her evening tea ready for her. "Hello! How was work?"

she asked. "The usual", said Kathleen. "What's this? You have our tea ready - good on you, girl. I could eat a horse. How did your meeting with Jean go?" "Let's just say she got a shock. I told her I want £9,000." "Wow!" said Kathleen. "What did she say to that?" "She said that they don't have that amount of cash about them to which I said, 'That's my offer, take it or leave it. I can put her up for adoption'." "You said that? No bother to you, Cissie. Well done." Cissie then asked Kathleen, "How would you like to go to a wedding in October?" "Who is getting married?" asked Kathleen. "My brother Matthew. This letter came today from my mother. It nearly gave me heart failure." "Why?" "In all my years away from home not once did I receive a letter from Mum. I thought the worst straight away." "You must have got a shock alright", said Kathleen. "Anyway, what do you say?" asked Cissie. "Yes, of course", said Kathleen. "I would love to. It will be really nice to see your home place and your family." "Brilliant! So we can book our holidays for October then", said Cissie. "Might not have to", said Kathleen. "The place could be sold before then." "That's true. Nevertheless, we will still book them with Michael tomorrow at work." Next day at work, when the girls got a chance to speak with Michael, they booked their holidays for October. "Are you going somewhere nice?" Michael asked. "My brother is getting married and he wants me over for the wedding. I've asked Kathleen to come with me", said Cissie. "Very nice. Is he older than you?" asked Michael. "No, he is younger." "He is younger? Gosh, you are only nineteen. He is getting married young." "I know. He is only seventeen but Mum got married when she was only eighteen." "What does it matter? As long as they love each other that's the main thing", said Michael. "Too true", said Kathleen. With the holiday now booked for the wedding, the girls decided to go shopping for a dress each on the upcoming Saturday, and when they got an hour off work on Saturday, they did just that. Kathleen bought a polka-dot dress and Cissie bought a green floral one. With their dresses purchased, Cissie suggested that she should now buy a wedding present for her brother Matthew. "What will you buy him?" asked Kathleen. "Do you know something, Kathleen? I have not got a clue. It's been that long since I have seen him I don't even know what he would like, but then again it's for both of them so I am thinking of buying them blankets with 'Olympic Games 1948' printed on them - they are half price now in that shop where you and I saw them last month." "Good idea. Whenever they go to bed they can think of our time at the Olympics", said Kathleen. "They sure can, and if they don't believe that we were there then we can bring proof with us." "Oh yes, the newspaper. Good thinking", laughed Kathleen. The girls made their way over to the department store to buy the blanket at half price. Inside the store, they couldn't see any of the blankets they were looking for. Just then one of the shop assistants came over. "Are you okay here, girls?" he asked. "We were in here last month and we saw blankets with the Olympic Games on them", said Cissie. "They are all sold", said the assistant. Then another worker came over because he had overheard the girls explaining what they were looking for. He said, "Excuse me, but I heard what you said. I believe you are looking for the blankets that have the Olympic Games printed on them." "That's right", said the first assistant, "but they are all sold." "Not really", said the second assistant. "A woman left a deposit on two blankets yesterday but she came back into the store today looking for her deposit back because she had changed her mind and no longer wants to buy them because when she went back home last night her husband already had a set in the house. He had bought them for her as a present and wanted to surprise her. She told me today that she was planning on doing the same for him but she just didn't have enough money on her yesterday to buy them there and then so that's why she put a deposit on them and was going to call back today and buy them outright." "Now there is a stroke of luck, girls", said the first assistant. "Tell us the truth", said Kathleen jokingly, "you were just hiding them all along, weren't you?" "That's what it looks like, I know", said the first man. Then the second assistant went over and collected them from behind the counter, and said, "You are lucky. I was meant to put them back out on display again but it slipped my mind." "Looks like we were meant to get them", said Kathleen. Cissie bought one of the blankets. Kathleen said, "You know what? I think I'll buy the other one. It will remind me in years to come of our time at the Olympics." "Kathleen, do you know what I'll do?" said Cissie. "I think I'll buy them something else for the wedding and keep the blanket for myself. I think your idea is good. I want memories of the Olympics in years to come, too. We'd better hurry now - we are due back at work in less than ten minutes." The man listening to the girls suggested, "Why don't you buy this type of blanket? It has London Bridge printed on it, and it, too, is half price for this week only." "Let me take a look", said Cissie. "I like it. Okay, I'll buy it but more than likely my brother would prefer a sheep on it, or a cow." "Ha ha, sheep or cow", laughed Kathleen. The girls each bought blankets and left to return to work. In the restaurant there were two visitors. Jean was there and she had taken Molly along with her in her pram. "Michael was just telling me that you two are going on holiday to Ireland", said Jean. "Yes, my brother is getting married", said Cissie. "That's great news", said Jean. "Is he the first one to get married." "Yes, he is the first one to be getting hung." "Hung? I never heard that expression before", said Jean. "Have you, Michael?" "No! Can't say I have." "Well I have", said Kathleen. "It's an old Irish expression." "Anyway", said Jean, "the reason I am here, Cissie, is ... do you want me to collect you tomorrow to go to church with me?" "Yes! That would be great." "What about me?" asked Kathleen. "You didn't ask me did I want to come along", but before Jean could answer, Kathleen said, "I am only pulling your leg. Tomorrow is my lie-in day." "If you want to come along, Kathleen, then you are more than welcome but I sort of knew myself that you wouldn't", said Jean, and continued, "Right then girls, I must get this little one back to the house. It is nearly time for her feed. I'll see you in the morning, Cissie. Come on, my little princess, let's go. Oh Michael! I nearly forgot..." Jean called Michael over to one side and told him, "There was a phone call for you today. There is a couple interested in the restaurant." "Funny! We haven't even put up a 'For Sale' sign yet", said Michael. "We were doing a lot of talking, though, about selling it. Someone, somewhere, somehow, must have got word through the grapevine", said Jean. "Did they leave a name and number?" asked Michael. "Yes, said Jean, "but I wanted to consult with you first. They said you were to ring them when you get home later as they were going away for the day and they wouldn't be home until eleven tonight." "I'll ring them later then", said Michael. Kathleen said, "Before you go, Jean, take a look at our dresses." "Let me see them quickly then", said Jean. The girls showed Jean the dresses. "They are beautiful, girls. I like your taste. All the men will be admiring you over in Ireland." "We can't help it - we are beautiful", laughed Kathleen. "Ha ha, very good", said Jean. "Honestly, girls, I must dash. Have a nice day. Bye." "See you tomorrow", said Cissie, "and don't be late."

That night when Michael came home from work Jean said, "You can ring that couple after you've had your tea." When Michael had finished his tea he rang the number and a man answered,

"Hello." "Hello! This is Michael Smith. I believe you talked with my wife earlier in connection with our restaurant?" "Yes, Hello, Sir. My name is David Taylor. My wife and I were hoping you could show us round your restaurant one day. We are hoping to make an investment." "We are closed on Sundays until the afternoon", said Michael. "Do you want to take a look around tomorrow? You will get peace to view it." "Yes, tomorrow will be fine", said David. "Great! Shall we say 10:00am?" said Michael. "Ten will be perfect. I'll see you in the morning. Goodnight." Jean asked Michael, "Well? What did you say to them?" "His name is David, and he and his wife want to view the place, so I told them to come and take a look around tomorrow as we are not opening until lunchtime." "What time are you meeting them there?" asked Jean. "Ten o'clock. That gives us plenty of time", said Michael. "You will need to leave a bit earlier", said Jean. "I promised Cissie that I would drive her to Mass - you can drop us off at the church first." "Fair enough", said Michael, "but you might have to take the bus back as I could be late getting away." "Not a problem", said Jean. "Cissie and I will take the bus home. Maybe they will make you an offer tomorrow, Michael. Have you a price in mind?" "We agreed that we would sell for £15,000, didn't we?" said Michael, "but we might need to have a nearest offer price too." "Like what?" asked Jean. "I am not going to settle for any less than fourteen grand. What do you think?" "Yes", said Jean, "don't settle for any less, Michael. We will need it, especially now that Cissie wants £9,000 from us for Molly." "We discussed this last night, remember?" Michael said. "I thought we agreed to offer her £5,000 and not a penny more." "I'll just have to see tomorrow if I can bring her down a bit", said Jean. "A bit? You need to bring her down by almost half. We can't afford that - well, we can but there is a principle involved", said Michael. "Never mind all that now. Let's open a bottle of wine. It's Saturday night, after all, and Molly is fast asleep", said Jean.

Over at the flat Kathleen was preparing to go out. "Where are you going at this hour of the night?" asked Cissie. "I am meeting Rob. His parents have gone to Cornwall for the weekend." "Naughty girl", laughed Cissie. "What price will you accept for Molly tomorrow if they don't want to give you the nine grand?" asked Kathleen. "Maybe I'll come down to eight but no less", Cissie said. "Stick to your guns, Cissie. If they want her then they should be prepared to pay you. They have plenty after all." "She will be here in the morning to collect me for Mass. When we come out, no doubt she will invite me round for dinner, but I was planning to go to that little cafe on the square to have dinner on my own tomorrow for a change. We can negotiate a price in the car on the way back." "I couldn't stomach sitting in their house one more Sunday, pretending to be polite ... thank you for this, thank you for that", joked Kathleen." "That's what I mean. I just want my own space for a change", said Cissie. "I don't mean you, Kathleen, don't get me wrong." "Of course, I know what you mean. Besides, I'll be eating out tomorrow myself and Rob will be buying", Kathleen laughed. "Proper order. Let him see who wears the trousers. Right, enjoy your night of passion. I'm off to bed", said Cissie. "I'll see you tomorrow evening, Cissie, and remember to stick to your guns! Don't take no for an answer." "Don't worry, I won't."

On Sunday morning, Jean and Michael called round for Cissie. "Before we set off for church", said Cissie, "I won't be coming round for dinner. I just want to let you know that early - I have plans." "Very well", said Jean, "with anyone I know?" "No! Nothing like that, just a little me-time, that's all." "Time on your own now and again - there is nothing like it", said Jean. "You took that well", said Cissie. "Not a problem, Honey. I like time on my own too." "Ahem! I am beside you, Jean", joked Michael. "Not you, Darling. I love time with you." "Are you going to church, too, Michael?" asked Cissie. "No! Me and this little one are going over to the restaurant for an hour or so ... a time for bonding." "Did you bring Molly's pram?" asked Jean. "Yes, it is in the boot."

After Mass Jean said to Cissie, "We will have to get the bus back as Michael has the car." No sooner had she said that than Michael turned up at the church. "You got away early", said Jean. "Yes! It went better than I expected", he said. "I'll tell you about it later. We'd best get back to the house. I am starving." "Cissie won't be joining us", said Jean. "She is eating out today." "Oh, that's right. So will we have a quick talk before you go then, Cissie?" suggested Michael. "Can't see why not", said Cissie. "Listen, I'll make it quick and I'll get to the point. I asked Jean for nine thousand, and that's my price." "That's a bit steep, Cissie", said Michael. "We were thinking more on the line of £5,000. That's all we can afford. If you want more than that then we will have to adopt somewhere else." "I see", said Cissie. "Tell you what, I'll settle for eight but not a penny less." Jean, seeing how serious Cissie looked, intervened and said, "Let's be reasonable here, Cissie. You know how Michael and I love Molly. We will offer you £7,000 but we can't go any higher, honestly we can't." Cissie was now feeling guilty and saw how sad and desperate Jean looked. "Very well then, seven it is", and they shook hands on the deal. Cissie left to walk away. Michael shouted to her, "Don't you want a lift?" "No. I want to walk. It's only a five minute walk to the cafe from here." "That's fine. I'll see you at work in the morning", said Michael. "How was my little darling?" said Jean, as she took Molly in her arms, "I missed you so much. Mwah! Come on, let's get this princess home. Then you can tell me all about your meeting with the Taylors." Back at the house, Jean changed Molly's nappy, made some coffee, and then asked Michael, "How did it go then with the Taylors?" "You know how we both agreed that we would settle on a deal for £14,000 for the restaurant?" said Michael. "Yes." "Well", said Michael, "I have news." "Good news I hope?" said Jean. Michael said, "Margaret, his wife, loves the place and so does David - so much so that I read it in their body language and faces." "Did they make you an offer?" Jean asked. "They did", said Michael, "and you won't believe this - David had assumed that the restaurant would be worth around about £14,000." "He never!" "Yes!" Michael said, "So, using my head, I said 'you are close'. He said 'Why?' I told him, 'My asking price is £14,750'. Margaret looked at David in a way that to me suggested she was prepared right there and then to make the deal. David, however, now a bit annoyed with his wife for revealing too much information by the look on her face, said 'Tell you what, Michael, our budget was £14,000. We could meet you at £14,250 but that's as far as we could go'." "What did you say to that?" "I said, 'Folks, here is what I am prepared to do. I'll come down to £14,500 - anything less and I'm underselling'." David then took Margaret to the other side of the room, which left me feeling like I'd blown it. Then they came back after they had talked for three or four minutes, and David said to me, 'Michael, my wife and I have both agreed on an offer. The most we can pay you is £14,300 but that's as far as we are going'." "What did you say to that?" "My hand went out to David first, and then his wife, and we shook on the deal." "Fantastic!" said Jean. "You know what? That's our second deal in one day. I'm impressed with you, Honey. We wanted fourteen grand and you got us an extra three hundred. You'd make a good salesman. I'm so happy." "Let's go out and celebrate tonight", said Michael. "I would love to, Michael", Jean said, "but you are forgetting someone. There is nobody to look after Molly." "We can ask Cissie over here to babysit her. After all, she hasn't looked after her once in almost eight months", said Michael. "Do you think she will, Michael?" "Why not? It won't kill her for one night. Kathleen can come over here too - surely one of them will help."

Over in the cafe, Cissie was feeling good about things too. She was forgiving herself for selling Molly, even though she hadn't actually received any money yet. She was thinking to herself: God will forgive me. It can be my reward for carrying a rapist's child. "Yes! I am right", she said in a loud voice, then looked around quickly to see if anyone had heard her, but no one had. After eating her food, instead of catching a bus, Cissie made the half hour walk back to the flat where she saw Jean's car parked outside. "What does she want now?" she thought to herself. As Cissie approached, Jean saw her in the mirror of her car and stepped out, "Hi Cissie, you're probably wondering why I am here." "Yes! What is it? Is everything alright? "Yes, everything is fine. Michael and I were just wondering - well, hoping - that you might be able to look after Molly for us tonight?" "Can't see why not. Are you both heading out somewhere?" "Yes, we are going celebrating." "What are you celebrating? I hope I haven't undercharged you", joked Cissie. Jean didn't see the funny side of that, and Cissie quickly realised it so she quickly said, "No, I'm only joking. I am happy enough. Yes, I will look after her, Jean. It won't be a problem. What time do you want me over there?" "Well, I was hoping you could come over at seven." "That's dead on. I'll see you all at seven." "Thank you Cissie", said Jean. "I'll see you later. Oh! Before I go - do you want me to come and collect you?" "That would be very kind, Jean. I am after walking back from the cafe, and I don't know if I could walk another inch." "You walked the whole way back? Are you mad? That must be two miles easily." "It is a beautiful day so I thought - what the heck." "Rather you than me", said Jean. "Okay, I'll come over and collect you at 6:45pm."

At 5:00pm Kathleen arrived back at the flat. "Look at you", said Cissie, "away all night gallivanting." "Ha ha", laughed Kathleen. "How did you get on with Michael and Jean? Did you get your asking price of £9,000 for Molly?" "I'm afraid not", Cissie said. "Why? What happened?" "It is a bit much, to be fair", said Cissie, "so I settled on £7,000." "Not bad, though", said Kathleen, "nearly fifteen years wages when you think about it." "True", said Cissie. "Hey! While we are on the subject of Molly, I have to babysit tonight over at the Smiths." "Why? Where are they going?" asked Kathleen. "They are going out to celebrate." "Probably to celebrate saving £2,000", said Kathleen. "More than likely. I did crack a joke about that but Jean looked through me and I changed my tune." "Why don't I come with you?" said Kathleen. "That would be great", said Cissie, "but we haven't got much time as she is calling over here at 6:45pm so if you are going to make dinner or tea then you'd better hurry up." "No, I am not hungry. I had a big dinner earlier. Seriously, though, what are Michael and Jean going to celebrate?" asked Kathleen. "I'm assuming it's because they are to become parents officially", said Cissie. "Not too official, if you ask me", said Kathleen. At 6:45pm Jean arrived to pick up Cissie for babysitting. "Are you ready, Cissie?" "Yes, Jean, I'll be there in a second. Kathleen is coming with me." "Great! Molly will be spoiled tonight ... well, if she isn't asleep. She was nodding off when I left the house", said Jean.

When the Smiths arrived home after their night out they were pretty tipsy. Jean told the girls, "Michael and I are finally getting out of the food business." Kathleen said, "What do you mean?" Michael said, "Don't listen to her." Jean said, "Ah Michael, they are going to find out sooner or later anyway." "Find out what? I take it you have the restaurant sold", said Cissie. "Correct", said Jean. "When were you going to tell us?" asked Kathleen. "We just did", said Jean. "Only because you are drunk", said Kathleen. "Look, girls", said Michael, "I will have a word with David during the week. I am sure he will keep you girls on as his employees. He and his wife are coming in for a meal on Wednesday night so you will have a chance to impress him." "That will have to do", said Cissie. There was a horn beeping outside the house. "The taxi man is honking his horn", said Michael, "I paid him to drop you girls over to the flat. As you can see, neither of us two is capable of driving." "We have noticed", Kathleen said. "Was Molly good?" asked Michael. "Yes, she was great", Cissie answered. "She only woke up once so we fed her and changed her." The horn beeped again, "We'd better go, Kathleen, or we will be walking", said Cissie. "Safe home, girls, and thanks so much", said Michael. On the way home in the taxi, Kathleen and Cissie were talking. "Do you think this David man will keep us on at the restaurant?" asked Cissie. "Jeez, I hope so, Cissie. I've been working there a long time and I am sort of attached to the place." "I wonder will they change the name of the place", said Cissie. "More than likely ... I can't imagine his wife would want it named after Jean."

On Wednesday evening the Taylors arrived for their meal at *Jean's Restaurant*. Michael introduced the girls to them, "This is Cissie." "Hello, Cissie." "And this is Kathleen." "Hello, Kathleen." "They are great workers, as you will see for yourselves as the night goes on", said Michael. Margaret Taylor, a very witty woman, cracked a joke with the girls who were about to serve up lamb chops, "Now girls, if you make a mistake with these chops, I'll give both of you the chop", and then she laughed it off, saying, "Michael told me all about both of you, and if all that he said is right then that's good enough for us." When the Taylors were about to leave they sent for the girls who were in the kitchen. Kathleen and Cissie came into the dining area. "You sent for us?" said Kathleen. "We did indeed. David and I were wondering - would you like to stay on here and work for us when we take over the restaurant in a month or two?" "Would we what!" said a delighted Kathleen, "Of course we will - isn't that right, Cissie?" "Are you crazy? Of course!" said Cissie. "Brilliant! We will be in contact", said Margaret, and she left a tip for the girls. "This calls for a little celebration of our own", said Kathleen. "We don't have to work until dinner time tomorrow", said Cissie. "Let's call into the pub on our way home for a few. We can lie in tomorrow morning." "You are on! Come on, let's get a head start on these dishes, and get them washed up as fast as we can", said Kathleen, "I'm dying for a good stiff drink." "Me too", said Cissie, "but I stink of food." "We are working girls, calling in for a drink on our way home. If they don't like how we smell, then they can stay away", said Kathleen. "Yeah, fair enough, let's go", and they celebrated holding on to their jobs into the small hours.

Six weeks later, Cissie and Kathleen were still working for the Smiths. "When are the Taylors ever going to take over here?" asked Cissie. "These things take time", said Kathleen. "You know, we will be going to the wedding in less than two weeks", said Cissie. "I can't wait", said Kathleen. While the girls were serving out dinner, David Taylor came into the restaurant with some paperwork that needed signing. Michael took him into the office. About an hour later David left the restaurant. The girls approached Michael. "Well? Is he taking over soon?" asked Cissie. "You will be working for the Taylors on Monday 25th October", said Michael. "Flip! We will be at the wedding the weekend beforehand. My brother gets married on Saturday the 23rd", said Cissie. "You did tell them about the wedding, didn't you?" asked Kathleen. "No", Michael answered, "because I thought we would have had about three or four weeks working for the Taylors clocked up by now, and I was going to leave it for a week before telling them." "What the heck!" said Kathleen. "Why didn't you tell them straight up at the start, when we knew they were going to be our new bosses?" "Listen! Don't worry, I'll have a word with them tonight. If the worst comes to the worst, and you can't make it back in time from the wedding, then Jean and I will help out. We can take turns looking after Molly, and Susan will be here too. We are not heading away until after Christmas so don't panic - there is plenty of time for me to sweeten them up." "Thanks Michael, we appreciate it, don't we, Cissie?" said Kathleen. "Yes, sure. Thanks Michael. Where are you meeting them tonight?" Cissie asked. "We are going for a meal, and then we are going on for a drink."

Later that night, the Smiths and the Taylors met up. A few hours into the evening, Michael revealed to David and Margaret that the Cissie and Kathleen would be attending a wedding in Ireland on October 23rd. "My, my. When will they be coming back?" asked David. "They will be back late on the Monday." "That's when we open", said Margaret. "We will need them." "Jean and I will help out on your first night, and Susan will be there too. I hope you don't mind a little one being present though", said Michael. "Why! Who else will be there?" asked Margaret. "My little princess, Molly", said Jean. "Here is what we will do, Michael - and I think I speak for both of us", said David. "We can leave it for a day or two. We can take over on the Tuesday or Wednesday. One day won't make much difference." "Yes, I agree", said Margaret. "That's okay", said Michael. "We will manage one more night, won't we, Darling?" "Yes! One more night won't kill us", said Jean. As Margaret Taylor hadn't had anything to drink she drove everybody home.

Inside the Smiths' house, Jean said to Michael, "Did you hear that? Once I mentioned the little one, they suggested they should open the following night or the Wednesday." "I heard them", laughed Michael, "I don't think they are prepared to let babysitting take place." "Snobs! Our little darling wouldn't get in their way", said Jean. "You know what, Jean? We have our extra staff arranged for the weekend that Kathleen and Cissie are off but we have nobody for that Monday, unless we ask the new girls to work that Monday too." "Don't worry about it, Michael. We should just close that Monday. I'll be glad to see the back of the place - we can make that our final weekend", said Jean. "Too right! That's settled then. We will finish up that weekend", said Michael. "You know, when I think about it, Jean, it's all for the best that they didn't take us up on our offer", said Michael. "Why?" Jean asked. "Well, the fewer people who know about Molly the better. You never know who might see her in the restaurant on that Monday." "We don't have to worry about that now", said Jean, "but I know you are right, although nobody would have seen her out the back."

On Thursday October 21st, the girls finished work early. They had a boat to catch that night, the late sailing from Holyhead. "My heart is pounding already, Kathleen. I haven't seen my family in nearly two years - well, it will be approaching two years now at Christmas." "That's right. You had Molly last Christmas", said Kathleen. "You will be so glad to see them." "You bet! And, if things work out well then, according to my plans, I'll be returning again two months later for Christmas", said Cissie. "Oh, that's what I meant to ask David", said Kathleen. "Ask what?" said Cissie. "Jean and Michael always closed during Christmas week but David and Margaret might want to keep it open that week. If so, then we might not get time to go to Ireland for Christmas and be back in time. I'm assuming they will be closed on Christmas Day but that might be the only day." "I see what you mean", said Cissie. "Let's just wait until we get back from the wedding. We can talk to them then about it." "Now", said Kathleen, "let's get back to the flat and finish up our packing. My dad is jealous of me going over to Ireland but I told him, 'Look, you will be going over yourself in two months time for Christmas'." "So, you and your family are going over this year again", said Cissie. "Of course. Granny looks forward to that time of the year. Dad makes sure we get over to see her for Christmas."

"Michael said he will drive us to the station, Cissie", said Kathleen. "That's great! What time did he say he would call for us?" "There is a train leaving at five o'clock. That's what I told him, and he said he will collect us at half past three so we can get on our way so as to make sure we will be there on time." "Perfect. Let's get a move on then", said Cissie, "I can't wait to get on our way." Michael arrived at the flat on schedule. The girls made their way out to the car. "Are you all set to go?" he asked. "Yes! We are ready to roll", said Kathleen. "Did you bring the wedding present, Cissie?" asked Kathleen. "Yes!" said Cissie. "Right", said Kathleen, "a quick double check ... wedding present packed, my dress is packed, and extra clothes for Friday and Sunday ... looks like we are set to go." The girls arrived at the station with plenty of time in hand. "How about a couple of coffees?" said Kathleen. "I'll have one, yes. Gosh! I can't believe we are just hours away from my home", said Cissie. Kathleen brought over two coffees, and then asked Cissie, "When are you getting your £7,000 from Michael and Jean?" "They said whenever they sell the restaurant, but that the transaction might take a while. They told me it would be no later than early January next year - maybe before Christmas yet, fingers crossed", said Cissie. "That seems weird", said Kathleen. "They have the money - the sale has been done ... ah, maybe it takes a while, should be no problem - provided they are still there when we get back. Cissie, it's ahead of you, that's the main thing." "You know, you are joking about them being gone before we get back, but that thought did enter my head", said Cissie. "No! Don't think like that. I can't imagine they would do that. After all, they are genuine folk", said Kathleen. "Nah! I'm just being silly. I know they are sound people", Cissie said and then laughed, "I hope ... should be no problem."

A worker came into the little coffee room, "The Holyhead train is leaving in five minutes. "Do you hear that, Kathleen? I am so excited I could nearly swim the Irish Sea. Kathleen laughed, "You can swim if you want to, Cissie, but I am taking the boat." Several house later, the girls boarded the boat to start their journey to Ireland. "This is real bliss. Mum! Here I come", shouted an excited Cissie. "I am excited for you, too, Cissie. It will be great for you to see your family. Come on, let's find somewhere comfortable so we can lie back and relax. We have a long trip ahead of us." A few hours later the girls arrived at Dublin Port, and caught a bus to the city centre. It was after eight on the morning of Friday 22nd of October.

Kathleen and Cissie found a place to have some breakfast before starting the next leg of the journey up to Donegal. "This cafe looks good, Cissie, and it's fairly cheap too." "Yes, let's go in here", said Cissie. The girls ordered a full Irish breakfast each. "Now this is what I call a breakfast!" said Kathleen. "Hard to beat the Irish grub", said Cissie. Kathleen said, "We should look for the next bus up to Donegal when we've eaten this, Cissie." "I agree, Kathleen, we can ask someone about the bus departures." "Did you go to Scotland from here?" asked Kathleen. "No. I went from Northern

Ireland. It seems like ages ago now since the last time I came through Dublin, though. Flip, that's nearly two years ago." "What bus did you get up to Donegal back then?" asked Kathleen. "I can vaguely remember. I think I got one that was leaving at 12 noon, but I really can't remember. It might have been one o'clock. I was in Manchester at that time with my friend, Annie. She was down visiting her auntie and she asked me to stay with her, and she suggested I travel over to Ireland then from there, so I agreed." "That must have been a longer route for you", said Kathleen. "Yes, it was, but by the time I'd have travelled back up to Scotland to catch the boat there, I thought, what the heck - it's just as close now from Manchester." Outside the cafe, the girls got talking to an elderly man. "Do you know what time the next bus is leaving for Donegal?" asked Cissie. "I'm not really sure", said the man, but I think there is one leaving at noon. It will be displayed on the billboard in the bus depot. You can check it to make sure." "Thank you, Sir", said both girls. The girls made their way to the bus depot. "Look, Cissie, the next bus is leaving at 12:30. We have a few hours to kill before that."

A few hours later, after looking around the shops, the girls got on the bus bound for Donegal. "This will be my first time in County Donegal", said Kathleen, "I'm really looking forward to it." Nearly five hours later, the girls arrived in Donegal. "Now comes the tricky bit", said Cissie. "It may be hard to find a bus going to my town as it's so small, but if McGettigans' bus is still operating then we might be in luck - that's the one I got back at Christmas time two years ago." She asked a girl outside the station, "Excuse me, Miss! Do you know if there is a bus going to the town of Mulldish anytime today?" asked Cissie. "Yes! There is a minibus leaving here at 6:30", said the girl. "Great! Oh, do you know what the name of the bus is?" "Certainly, it's McGettigans." "Thanks very much." "You are welcome."

The girls finally arrived in the town of Mulldish, and a very excited Cissie was greeted by an equally excited Agnes. "My baby! Aw, it's so great to see you. It's been so long", said Agnes. "You look great, Mum", said Cissie. "This is my mum, Kathleen. Mum, this is Kathleen." "Pleased to meet you, young lady. Cissie told me all about you in the letters", said Agnes. "Nice to meet you, too, Mrs McGinley." "Call me Agnes, and come on in and make yourselves at home." Inside the McGinley home Cissie had more introducing to take care of. "Look at you!" Cissie couldn't believe her eyes as she met her youngest brother, Joseph, "My, you have grown. This is Joseph. He is the baby." "Nice to meet you, young man", said Kathleen. "This is Bernadette and this is James." "Nice to meet you." "And this is Mary". "Hello Mary." "And finally, the man himself - Matthew." "It's great to meet you all", said Kathleen. "Right! That's my family. Let's get this stuff unpacked, Kathleen." "I'll show you to the room", said Agnes. "When you get unpacked, girls, come into the kitchen and I'll give you some dinner." "Okay, Mum. Thanks."

"Irish stew! Yummy, it's been a long time since I had this", said Kathleen. "Mmm, this is delicious." "Eat up girls. We'll need our stomachs well lined for later", said Agnes. "Why? What's in store for us later?" asked Cissie, "or should I ask?" "We are going over to the pub for a few drinks. We can meet the bride-to-be over there. The lads are going to *The Mountain Bar* for a few." "A few?", laughed Cissie. "You know yourself", Agnes laughed.

While the girls were eating dinner, a car pulled up outside the cottage. Tommy Murphy stepped out of the car. Agnes went out to meet him and greeted him with a kiss on the lips. Cissie noticed it, and she started to wonder what was going on here. Tommy came inside and he told Matthew, "I will collect you tomorrow at 12 o'clock sharp. The wedding starts at one but, knowing you fellas, tonight might become a session over at *The Mountain Bar*, and we won't want you sleeping in." Then, seeing Cissie, he said, "Hello! It's been a long time, Cissie. "How are you, Tommy?" said Cissie, "I see you have a new car." "Yes, I just bought it last month. I'll be driving Matthew to the chapel tomorrow. That's why I'm here, to remind him not to be overdoing it tonight over at *The Mountain Bar*. And who is this young lady?" asked Tommy. "This is Kathleen Murphy", said Cissie. "Ah! Murphy - great surname." "I take it you are Murphy as well", said Kathleen. "I sure am. You have an English accent - where did you get the great surname from?" laughed Tommy. "My dad is Irish, he is from Cork." "Thought so", said Tommy. "Anyway, girls, I'll see you all tomorrow. I have things to do now. Nice seeing you again, Cissie, and nice meeting you, Kathleen." As Agnes walked Tommy out to the car Cissie was peeping out the window. Once again Tommy kissed Agnes on the lips, and this time it was accompanied by a loving embrace. Cissie was left scratching her head, "What the heck is going on?" she mumbled. "What is it, Cissie?" asked Kathleen. "Them two. What's this kissing on the lips all about?" said Cissie. "You mean, your mum and that man Tommy, who just came in here?" "Yes! I'll have a talk with Mum later", said Cissie. "Maybe they are just being friendly", said Kathleen. "Kissing on the lips? Hmm ... I'm not so sure", said Cissie.

Later that night the girls headed out to *The Oyster Bar*. Inside the bar they met the bride-to-be, along with her mother. Agnes introduced Cissie and Kathleen, "This is Maisy. She will be my new daughter tomorrow. Maisy, this is Cissie. She is my oldest child." "So nice to meet you", said Maisy. "You, too", said Cissie. "This is Cissie's friend, Kathleen." "Nice to meet you, Kathleen." "Nice to meet you, too." "This is her mum, Delores. "Nice to meet you, Delores." "You will meet her father, Bernard, tomorrow - he is out with the lads." "So Maisy! How long have you been seeing Matthew?" asked Cissie. "We met two years ago", said Maisy, "at a horse fair in Armagh." "Are you from Armagh?" asked Cissie. "No, I live two miles from here. I am Seamus McDonagh's daughter." "Ah, yes, I know Seamus. He is a farmer, right?" "That is right", said Maisy. "We keep horses too."

The night started to warm up. There were traditional musicians over in the corner of the lounge. The drinks were coming from all directions, and the girls were getting tipsy. Agnes was tipsy too. "I see you and Tommy are getting on well", said Cissie, a little sarcastically. "Yes. He has been very good to me ever since your father died." "How good, exactly?" enquired Cissie, "I saw you two kissing on the lips." "Were you spying on me out the window?" asked a stunned Agnes. "We were eating dinner, and I just happened to look out the window", said Cissie, "and I saw everything." "Look Cissie, I won't lie to you. Tommy and I have been an item since last year. It started out as pure friendship but one thing led to another. I tried to fight off my feelings but I couldn't any longer." Agnes began to sob. Cissie gave her a hug. "Hey, Mum, it's okay ... Dad is dead a long time now. Tommy is a great man, and I'm sure Dad would want you to be happy." "Do you think so, Cissie?" "Yes, Mum, I'm sure." "I still love Frank", said Agnes, "I'll always love him - he was a great man and a loving father. I'm sure he will understand." "Of course Dad will understand. He will want happiness for you, Mum. I wish you had told me earlier, that's all." "Sorry, my dear, I just didn't know how to", said Agnes. "Never mind", Cissie said, "I know now, and it's fine, honestly." "Thanks, Honey. Now let's get hammered - I haven't seen you in nearly two years, and I want to make the best of our time together", said Agnes. Cissie asked Agnes, "Why don't you write any letters to me, Mum?" "I know, Darling. I was going to write to you numerous times but you know how it is with this lot. If it's not one thing, it's another." "I understand, Mum. Finding time with this lot can't be easy." "It's down to four now, Cissie. After tomorrow, Matthew will be gone too." "Where is he going to live, Mum?" "They have a caravan over in one of Bernard's fields. It's a lovely spot ... great view ... I'll show you on Sunday." "That's great! Maisy seems very nice." "Yes, she is a wonderful girl, and a great worker. Oh! I'll be able to phone you now - Tommy got a phone installed." "Did he? Yes, that will be fantastic, Mum. I'll give you the number of the restaurant. You can ring me whenever you want." "I will indeed, Darling. Right, girls, more drink." "Your mum can put them away", laughed Kathleen. "She certainly can", said Cissie. "Is Maisy from around these parts, Cissie?" asked Kathleen. "Yes, she lives two miles from Matthew. She is from the traveller community too." "That's great. He doesn't have far to go to see her", said Kathleen. The girls partied into the early hours of Saturday morning.

Next morning, everybody rose early, feeling jaded and hungover. "I'll stick on some breakfast", said Agnes, "it might help soak up some of the booze." "Blimey! My head is aching", said Kathleen. "Mine too", said Cissie. "Matthew came downstairs; he was hungover, too. "There he comes. Enjoy your last few hours as a free man", joked Agnes. "You will be a good husband", said Cissie. "Thank you, Sister. I hope you are right", laughed Matthew. Over at the McDonaghs' place, Bernard was getting the horses fitted up. Maisy would be going to the chapel by horse and carriage. There would be six big horses pulling the carriage.

Back in the McGinley home, Matthew was starting to feel the nerves. "Everything will work out fine", said Agnes. A couple of hours later the time had come. Maisy arrived at the church on a carriage, pulled by the six horses which were decorated with flowers, and bows and ribbons. The sight resembled royalty. The wedding went like clockwork. Young Joseph was a pageboy, Maisy's young niece was flowergirl and her three sisters were bridesmaids. Everyone looked beautiful as Father Sweeney conducted the wedding ceremony.

After the service, the family and guests made their way to the McGinley cottage. Agnes had arranged for a few friends to prepare food for the reception which was held in the McGinley cottage. There were big silver pots of mashed potatoes, roast goose, chicken, vegetables and sauces, with soup for a starter. "This is amazing, Cissie", said Kathleen. "I have been to a few weddings in my day but this is a great idea, having a reception at the home place. I love it." "Yes, it is going well", said Cissie. Agnes and family members had cleaned up her shed, and the band were setting up inside. After dinner, the guests made their way outside and over to the shed for a good old knees-up. There were crates and crates of drink. Two hours into the celebrations, there was a commotion going on outside. Cissie and Kathleen went out to investigate. Barney McDonagh was having a bare-knuckle fight against Jake Boyle. "What are they fighting about?" asked a frightened Kathleen. "It's probably something silly", said Cissie. Before long, all of the guests came out of the shed to watch the fight; even the band members came out. The guests were cheering like mad. "Can't anybody stop this?" asked Kathleen. "Don't worry, Dear", said Agnes, "this is our tradition." "I don't understand", said Kathleen. In round seven, Barney McDonagh knocked Jake Boyle to the ground, and the fight ended. Barney helped his defeated opponent up of the ground. The men hugged each other and turned around to the guests. "Right, everybody back to the dance floor. I won the bet", said Barney. The guests headed back into the shed and carried on dancing, as if nothing had ever happened. "I'm gobsmacked", said Kathleen. "Those two men were fighting but now they are hugging each other and joking together." "There is a lot to learn about our traditions, Kathleen", said Cissie. "Come on, let's get back inside."

The guests danced it out, drank their fill, and when the band finished up they started a singsong. Agnes made breakfast for those who had stayed up throughout the night and hadn't gone home. When she finally got rid of them it was nearly 9 o'clock. Cissie and Kathleen had gone to bed at 5:30am but Cissie got up again at 9:15am. "You're up early, Darling", said Agnes. "Yes, I want to go to Mass, I won't see the chapel again until Christmas - that's provided we get time off work." "Oh, I hope you do, Honey", said Agnes. Cissie said, "We will be working under new management when we get back. If we do get it off, imagine - I will be back in two months." "That's great! Two months from today will be Christmas Eve. I'll make you some breakfast now", said Agnes. "No! I couldn't face eating, Mum. My stomach isn't the best." "What about Kathleen? Will I bring her some down?" "No, just let her lie on. This is her usual lie-in day." "I take it she is not a church goer", said Agnes. "Sometimes she goes, but not very much." After Mass, Cissie and Agnes came back to the cottage, and Cissie helped her Mum to make the dinner. When they'd finished their dinner, Agnes, Cissie and, Kathleen went to the cemetery to pay their respects to Frank. Kathleen exclaimed, "God, your father was young when he died! Poor man, he was only thirty three. You must have been devastated, all of you." "We sure were", said Agnes.

The next day, the girls rose early as they had to make their way back to Dublin. Agnes was emotional. "Make sure you come back here for Christmas, Cissie", she said. "I'll do my best, Mum." "And you are welcome here anytime, Kathleen." "Thanks for everything", said Kathleen, "and I hope to see you all again." Tommy Murphy assisted with the first part of their travels. He drove the girls to the bus depot where they were pleased to find out that the next bus to Dublin would be leaving in six minutes. "This is fantastic", said Kathleen. "I hate waiting around." "Let's pay a quick visit to the toilet", said Cissie. "It's a long journey." "Good thinking." The girls made it to Dublin with two hours to spare before the next sailing to Holyhead. Michael told me to ring him at home before we board the boat; he said he would judge our arrival in London the best he could, and that he will wait at the station for us in the car", said Cissie. "Good! Let's just pray he doesn't fall asleep", said Kathleen. "Even if he does, we can walk around and check all the cars. We should find him parked somewhere", said Cissie.

The girls boarded the boat and set off on their journey. When they finally arrived at the railway station in London, Michael was waiting for them; he had been waiting a couple of hours. When the girls got off the train they set about looking for Michael. It was Michael who spotted them and he beeped the horn at them. Kathleen saw him, "Look! There is Michael parked over there." "Great!" said Cissie. "Let's get going. Heaven knows how long he has been waiting for us."

"Well? How was the wedding?" asked Michael. The girls told Michael all about the wedding on their way home. "Jean asked me to bring you to the house for a cup of tea before you head back to the flat, if that's alright with you two." "Sure! Why not?" said Kathleen. Jean met the girls outside her home with a big hug for each of them. "Come in and tell me all about the wedding." After the girls had told Jean all about the wedding, they had to get back to the flat. "Thanks for the tea, Jean, and thank you again, Michael, for collecting us at the station." "Not a bother", said Michael, "I might as well finish the job now and drop you over to the flat." On the way over to the flat, Cissie said to Kathleen, "I am not looking forward to our first day at work tomorrow for the Taylors." "Me neither", said Kathleen. "That's right!" said Michael, "I meant to mention that to you. The Taylor's won't be opening until Wednesday." "Why? I thought they were opening tonight." "No! They said they would wait a few days." Both girls erupted with excitement. "Yes, yes! I'm so tired", said Kathleen, "the thought of working tomorrow is horrifying." "Best news I'll hear all day", said Cissie. "I'm wrecked too." The girls enjoyed their day off work.

The following day was their first day working for the Taylors, and things went as smoothly as a bald man's head. The restaurant was packed to the rafters. The Taylors had a very profitable first night. Every night was the same for the next six weeks. With Christmas just a fortnight away, the girls thought it was time to pop the question to the Taylor's about the restaurant arrangements during Christmas week. The girls came into the office during a quiet spell. Kathleen said, "David, my family always go over to Ireland for Christmas." "Yes", said David. "You see, the thing is … I always go with them. We go over to Grandma's house." "I see. Well, here is the thing", said David. "You know we are up to our necks with Christmas party bookings." "Yes", said Kathleen. David continued, "Michael and Jean assured me that Christmas week was always closed, with reopening taking place on New Year's Eve." "That is correct", said Kathleen. "Here is the news", said David. "This year will be no different." "Wow! Does that mean we can get time off work?" said Kathleen. "Unless you and Cissie want to open for business yourselves", said David. "Fantastic news!" said Cissie. "This means I can go and spend Christmas at home." "You are going over to Ireland too?" asked David. "Yes, I am", said Cissie. "Well, girls, now that we have cleared that up … I must inform you … I need you both back here for New Year's Eve." "We promise", said Cissie. "That's a promise, David", said Kathleen. "Now back to work. We have a couple of tough busy weeks ahead with parties", said David. Cissie and Kathleen worked the remainder of the night with big smiles on their faces. The thought of getting Christmas week off filled them with glee.

The girls couldn't believe their luck; getting Christmas week off work was just brilliant. The partygoers came and went, and it was a very busy period in the restaurant. One day at work, Cissie used the phone to ring her mum to tell her the great news that she would be coming home for Christmas. Tommy answered the phone. Cissie's mum wasn't there but Tommy said, "I'll tell her, Cissie. She will be delighted with the news." "Thanks Tommy. See you all soon." On the last week before Christmas Jean and Michael came into the restaurant; they had a serious look on their faces. Cissie was curious to know why they were there. She still hadn't received her £7,000. Michael and Jean came back out of the office and came over to say hello to the girls. "We believe you are getting the week off for Christmas." "Yes, we are", said Kathleen. "It's great." "If you want, I can drop you both to the station whenever you are heading over to Ireland", said Michael. "No. It will be fine, Michael, thanks. Dad will be driving over, and we will take Cissie with us." "That's right", said Michael, "I forgot about your mum and dad - they always go over. Okay then, girls, come over and visit us before you head off to Ireland." Jean was very quiet. She looked as if she was hiding something; however, she did say goodbye to the girls. "Did you ask your father would it be alright for me to get a lift to the port, Kathleen?" asked Cissie. "Don't need to, Cissie. "He will be glad to. Did you notice Jean? What about her! She was very stand-offish - for want of a better word - don't you think?" said Kathleen. "She was very quiet, now that you mention it. Maybe it's her time of the month", said Cissie. "Probably! Well, she did say goodbye."

The girls were unaware of the fact that Jean and Michael had called around to the office for the rest of their money for the restaurant. Outside the restaurant, before getting into the car, Michael said to Jean, "Will we invite Cissie over for tea tonight so we can pay her the money before she heads over to Ireland for Christmas?" "We can pay her when she gets back. She will only be gone a week", said Jean. "She might want to give her mum some money for Christmas though", said Michael. "We can discuss it at home", said Jean, "I'm still not very happy with the amount."

Back at the Smiths' house Jean put Molly into her cot; the trip home in the car had left her sound asleep. Jean came back into the sitting room. "Now my dear, sit yourself down", said Michael. "We need to discuss Cissie and the money." "Fair enough, but you might not like what I am about to say." "Try me", said Michael. "Look", Jean replied, "we have the restaurant sold, we have the money, we have Molly. Let's just clear off with everything." "Do you mean Cissie's money as well?" "Yes", said Jean, "I do. We have been looking after Molly for nearly a year now. We are her parents so I think that's a good enough deal for Cissie." "Hold on, Jean. You love Molly. The only reason you have her is because Cissie is selling her to us. When she finds out we are gone with her money she might blow up and come after us. She might inform the police! We could be prosecuted for kidnapping", Michael said. Jean replied, "That's a risk I'm willing to take. Besides, nobody will know we are gone. I'm tired of hiding Molly all the time - I want to be able to take her everywhere. I want us to start afresh in a new country." "Like where?" asked Michael. "My sister, Diana, is expecting us over for New Year's Eve. I told her all about Molly. She said she would put us up for a month or two until we find a house of our own to buy." "Your sister Diana lives in San Francisco." "Yes, she does. It will be perfect, Michael - a life we always dreamed of." "What about this house?" asked Michael. "We can give it to Cissie - it's the least we can do." "How exactly?" "We leave a note through their letterbox when they are gone to Ireland. I mean, come on, this house is worth a fair bit. She can sell it if she wants. We need the money if we are going to buy a house in America, and I don't want to wait around here for another possible six months before we sell it. With the £7,000 ready cash, we can use that to buy our new house. It's not like we are not paying her - well ready cash - she will have it in property." "Let me think it over, Jean. This is all a bit sudden." "What is there to think about? We have the restaurant cash - we keep Cissie's cash. She has the house - which is worth more than £7,000 - and she can sell it. She might be angry for a while but when she adds it all up in her head then she will be satisfied enough. I can't wait any longer", Jean said. "Alright, Dear, you have convinced me", said Michael. "No need to think about it any more, we will do it. Let's get a move on though - we need to book the tickets for San Francisco." "No need", said Jean, as she went to the sideboard and brought out tickets. "I already have them." "When did you purchase them?" "I bought them the other day. I took a gamble on persuading you to agree with my way of thinking. I'm sorry for doing that but we need to be ahead with things." "Very cheeky ... but I suppose I'll forgive you", said Michael.

When the girls had finished their last shift before their holidays they headed over to the Smiths' house for tea. "Are you all set for Ireland?" asked Michael. "Yes, I'm so excited", said Cissie. "I missed them so much last year." "This time last year you were like a balloon", laughed Kathleen. "That's right", said Jean. "Look at her now." As Jean took Molly in her arms she looked and spoke tenderly to her, "You will soon be one!" Kathleen said, "It will be horrible for Molly in years to come, don't you think? I mean, imagine having your birthday on Christmas Day, the one set of presents covering everything." "We will just have to get you extra ones, Molly", said Jean. "On the subject of presents", said Cissie, "I have one here for Molly." "Thanks, Dear", said Jean. "Thank you", said Michael. "And this is from Kathleen and me, for the both of you." "Thanks very much, girls." Michael handed each a present, "This is for both of you." "Thanks Michael. Thanks, Jean."

After everybody had exchanged presents and their goodbyes and wished each other a happy Christmas the girls went back to the flat. "Have you everything packed, Cissie?" "Yes, I have. I can't wait to see my family again, even though it's only been two months. There is something special about Christmas - I can't wait." "You know, that is so true. Christmas without your family wouldn't be the same", said Kathleen.

Meanwhile, in the Smiths' house, Jean said, "That was a bit awkward. I found it hard to look Cissie straight in the eye." "A bit weird alright", said Michael. On Christmas Eve morning at 5:00am the Murphys arrived at the flat to collect the girls. They made their way to Holyhead for the sailing to Ireland. In Dublin they went their separate ways, the Murphys to Cork and Cissie to Donegal. When Cissie reached home, it was nearly nine at night. Agnes gave her a big welcoming hug, "My darling!" "Oh! That smell", said Cissie. "It must be goose. I can remember that smell just like yesterday." "It's goose, and I have turkey too", said Agnes. "Roll on tomorrow", said Cissie, "a big tasty dinner with my family! I can't wait", as she broke down and cried. "Don't cry, Honey", said Agnes. "You're home now, and it's going to be a very special Christmas." "I'm so happy, Mum - that's why I am crying." "I know, Agnes said. "Listen, do you want to go to Midnight Mass tonight? You could have a lie-in then tomorrow." "Yeah! That sounds good", said Cissie.

Christmas morning 1948. Molly was one year old. The Smiths were celebrating her first birthday and her first Christmas. Cissie was enjoying Christmas with her family. When the rest of the family had gone to bed Cissie and Agnes sat down and talked. They talked into the small hours and they drank porter. "You know, Cissie, you don't have to send me money any more", said Agnes, "Tommy and I are doing just fine now." "Are you sure, Mum?" "Yes", said Agnes, "and I'll remember what you did for this family for the rest of my life. I can't thank you enough. If you ever need anything or tell me anything then I'll be here for you." When Agnes spoke these words, Cissie broke down crying. She couldn't hold back her guilt any longer. "What is it, Darling?" asked Agnes. Cissie told Agnes all about Molly. She even showed her the newspaper which had the report of the rape case in it. She told her she had sold her to the Smiths. Agnes could hardly breathe. "You mean to tell me I'm a granny and I didn't even know? Oh Cissie, you should have told me." "I thought it best, Mum, not to as I didn't want to keep her because I'd been raped." "Poor baby, come here." Agnes cried and consoled Cissie. "If only I'd known", she said. "When was she born?" "She is one year old today, Mum." "She was born on Christmas Day!" said an excited Agnes. "That explains why you didn't come here last year." "Sorry for lying, Mum, but I didn't know what to do. I lied about the work drying up in Clydebank, too, because everybody wanted me to have an abortion so I pretended I was going to London just to do that, and I didn't return." "Come here", Agnes said, and began to cry. "I'm so proud of you. That is so brave. I brought you up well - you are a very special girl." "I didn't let myself love Molly, Mum, and now that I know how you feel I'm starting to regret it already. I shouldn't have sold her." "Did you get the money yet?" asked Agnes. "No, not yet. They said they would pay me in early January." "Well", said Agnes, "that's alright then ... here is what we will do ... I will come back with you to London, and I'll take Molly over here to live with us. If you want to come back too, then, better still. Tommy needs help with work - I can help him out, and you can let your guard down and you can start loving your daughter." Cissie hopped off her seat. She hugged her mum and cried very hard, "Oh, Mum, thank you! I do love Molly. I was just afraid to." "When are you due back in London?" asked Agnes. "We have to work on New Year's Eve so we are going back early on the 30th." "Right", said Agnes, "we will go over and get Molly. You can work a few weeks notice for your employers and I'll stay in London with you for a fortnight until you do and we can come home, all three of us." "Cissie sobbed, "Aw, Mum, I love you. I've wanted to come home ever since I left years ago. I hate the city life - I'll never get used to it." "We are financially okay now, Cissie", said Agnes "so let's go and get my granddaughter and your daughter. My girls are coming home. Raise your glass." They raised their glasses filled with porter. Agnes said, "To my girls."

The Christmas week passed quickly. On December 29th Cissie has her bags packed early for the journey ahead, and so had Agnes. Tommy Murphy, who now knew about Molly, came into the McGinley home. Agnes told him that he would have to look after the family while she was away in London. Tommy was not to mention a word to the rest of the family about Molly's existence; she was to be a surprise.

Meanwhile in London, at the Smiths' house, Jean had the letter written for Cissie, informing her that they had gone, but she didn't say where. The following day, Tommy drove Agnes and Cissie to the bus depot. When they reached Dublin, the Murphy family were already there. They would all be going over in the same boat. "Nice to see you again, Agnes", said Kathleen. "Did you come down to Dublin for the trip, to see Cissie off?" "No! She is coming with me to London", said Cissie. Cissie then whispered to Kathleen, "Mum knows all about Molly." "Oh. I see", said Kathleen. "We are going over to take her back", Cissie continued, "I didn't think Mum would be so understanding. I love Molly." "Do you mean you are leaving London?" asked Kathleen. "Yes, Kathleen, I am." "I will miss you so much", said Kathleen. "Won't you reconsider?" "No", Cissie said. "I want to come home to live. We can talk about it in the flat."

When they reached London the Murphys dropped the two girls and Agnes at the flat. "Nice to have met you, Mrs McGinley", said Patrick Murphy. "You too", said Agnes. "Enjoy your holiday in London", said Sally Murphy. "I will, as long as I don't get lost", joked Agnes. "You will be fine", said Sally. "Make sure you call over to our house for a cup of tea before you go home. Kathleen can bring you. "I'll take you up on that", said Agnes. The girls and Agnes make their way up to the flat and opened the door. Inside the door, there were a few letters on the floor that has been dropped through the letterbox. Kathleen said, "It looks like we have a few belated Christmas cards to open." "We can open them later", said Cissie. "Let's get some tea first and get the fire lit. It's freezing in here", and added, "Here Mum, I'll show you to your room. I'm going to use the sofa for a while." "Don't be silly, Cissie", Agnes said, "I'll use the sofa." "No! You are our guest, and you are my mum so you are using my room, no argument", Cissie said. "Okay then, Cissie, if you insist", said Agnes. After Cissie got the fire going and they'd had their tea the girls settled back on the sofa with Agnes. "Right, Kathleen, let's open up these letters." Kathleen opened three of the four letters; they were all late Christmas cards from friends. "Here, this one is for you, Cissie", she said. Cissie opened up the letter. After reading the first two lines, she nearly collapsed. "What is it, darling?" asked a worried Agnes. Cissie was speechless - so much so she handed Kathleen the letter. Kathleen read aloud ... "Dear Cissie, We are sorry for having to do this but we feel it's the best for everyone. We have taken Molly with us. We won't be back in England ever again. I know you are probably angry right now. We are taking the money we were going to pay you with us. We will need it to start a new life." Kathleen paused after reading that, and then continued, "All is not as it may seem. We are not stealing your money. We just need ready cash. We have left you our house. The keys and the paperwork are in the blue jar in the restaurant. David let me in earlier yesterday so I could put them in there. The house is worth more than £7,000 as you might well know. We hope you won't hate us but you know I love Molly, and nobody around here knows that she is now mine. I hope one day you can forgive us. All the best, Jean and Michael."

Agnes was crying her eyes out. Cissie was sobbing, too. Kathleen joined in the crying as well; she realised now that Cissie loved Molly and that up to now she had just been afraid to let herself love her.

"I don't know what to say to you both", said Kathleen. Agnes cried out, "Where do they live?" Cissie said, "What's the point? They will be long gone." "We can get the bus over there if you want", said Kathleen. "Come on then - let's try!" said Agnes. "There is no point but I suppose we can try", said Cissie. The three caught a bus and got off close to the Smiths' house. They walked the final 150 yards up to the house and knocked on the door but, to nobody's surprise, there was no one home; the house was empty. Cissie sat on the door step. Agnes and Kathleen joined her. Cissie cried out, "What have I done, Lord? What have I done?"

Two days later Agnes said, "I think I'll go home, Cissie. There is no point in me staying here now." "Stay for a couple of more days, Mum. You can go home then." "No. I'd better get back to my family." "You know, it might take a while now to sell the house, Mum, but when I do get it sold, I'll be coming home straight away", said Cissie. "That's fine dear. I understand." A few days later, Agnes phoned Tommy to tell him she was on her way home."

Cissie invited Kathleen to move into the house. "Look at it this way, Kathleen. At least we will be rent free for a while", said Cissie. "Well, thank you, Cissie. I'm glad you are inviting me to live with you. I will buy the food." "Don't be silly, we can share the food costs, and the bills", said Cissie. The girls lived like that for the next five months until Cissie finally got the house sold and she returned to Ireland.

CHAPTER FOUR

S AN FRANCISCO 1967. MOLLY HAD just finished high school and was contemplating leaving home. Jean and Michael were busy running the restaurant they had bought during the spring of 1949 which they named *Cornie's*. A few years later Molly worked there every evening after school, and she worked there fulltime during the summer months, all the holidays.

Molly really excelled at high school. Her exam results were outstanding, so much so that she was planning on entering university in early September - in New York City. However, Jean was very protective of her, and didn't want Molly to leave San Francisco.

The atmosphere in the house was getting a bit claustrophobic for Molly. She was starting to become very independent. She was eager to get out and get a place of her own; however, she was planning on working the summer in the restaurant first as she could do with the money. *Cornie's Restaurant* was very popular. The new chef, John, was famous for his special curry dishes which attracted people on a regular basis. When the restaurant finished serving food for the night the bar remained open. The Smiths had quite a large staff working for them. There were three waiters and there were four waitresses in the restaurant. There were five people working in the bar which Jean had decided to call *Sissy's*, a name she had chosen for two reasons, one: she wanted to remember Cissie, and two: she joked about spelling the name properly. Jean and Michael had fun when they named the bar. Michael and Jean would talk about Cissie and Kathleen every so often.

Molly knew about the reason for the naming of the restaurant; it was related to a chef who had worked there. His nickname was Corndog. Jean thought it would be a nice gesture to name it *Cornie's* in his honour because he was their original chef when they bought the place in 1949. That chef was killed in a motorcycle accident. Before it was called *Cornie's*, the restaurant was named *Harry's*. Molly was never told the reason for the naming of the bar. Jean just told her she liked the name and that's all that was said about the topic. Every night Molly made sure she went behind the bar to work. Working behind the bar was a great way of making extra money; people always left good tips which the bar staff split at the end of the night.

One morning Jean came into the kitchen as Molly was sitting eating cereal. "Molly", she said, "look at this newspaper. There is something in here I think you should read." "Give it here, then, Mom." Molly began to read it to herself. The article in the newspaper had a guide on all the courses and subjects in the San Francisco University. "Mom! We have been through this before", said Molly,

"We talked about it. I am not going to university here. I told you I am going to university in New York." "Why New York? All the subjects you can ask for are in here. Read it", said Jean. "I have read it, and you are right but I just want to go to a different city. I want to explore a new place", said Molly. "All I'm asking is that you consider it - that's all", said Jean. Mollie answered, "Very well, Mom, I'll give it some thought" "Thanks, Dear. You won't regret it", said Jean.

Molly worked in the restaurant and the bar for the next two months and had a lot of money saved up. She decided to take a mini break, given the fact that she would be entering university in five weeks time. Which university she would be choosing would need to be decided soon as the applications needed to be in within the next four days. She made a trip to New York City to visit Stony Brook University. When Molly went inside the university she made her way up to reception and asked for information about the courses and subjects beginning in September. She went over and sat down beside a table. She put the list on the table and she started to read it. As Molly was reading it she realised her Mom was right; the subjects were quite the same as the subjects on offer at the university of San Francisco. She was thinking aloud to herself. "Ah, you know what? I think I'll just choose San Francisco! I can move out of the house and get my own apartment. That way I can have my independence, and keep Mom happy at the same time." Sitting across from her at another table was a young man with looks to kill. He looked at Molly in a way that manifested to her that he'd heard everything she said. Molly realised this. She was thinking too loudly; her whispers hadn't gone unheard. The young man came over to her table, and he said these words to her ... "Why would you like to stay in a city named after a saint?" and then he walked away. As he was walking away Molly said to him, "Excuse me?" The man smiled and said, "I'll see you around", and then he left. She thought to herself "What a weirdo", though adding in a soft voice, "What a hunk."

In the Smiths' house Jean was waiting patiently for a phone call. She had told Molly to phone home when she reached New York. Finally the call that Jean was eagerly awaiting came. "Hello Mom!" said Molly. "Hi, Darling!" said Jean, "I've been waiting for you to call all evening. I was worried about you. Did you arrive safely?" "Yes, Mom", Molly answered, "I'm sorry I didn't call you earlier but I lost track of time. You know, Mom ... you were right - all the subjects here are the same." "Does that mean you are going to go to San Francisco University?" asked a hopeful Jean. "Yes, Mom. I suppose it does." Jean exclaimed, "Yes! Oh, Molly, this is great news." "When I get home, though, we have to talk", said Molly. "Fine, Dear, whatever you say. When are you coming home?" asked Jean. Molly replied, "I want to visit a few places first so I am going to stay two nights in a youth hostel. I'll see you on Tuesday night." "Okay, Darling", said Jean, "stay safe, love you." "I love you, too, Mom. See you soon. Bye bye." Molly visited as many places as she could while in New York. She went to museums, to the zoo, parks, and lots of places of interest. Sitting in a cafe eating hamburger and chips, Molly thought about the words that the weirdo hunk had spoken to her the day before, "What the hell did he mean when he said, 'Why would you live in a city named after a saint?' and how did he know I lived there? Ah, maybe he heard me saying it." Nevertheless, the whole experience upset Molly; it left her feeling very uncomfortable. On the last night of her stay in New York, she went to a concert. The band played music from the fifties era, and they were brilliant. The lead singer was a female, and she was outstanding. Molly thought to herself, "Gosh, what would I give to be able to sing like that?"

From behind where Molly was sitting came a voice. It was like a voiceover from thin air. Molly heard it plainly; the voice said "I can think of something that you could give." She swung around in her seat to see who had said it, saying to herself, "What the heck?" To her surprise, there was nobody there. She turned back again to face the band. While listening to the band she thought to herself, "What just happened then?" She shrugged her shoulders and thought, "Ah, maybe I'm imagining things." The band played for two hours, and Molly was entranced from start to finish. When they finished playing, everyone stood up and gave them a huge round of applause. The lights came on in the floor area, and people started making their way to the exit doors. Just when Molly was about to step outside a young man caught her attention. He was just about to go out of another exit door when he stopped still and glanced over at Molly. She felt uneasy and said to herself, "That's the same weirdo who was at the university the other day!" She was thinking, "What is he doing here?" and then she thought, "This is a crazy coincidence." She walked on outside and flagged down a taxi which brought her back to the hostel to spend her last night in New York City.

Molly had trouble sleeping. Eerie thoughts kept entering her head. Where did that voiceover come from? Why was that weirdo at the concert? And why was he staring at me? After a lot of tossing and turning, she eventually fell asleep. Bright and early the next morning, Molly left the youth hostel. She would start out on her journey home after breakfast. While in a cafe Molly asked the waitress, "Can I use your phone please? I will pay you. I want to call my mom." The manageress comes over, "Sure, dear. Feel free." Molly phoned her mom, "Hello Mom." "Hello, Darling. Where are you now?" Jean asked. Mollie answered, "Mom, I can't stay on the phone long. I'm in a cafe. I'm calling to tell you ... go into my room - my application form for the University of San Francisco is in the top drawer of my dresser. I need you to drop it in to reception first thing in the morning - or today if you have time." "Of course, Darling", Jean said, "I'll drop it in now on my way to work. When will you be back?" Mollie replied, "Well, I'm taking the train. It could be nearly three days so I'll see you when I see you. Okay, I have to go." "See you soon, Honey. Safe journey home." Molly went to pay the lady for the use of her phone. "How much do I owe you, Miss?" "Don't be silly, young lady. It's okay." "Thank you so much", said Molly.

Back in San Francisco, Jean was on her way to the university to leave in the application form for Molly. "You are cutting it fine", said the receptionist. "Why?" asked Jean. "Today is the final day for receipt of the application forms." "You are not serious?" said Jean. "Goodness. Thank God Molly called me! I thought tomorrow was the last day. Molly must have got the date wrong." The receptionist smiled, "Better late than never." "It was a last minute decision", said Jean. "She was going to go to university in New York City but thank God she changed her mind." "You know young girls, and what they are like", said the receptionist. "Too right", said Jean, and she left.

Jean was talking to herself on her way to work, "How lucky was that! I was going to leave the application form until tomorrow morning. Whoosh!" She wiped her brow and said, "Was that close or what?"

In New York Molly had just boarded the train bound for San Francisco. She took her stuff into her cabin on the train. It was a bit cramped but she managed. She lay down for a few hours, then she got up off the bed and made her way into the seating area. After a day on the train, a young girl got on board at one of the stations. It just so happened that she was on her way to San

Francisco. At first, she sat across from Molly. About twenty minutes later, when the girl realised that Molly was travelling alone, she came over and introduced herself. "Hi! My name is Viola ... do you mind if I sit beside you?" "No! Sure, sit down. My name is Molly. That's a lovely name you have", said Molly. "My father named me after his mother. She is from Kenya in Africa." "Is your dad from Africa, too?" asked Molly. "No. Dad was born in Chicago. My grandma came over to the USA a long time ago. Dad grew up in Chicago but then he moved to San Francisco - that's were I was born." "So, are you on your way to San Francisco now?" asked Molly. "Yes, I am", said Viola. "What about yourself? "Whereabouts are you headed?" "I'm going to San Francisco too", said Molly, "I live there. My parents own a bar and restaurant there." "That's great. What is the name of the restaurant?" asked Viola. "The bar is called *Sissy's*, and the restaurant is called *Cornie's*." "You know, I have passed by that restaurant a few times but I have never actually been inside it", said Viola. "Well, next time don't walk past it", joked Molly, clenching her fists in a joking manner." "Ha ha, I won't, said Viola. "So, Molly, do you work in the restaurant or the bar?" "Yes. I work in both parts. I do waitressing first, then I do bartending." "Very good", said Viola. "I got paid off last week. My boss ran off with another woman, then his wife sacked us all and she closed the cafe." "Flipping heck! Why did she do that?" asked Molly. "It was one of the girls who worked for them who was having an affair with her husband. Unfortunately for us, we all had to take the rap for it", said Viola. "That's a bit harsh, don't you think?" said Molly. "Well, I suppose the way she looked at it ... we were all in on the secret", said Viola. "You see, we all knew about it." "Nevertheless, there was no need to take it out on the rest of the girls", said Molly. "I know what you mean, said Viola. "I think she saw us all as a potential threat." "A bit stupid though. I mean, he is gone now, so there is no need to worry anymore", said Molly. "She probably thinks he will be back", said Viola, "and doesn't want him getting tempted again." "Maybe he will, but I don't know the man so I really can't predict anything", said Molly. "Thing is, if I know Annabel the way I think I do, he will be back. Her track record is predictable", said Viola. "So, is that the name of the girl that he ran off with?" asked Molly. "Yes. She thinks he has money", said Viola. "The thing is, his wife deals with all the money, and now that he has run away with another woman he might get hard done by in a court of law, assuming it goes that far. His wife is very steadfast. I reckon she will divorce him, and when Annabel realises he hasn't got much money left she will leave him." "He will deserve it", said Molly, "Is he much older than her?" "Annabel is twenty two and he is forty five", said Viola. "Dirty old man", joked Molly. It was day two on the train. At 10:34pm, Molly said, "I'll see you in the morning, Viola. I'm going to lie down." "I think I will lie down myself, Molly", Viola said, "I'll meet you for breakfast." The two girls went to their cabins for a good night's sleep.

At breakfast the two girls met again. "Good morning, girls. Enjoy your breakfast", said a conductor. The girls said "Good morning." "Do you know how long it will take us to get to San Francisco now from here?" asked Molly. The conductor replied, "You will be there in roughly three hours." "Great! My bum hurts from sitting", said Viola. "Mine too", said Molly. "We must get together in San Francisco one night", said Viola. "We will", said Molly, "why don't you call over to the restaurant one night, or maybe even to the bar for a drink." "Good idea, Molly. I think I will. What nights do you work in the bar?" "Usually the lot ... the tips are good, and I need the money for my new apartment, and I have very little time left before I start university." "You are going to move into your own apartment?" said Viola, "That's great. I hope I can find work again soon. I want to move out of the house myself." "Hey! Tell you what - why don't you work for my mom and dad?" said Molly. "Do they have a vacancy?" asked Viola. "Well, I'll only be able to work Fridays and Saturdays from now on. I will be up early for university during the week and I'll need my rest. You could do my shifts during the week - I'll put a word in for you." "Would you? Oh! That would be brilliant. Thanks, Molly." "Call in on Saturday night for a drink. I'll show you some bar skills", said Molly. "I will, Molly. I've always wanted to work in a bar."

A few hours later the girls arrived in San Francisco. "Let's go for a coffee somewhere. I want to find a phone so I can ring Mom", said Molly. "Yes, cool. A coffee would be nice." The girls found a coffee shop nearby. Molly called the restaurant, and her mom answered. Molly said, "Mom! I'm in a little coffee shop called *Steve's*. Can you come and collect me?" "Sure, Darling, said Jean, "I'll be there in ten minutes. I know the cafe well. Your Aunt Diana goes there often and I join her sometimes." "Lovely. I'll see you soon, Mom." Jean arrived at the cafe. Molly asked Viola, "Whereabouts do you live? My mom might know where it is - she knows the city well." Viola told Molly where she lived. "Come on out to the car. I'll ask Mom if she knows that area ... Hi Mom!" "Hello, Honey. So glad to see you", said Jean. "Mom, this is Viola", Molly said, "I met her on the train. I'm hoping you know the East Bay Area well - I've offered Viola a ride home." "How are you, Viola? Yes, I know it fairly well", said Jean. Viola told Jean the exact address. "Yes. I know where that is. Of course I'll give you a ride home, Dear." Molly and Viola got into the car. On the way there, Molly put a word in for Viola in connection with the vacancy that would arise when she started at university. "Mom! Viola and her co-workers were all laid off work." Molly told Jean every single detail.

"Where are you going to work now, Viola?" asked Jean. Molly intervened, "Mom! I was suggesting to Viola that she could take my shifts during the week while I'm at university, if that's okay with you? She has waitressing experience." "What about bar experience?" asked Jean. "Unfortunately, I never worked in a bar", said Viola, "but I'm willing to learn." "I told her to call in for a drink on Saturday night and I'll show her some bar skills", said Molly. "Saturday nights are busy, Molly. Wouldn't it be better to call during the day on Saturday when it's quiet behind the bar? That way you would have more time", said Jean. "What do you think, Viola?" asked Molly. "Does that suit you?" "Fine by me. I will come round on Saturday after lunch", said Viola. "Does this mean you will consider giving her a job, Mom?" asked Molly. "We will know better on Saturday", said Jean. Six minutes later they reached Viola's home. "Well, here we are", said Jean. "That was quicker than I expected", said Molly. "We are only two miles away from my restaurant", said Jean. "It's closer than I thought", said Viola. "You could almost walk to work from here - provided Mom hires you", laughed Molly. "That won't be a problem. If I'm fortunate enough to get accepted, I'll walk it, no sweat", said Viola. After they dropped off Viola, Jean and Molly went home. "I'll be so happy to see my bed tonight", said Molly, "that bed in the cabin was so uncomfortable." "Why don't you lie down for a bit now?" said Jean. "Sounds like a good idea, Mom. I'll get a proper cup of coffee first, though. The coffee in that cafe tasted like tar."

"Molly, you were cutting it fine with the application form for the university." "Why? Was there a problem?" "No. But, one day later and there would have been. I got it in on time, by the skin off my teeth. You got the date wrong by a day." "Flip! Ah well, it's in now. Thanks, Mom." "I'm so glad you changed your mind about New York", said Jean. "So what is it you want to talk about now that you are back?" "I'll talk with you later tonight", said Molly. "I want to take a nap first." "That's okay, Honey", said Jean. "You must be shattered. I'll talk with you later. Get some rest now."

Molly had a few hours sleep. When she got up she met her mom who was in a hurry. "Where are you going, Mom?" "Michael wants me to come over to the restaurant. One of the girls called in sick." "Just when we could be having our talk", said Molly. "I know ...can we talk when I get back?" asked Jean. "Mom, I'll be frank ... I am moving out of the house - I'm getting my own flat. Sorry for being so brief but I won't be able to concentrate on my studies if I stay here." "Don't say that, Honey. Listen, I gotta go. I'll see you when I get back - we can talk about this properly then." "Mom, I know you are in a hurry but there is no more to talk about. It's either the flat here or I'll head back to New York." "Very well honey. I'll see you later", said Jean, with a look of disappointment on her face, "I'm off - no need to wait up."

Over at the restaurant things were really busy. "Did Molly make it home safe?" asked Michael. "Yes, she had a few hours sleep", said Jean. "It's a pity she is tired. We could be doing with her in the bar now that Simone has called in sick", said Michael. "She met a girl on the train called Viola who has been laid off work. Apparently, she did restaurant work before", said Jean. "Where is she tonight? We could be doing with her", said Michael. "You will get to meet her on Saturday. She is coming in to train in the bar. I asked her over. If she is impressive then we can hire her." "We can be doing with someone else", said Michael. "Yes. We will be losing Molly during the week when she starts university - worse still, we will be losing her at home, too", said Jean. "Why? What do you mean?" asked Michael. "She is moving out of the house. She wants her own apartment." "When did you two discuss this?" asked Michael. "We didn't really", said Jean, "I wanted to sit and talk to her tonight but when you rang me to come in to work then I never got the chance. Then, when I was just about to leave she dropped this on me. I didn't even get a chance to talk with her properly." "Maybe she will still be up when we get home", said Michael, "we could both talk to her then - see if we can talk a bit of sense into her." Jean said, "No! That's not a good idea, Michael. She more or less told me it's not up for negotiation. She said it's either the flat or she will move to New York, and I don't want her moving to New York, no way." "Well, if she gets an apartment close by then maybe we can visit her often", said Michael. "It will be okay ... I hope", said Jean.

After a busy night at the restaurant Jean and Michael arrived home and Molly was still up. "Great to see you back", said Michael, and he gave her a big hug, "Jean tells me you met a new friend." "Yes. I met her on the train on our way home. She lives with her parents, just two miles away from the restaurant. She was laid off work..." "I'll stop you there", said Michael, "Jean told me everything about her. I believe she is coming in on Saturday to learn a few bar skills." "Yes. I told her to call over - well, Mom did too - on Saturday. She has waitressing skills so if she gets the hang of the bar I reckon she will be an asset." "Let's hope you are right", said Michael, "Simone isn't very reliable." "Ah! Simone is a good worker though", said Molly. "I know she is", said Jean, "but what's the point in being a good worker if she isn't turning up for her shifts? "You know, she just split up with her boyfriend, though", said Molly. "That's unfortunate, I know", said Michael, "but what goes on in my employees' private lives shouldn't be affecting their work." "Probably not", said Molly. "Anyway ... I hear you are moving out", said Michael - as Jean gave him a poke in his ribs - "and before you answer me, I want you to know: Jean and I are fine with it - provided we are welcome to visit." "Aw, Dad, thanks! Of course you can visit, as many times as you like", said a delighted Molly. "Right! I don't know about you two but I am going to bed", said Jean. "Me too", said Molly, "I am so tired." In the bedroom Jean said to Michael, "I thought you were going to try and talk Molly out of moving out! I nearly fainted." "My ribs can verify that", said Michael. "Sorry about that, Honey. I just panicked. You know, it just seems like yesterday when we were putting her down in her cot", Jean sighed, "where does time go?"

On Saturday afternoon, Viola came into the restaurant. "Hello there! Come through", said Molly. "You met my mom. This is my father." "Hello! Viola, I believe?" said Michael. "Yes. Nice to meet you", says Viola. "Right, you know my wife's name. My name is Michael. Molly will show you around." After Molly showed Viola the ropes she took to the bar work like a duck to water. Viola was so impressive behind the bar Michael asked her to try the busy Saturday night shift. Saturday night in the bar was very busy. Viola stayed on and worked the shift, and she coped with the pressure, no problem. When all the customers had left the bar, the girls cleared the tables, washed the glasses, and then they split up the bar tips four ways, Viola, Molly and the other two girls getting equal shares. Michael had decided to sit on the other side of the bar, as a customer. This way he could observe Viola to see what sort of barmaid she was. Michael came over and said to Viola, "Well! What can I say? You are a natural bartender." "Does this mean you will keep her on?" asked Molly. "Certainly", said Michael. "You can have as many shifts as you want." "Thank you so much. This means so much to me", said Viola.

A few weeks later Molly made her way to university for her first day. She would be focusing on medicine; she wanted to become a pharmacist. Viola finished an early shift at the restaurant and decided to go home for a couple of hours, and she would be coming back later to work in the bar. When she arrived home, there was a big red car parked outside her home. "I wonder who this could be, parked at our house", she thought. When she went inside the house her parents were standing in the sitting room with smiles on their faces. "Who owns the car parked outside?" asked Viola. "There is only the two of us here", said her father Isaiah. It didn't take long for it to register with Viola. She shouted, "Whoopee! You bought a car?" Her mother, Jenoye said, "Yes, we have, Baby! We can give you a ride to work now." "Brilliant! You can take me over to the bar later", said an ecstatic Viola. "Mom and Dad, this is so great."

With six or seven shifts on offer every week, Viola was able to save plenty of money. Before long, she started taking driving lessons from her father. She was planning on buying her own car; however she might have to wait a few more weeks because Molly had a proposition for her.

On Saturday evening Molly came into the bar to start her shift at seven o'clock, and Viola came in at nine to start her shift, having worked in the restaurant earlier. When the girls got a little quiet moment Molly asked Viola a question, "How do you feel about moving into an apartment with me on Monday?" "Monday? That's a bit of short notice, isn't it ... wow, I don't know ... maybe I should just say yes straight away. Flip! Why not?" said a pretty unsure Viola. "You should see it, Viola. It is beautiful", said Molly. "When did you see it?" asked Viola. "I saw it today earlier. This girl at university told me her father had an apartment to rent. When she found out that I was enquiring about an apartment she approached me and told me about the one her dad was going to lease. She took me around to see it - she showed me all around it. It's so perfect, you should see it!" said Molly. "We could go and look at it tomorrow", suggested Viola. "Good idea! You will love it", said Molly, "thing is ... they want the deposit before we move in. "Awk! I was planning on buying a car for work", said Viola, "I have quite a bit saved now." "Don't worry, you will only need to walk 300 yards to work from now on", said Molly. "Is it that close?" asked Viola. "Yes! Just a couple of minutes walk from here. You can brush up on your driving - plenty of time to buy a car. Besides, the cars are 15% cheaper in January - so my dad reckons", said Molly.

At the end of the night the mood was dampened when Molly informed her mom and dad that she was moving into an apartment on Monday, but when they were told how close the apartment was to the restaurant Jean and Michael felt a bit better. On the way home, Michael and Jean dropped Viola off at her house. Jenoye was still up. "Why are you up so late, Mom?" asked Viola. "I couldn't sleep, Dear. I came down for some milk, and then I started to read the newspaper. I couldn't believe the time when I heard a car pull up outside and I looked at the clock. It's after three in the morning." "You should go back to bed, Mom. You might be able to sleep now." Jenoye said, "That bar work involves very late hours, Viola. Why don't you get a day job in a cafe or a shopping store?" "I'm working in both places just for now, Mom. After I get enough money for my car I'm going to work in the restaurant only." "So! You are buying a car?" said Jenoye. "Yes", said Viola, "but it will have to wait. I need money upfront for the apartment." "What apartment?" asked Jenoye. "Molly and I are moving into an apartment on Monday." "Are you indeed?", said Jenoye, "well, I stand by your decision, Dear." "Gosh! You are very understanding", said Viola, "Molly's parents were pretty upset." "What's the point in getting upset? Isaiah and I predicted you would leave one day soon." "Oh! Why is that then?" Viola asked. "You have my personality, Honey. I moved out of my home when I was two years younger than you are now." "I'm glad that you are okay with it, Mom, thanks! Now, get to your bed", said Viola. "Alright, Darling, see you in the morning." The next day Viola and Molly went over to look at the apartment. Inside the apartment Viola said, "This is so lovely." Molly said, "I told you so! Well? What do you reckon? Do you want to move in?" "Yes, I do! I can't wait", said Viola. "Right", said Molly. "Let's get the deposit money organised. We can have it ready for them tomorrow." The following day the girls paid the deposit and moved into the apartment.

Jean missed Molly so much when she first moved out of the house, but she called round nearly every other day to visit. Viola's parents called round to the apartment, too.

The months passed by. It was after Christmas now, and nineteen year old Molly was behind with her studies. Instead of working two shifts per day, Viola decided just to work in the bar from now on. With the tips she received in the bar at night she was quickly saving the money for her car.

In late February Molly started her midterm exams - which she hadn't studied for - at university. She came into *Cornie's* later that night. Viola was working behind the bar. "What can I get you?" asked an excited Viola. "I'll have a double scotch", said Molly. "What's the occasion?" asked Viola, "and shouldn't you be in bed? You have exams." "Not tomorrow. It's a free day for studying - not that it's gonna make any difference", said Molly. "Why? What's the matter?" asked Viola. "It's too difficult. I'm not able to concentrate - I'd be better off working in the bar." "Don't say that. You will be fine ... maybe you are doing better than you think", said Viola. "No, It's no good. I'm going to leave university", said Molly. "where are Mom and Dad tonight?" "They left earlier. I have to close up later for them. They said they were going out for a meal somewhere." "Shucks! I wanted to see them. I'm going to tell them I'm leaving university. I know they will be mad but I'm not happy so I'm leaving. I want to work in the bar full time again", said Molly. Not long after Molly had spoken these words Michael and Jean come into the bar for a drink. "Look! Molly is here", said Jean, "let's go over and join her." Michael and Jean were already tipsy. "Hi, Darling! What are you doing here?" asked Jean. "Shouldn't you be in bed? You have to get up early for university?" "Tomorrow is a free day for studying. I thought I'd call in for a couple of drinks - it'll help me sleep." "If you are off tomorrow then what the heck. We had a few drinks ourselves earlier", said Michael. "I can see that", laughed Molly. "Look at the pair of you! You are half drunk. "We don't get out much, Honey, we are making the best of it", Michael said. Jean bought Molly a drink. She got a shock, though, when she asked Viola to give Molly the same again. Viola set up a double scotch for Molly at which point Jean's jaw dropped. "You are on doubles, my dear! Are you planning on getting plastered?" "That is the plan, Mom. I'm glad both of you came in - I want to tell you something." "What is it, Honey?" asked Jean. "Now ... don't over react ... I am leaving university." "You are what? Why? What has brought this on?" asked Jean. "I can't focus. I'm not cut out for university, and the course is so hard. I just want to work behind the bar fulltime again." "How long have you felt like this?" asked a stunned Jean. "For quite a while now", said Molly. "This is not good", said Jean. "Listen! If she wants to leave university and come to work fulltime in the bar, then why not?" said Michael. "Maybe she will be better off. After all, it's her decision." "You should give it more thought, Molly - that's all I'm saying", said Jean. "I have, and I'm leaving this week", said Molly "and that's final." "Looks like we will have our full team back", said Michael. "Look on the bright side, Jean. When we retire, at least we can come in here for a drink ... Molly can take over as the manageress." "I suppose", said Jean, as she threw back another shot of bourbon. After work Viola drove Jean and Michael home. "Come in for a coffee, girls", suggested a Jean. "No, I don't want to keep Viola waiting", said Molly. "She has been on her feet all evening, and the bar should have been closed an hour ago. The three of us kept her long enough." "True enough. Get yourselves home safe", said Michael, in a rather slurred voice.

Next morning, Molly woke up with a splitting headache. "My head! It's aching ...what the heck did I drink last night?" "Not just you, your parents were knocking them back too", said Viola. "Do you remember them leaving the bar?" asked Molly. "It was me who took them home", answered Viola. "can you recall what your dad said last night? "No, I can't remember very much." "He was talking about making you manageress of the bar." "Was he indeed? I might take him up on the offer", said Molly. "The bar is losing some of its custom lately", said Viola. "I know, we need to start booking some live bands for the weekends", said Molly. "Why don't you talk to your parents today?" said Viola. "Make sure what they said last night wasn't just the drink talking." "Good idea ... I hope it wasn't the drink talking, too. I'll have a word with them later."

Later that evening Molly called round to her parents' house. While having a cup of tea together Molly said, "Do either of you two remember what you suggested to me last night?" "Vaguely. I think I suggested making you the manageress", said Michael. "Correct. And I think I'll take you up on the offer ... that is, if you haven't changed your mind", said Molly. "No, we haven't changed our minds, have we, Jean?" "No. I think it would be a good move", said Jean, "I'm not totally over the moon with your decision to leave university but if you are coming back to work fulltime in the bar then why not? It could benefit our business." "Things are pretty slack at the moment", said Michael. "Maybe Molly might come up with some fresh ideas for the place." "So? Are you making it official then?" asked Molly. "Am I to become the new manageress?" "I guess so. Jean, what shall we say?" asked Michael. "Go on then", said Jean. "Let's do it. Let's make Molly our new manageress." "Brilliant!" said Molly. "I won't let you down, I promise. I'm gonna come up with some good ideas, starting from tonight."

Molly returned to the flat. "Viola! You are looking at the new manageress of *Sissy's Bar*." "Good for you, Molly! When do you take over?" "Well, I'm off tonight so it'll be tomorrow night. I must come up with some ideas ... have you anything in mind, Viola?" "What about making Monday night a quiz night?" said Viola. "Yes! Sounds good, and I think we should have a discount night for students - the number of students who head over to *Dina's Bar* every Wednesday night is unbelievable because they have a discount on that night. Our bar has a lot more space. I could put up flyers on the university billboard advertising our night." "Would that be a good idea though?" asked Viola, "I mean, if we have our discount night on the same night then there is gonna be a clash." "I see what you mean. What about having our discount night on Tuesdays then?" said Molly. "Yeah, it makes more sense, Molly. What have you planned for the weekends?" "Live bands on a Friday night, the same on a Saturday night, and we can have a free jukebox night on Sundays", said Molly. "You will need to start looking up some numbers of bands", suggested Viola. "Yes I will", said Mollie. "I heard a fantastic band when I went to New York - they were amazing." "What was the name of the band?" asked Viola. "They are called 'Manhattan Sound'. Flipping heck! The lead singer, a girl - her voice is unreal! I remember thinking at the time that I would give anything to be able to sing like her." "How would you get in contact with them though?" asked Viola. "Maybe if I rang up that venue they might know their number. What am I saying? Of course, they will know their number - after all they have to know it, seeing that they booked them." "Go for it", said Viola. "Let's start off with some cheaper bands, though, just in case we are unable to cover ourselves moneywise." "You are right, Viola, we should build it up slowly but surely at first. Flipping heck ... I think you should be the manageress", laughed Molly. "Tell you what ... I'm going to make you my assistant manageress, Viola! You have a good head on your shoulders." "Fine by me, Molly", Viola laughed. "You know the old saying ... two heads are better than one." "Ha ha! Too right, Viola."

Molly and Viola worked together in perfect harmony. They had quizzes every Monday night which draws a big crowd. On Tuesday nights they had a reduction on all drinks; this brought lots of students in, and it brought a lot of locals too. And, as they had planned, they started with lower priced bands on Friday and Saturday nights. Things went like clockwork for weeks and weeks, so much so they had to turn people away at the weekends. Before long, Michael hired some skilled craftsmen to add an extension to the dance area. Two weeks later, the extension was completed. "You know, Molly, I think it's time to hire 'Manhattan Sound.' What do you think?" asked Viola. "Next month maybe ... we are going to have a big turnout this weekend, and for the next few weekends, especially now with our new venue." "Yeah! That's for sure", said Viola. "You have their number now, though, don't you?" "Yes, I have. It's in my diary. Perhaps I'll book them for next month just in case they require plenty of notice. Knowing my luck, they are probably booked up." Molly dialled the number, "Hello, I'm looking to book your band." Molly gave all the details to their manager. "How did it go? asked Viola. "Were we lucky or what?" said Molly. "They are booked up for the entire year." "How were we lucky then?" asked Viola. "They have a cancellation in three weeks time. It is a Saturday night so I booked them for that night. Oh I can't wait to see them again." "Me too! You have told me so much about them, I can't wait", said Viola. "Right! You know this is my night off, Honey. I'll call in later, though, for a drink. I'm going over to Mom now for a gossip. I haven't been over there for a while", said Molly. "Okay, I'll see you later then."

Later on that night Viola and one other bartender were able to cope behind the bar, Wednesday nights being pretty laid back. Just after ten that night, a young man came into the bar. He was on his own. He walked up to the bar and ordered a Bloody Mary. Unbeknown to Viola or the other barmaid, he was the same man who had spoken to Molly when she was in New York City five months earlier. Viola was a gifted spiritual person. It ran in her family; her mother Jenoye was a medium, and Viola must have inherited her gift. Even though the young man has striking good looks and was dressed in fine attire Viola was reluctant to serve him. There was something eerie about him that gave her the shivers. The young man was very politely spoken; nevertheless, he had a cockiness about him. The other barmaid was very impressed with him, and she kept flirting with him. He said to Viola, "No point in talking with you. You're not on our side." "What?" said a very uneasy Viola. "Whose side? What are you on about." "Nothing", said the young man as he walked away from Viola, and he walked over towards the other barmaid with a confident smile on his face and put a piece of paper into the pocket of her blouse. The young man finished his Bloody Mary and before walking away he turned around and said to Viola, "Tell Molly I dropped by." "Who shall I say dropped by?" asked Viola. The young man sniggered and said, "The man she wanted to sleep with in New York." Then he left the bar.

Viola had seen him put something into Vicky's blouse. "What did he put into your pocket", she asked Vicky. Vicky reached in and pulled out a piece of paper from her blouse pocket. She started to read. The note read, "naughty thoughts." "I like that! What the hell is he on about?" said Viola. Vicky froze for about three seconds. All during the time that the young man was in the bar Vicky kept having thoughts about sleeping with him. "What's wrong?" asked Viola. "You look like you have seen a ghost." "It's nothing", said Vicky and she ripped up the note and put it in the bin. While replacing an empty bottle of whiskey with a full bottle, Viola was thinking aloud to herself, "How does he know Molly?" Vicky heard her. "Well, you'll soon find out", she said as Molly and Jean came into the bar. "Why?" asked Viola, but she didn't need an answer as she turned around and saw Jean and Molly.

"It's so great to have the night off", joked Molly. "Stop teasing", said Jean. "What can I get you two ladies?" asked Vicky. The women ordered their drinks. "Not many about tonight", said Jean. "We had quite a few earlier", said Viola. "We are planning on staying on for a while later", said Molly. "You can stay on if you want", said Jean, "I have to be up early. Michael and I are going on a mini-break to Los Angeles." "Good for some", laughed Vicky.

Jean stayed in the bar until just after midnight when an old friend of hers offered to give her a ride home. Nearly everyone was gone by one in the morning. After all the customers had left, Vicky, Molly and Viola sat at the bar talking and drinking. "Anybody interesting in tonight?" asked Molly. Viola and Vicky looked at each other. "You tell us", said Viola. "Tell you what? How would

I know? I came in late", said Molly. "Is there anybody that you wanted to sleep with? ...that you met in New York?" asked Viola. "What?" Molly exclaimed, "What are you on about?" "We had a young man in here tonight. He was fantastically handsome and he said to me before he left, "Tell Molly I said hello." "Who was he? I didn't sleep with anyone in New York!" said Molly. "I didn't say you slept with him. I said you wanted to sleep with him." Molly paused for what seemed like ages and then said, "Flipping heck! What did he look like?" Vicky said, "He had piercing eyes, black hair and he is probably the best looking man I have ever seen." "If you ask me he is a creep", said Viola. "That sounds like the man I met alright", said Molly. "How did you meet him? asked Viola. "He came into the university when I was in New York. Then I saw him again at the concert. Strangely enough, he knew I was from San Francisco ... how did he know I wanted to sleep with him?" asked a confused Molly. "How did he know I wanted to sleep with him?" asked Vicky. "Why? What did he say to you?" asked Molly. "Nothing. He put a note into my pocket, then he left." "A note? What was on the note?" Vicky said, "It read 'naughty thoughts'. I like that! It's as if he could read my mind." "Looks like he read your mind, too, Molly", said Viola. "This is way too creepy", said Molly. "Let's change the subject, but before we do ... did you want to sleep with him, Vicky?" "Yes! At the time I did, but now I hope I never lay eyes on him ever again. Did you want to sleep with him, Molly?" The look that Molly gave Vicky and Viola spoke volumes, then she nodded and said, "Yes." "Right! Subject closed", said Viola.

"Yeah, too right", said Vicky. The girls polished off their last round of drinks. "It's home time", said Viola. "Can I stay with you girls tonight?" asked Vicky, "I don't want to stay in my apartment alone. "Sure you can, Pet", said Viola. "Yes, of course you can", said Molly. "We will have to get a taxi", said Vicky. "Are you mad?" laughed Molly. "It's only a three minute walk." Okay, but I need to hold someone's arm", said Vicky. "Come on, we will both hold your arms", said Viola. After Viola locked up the bar the girls set off on the short walk to the apartment. Inside the apartment Vicky said, "This is so lovely." "Why don't you move in with us?" suggested Molly. "I would love to", said Vicky, as she looked at Viola for inspiration. "That's a good idea", said Viola. "You are paying rent for that apartment on your own. If you move in with us you will be able to save a quite a bit of money. We will find it easier too." "Coffee for everyone?" asked Molly. "Count me in", said Viola. "Me too", said Vicky. While drinking their coffee the subject of the young man came up again. "Who was that creep?" asked Molly. "Not him again", said Viola. "Let's not talk about him. Besides, we will never see him again, I hope." The girls drank the coffee and got ready for bed. "You will have to double up with me, Vicky", said Viola. "We don't have any spare blankets." "That's okay, Viola. I'll promise not to snore", laughed Vicky." The next day Michael and Jean headed off to Los Angeles for a couple of days. Vicky informed her landlord that she was moving out.

A week later, Vicky moved into the flat with Viola and Molly. It was Wednesday night again. The girls worked every other Wednesday, and it was Molly's turn this week. Tony was on duty with Molly behind the bar. "Tonight is busy. This is not your usual Wednesday", said Tony. "Tell me about it!" said Molly. "I wonder what's brought them all out tonight. The place is buzzing." "It's because that bar is closed tonight", said Tony. "What bar is that?" asked Molly. "You know the one that has the price reduction?" "Yes. I do." "Well, there has been a death in the family. They are closed until Friday". "That would explain it then", said Molly, and added, "You know what I'm gonna announce?" "What?" asked Tony. "Just watch this." Molly rang the bell. The crowd all looked up; there was silence. "Alright everybody ... there will be a one-off Wednesday reduction night. I know my usual discount night is Tuesday but I've just heard about the unfortunate incident across the street, so the rest of your orders will be reduced." "Are you crazy? We will be run off our feet", said Tony. "It's only fair", said Molly. "Most of them are students - they were all prepared for a cheap night out, like they usually have on a Wednesday. They will all be heading to the *Scorpio Nightclub* soon anyway." The students were making the most of the cheap drinks on offer, so much so that Tony and Molly were under pressure. Viola and Vicky came in for a drink. They were shell-shocked when they witnessed the crowd. "What's the occasion tonight?" asked Viola. "Don't know", said Vicky. "Am I glad to see you two!" said a very busy Molly. "No need to tell us. We can see for ourselves", said Viola. Vicky and Viola went behind the bar to help out. Michael and Jean came in a short while after. "My goodness! Where did this gang come from?" asked Michael. Molly answered, "The bar across the road is closed. How was your stay in Los Angeles? I haven't laid eyes on either of you since you left. Are you keeping a low profile or what?" "We ended up staying a few more days. We only came back last night", said Jean. "Why not? You are both semi-retired - make the best of it" said Viola. "Thank you, Viola. I think you are right", laughed Michael. "I hear you have a big band coming soon", said Jean. "Yes! Not long now", said Molly. Michael and Jean only stayed for one drink as they were both very tired.

Around ten o'clock, a dark haired man came into the bar. He walked up to the counter and ordered a Bloody Mary from Tony. The girls behind the bar didn't notice him come in. Tony, who happened to be gay, was attracted to the man as soon as he laid eyes on him. About six or seven minutes passed before Vicky noticed him. "Look who I see", she said as she pointed in his direction. "Oh my word! It's that creep", said Viola. Molly was at the far end of the bar serving other customers. Viola went over to her. "You will never believe who is in the bar." "Who?" asked Molly. "Take a look over in the direction of that girl who is wearing the red dress and see if you can recognise anyone." "Blimey! Flipping heck, that's him. That's the man I met in New York! What is he doing here?" said a stunned Molly. "Maybe we will find out", said Viola. "He is talking with Tony, and by the looks of things, Tony is flirting with him." Before long, the crowd started to thin out. The students had left to move on to the *Scorpio Nightclub*. Only a handful of customers remained. With the bar now under control, Vicky and Viola sat on the other side. Vicky joked, "Well! That was a great night out - we both ended up working!" "I know", said Viola. "Ah well, at least we saved money, and earned at the same time."

The young man said to Tony, "Give those two girls who were working behind the bar a drink. I'm buying." Tony set up the drinks. "Where did these come from?" asked Viola. Tony pointed to the dark haired hunk, "That man bought them." Viola held up her drink and acknowledged him and said "Thanks." After all the customers had left the bar the young man was the only customer left. "It was last orders ten minutes ago", said Molly. "Alright. I can take a hint." He came over to Molly. The man put his hand out, "Long time no see, Molly." "Sorry? Do I know you?" asked Molly. "We met in New York ... don't you remember?" he asked. Although Molly had recognised him at first glance she played dumb. "No. I can't say I do." The young man gave her a cocky smile, "Never mind. It doesn't matter." "We are closing soon, Sir", said Molly. "Don't worry. I won't keep you", he said. "I just called in to see your premises." "And why is that?" asked Molly. "I believe you booked my band", he said. "*Manhattan Sound?*" "Crikey! Your band?" said Molly. "Yes. I'm their manager", he said. Molly didn't know where to look or what to say. "Forgive my manners. Yes, they will be here Saturday week, if all goes to plan", she said. "I'll make sure of that. You can count on it. Anyway it was nice meeting you again", said the man, with that same cocky smile on his face. Molly was now feeling a bit guilty. "By any chance, did I meet you in the university in New York?" she asked. The man, knowing well that Molly knew, just said, "Yeah, that's me. Thanks for your service - I'll leave you all to it", and left.

When he had gone Viola asked Molly, "What were you two talking about?" "Don't ask! Do you know who he is?" "No, but we know he is a creep", said Viola. "I'll second that", said Vicky. "Why? What's wrong with him?" asked Tony. "Never mind that! Who is he, Molly?" asked Viola. "He is none other than the manager of *Manhattan Sound*", said Molly. "You've got to be kidding", said Vicky. "No. He knew I'd booked them", said Molly. "He is probably bluffing", said Viola. "After all, there are flyers up in most windows advertising the band. He is full of crap." Just then Tony butted in. "No! He might not be bluffing. Take a look at this." Tony took out a little business card. "What's on the card?" asked Molly. "I haven't looked at it yet", said Tony. "Read what it says", said Viola. "Okay, I will … It says 'Manhattan Sound … New York City'." "Let me see that", said Molly, "Flipping heck! It does too." "What's his name?" asked Vicky. "It doesn't say … oh … hold on … there is something written on the back. It just reads 'Nick' and their phone number." "Well, now we know his name", said Vicky. "It would appear he isn't bluffing after all." "Why are you three so uneasy talking about that man?" asked Tony. Molly looked at Tony and asked him, "Did he put anything else in your pocket?" Tony blushed so that his face resembled a ripe tomato. "Why? What do you mean?" Vicky said, "No little notes? … 'naughty thoughts'?" Tony's face changed from bright red to pale white as he reached into his shirt pocket and produced a note. The note read … 'naughty thoughts.' "Are you psychic, Vicky?" he asked. "How did you know I had a note in my pocket?" Before Vicky could answer an embarrassed Tony said, "I'm going home. Goodnight." It only took one minute before Tony doubled back. The door sounded … "rap rap rap." "Who the hell is that?" said Molly. "It's nearly three in the morning." Vicky slid the blinds up and peeped out the window, "It's Tony. He must have forgotten something." "Let him in", said Viola. Tony came in. "Right! How did you know about that note, Vicky?" "It was just a guess, Tony", said Vicky. "Don't let it bother you. It's just some prank - he did the same with me one night." Tony felt a bit better on hearing that. "Okay. That's fine. I'm off this time officially", he said, with a forced smile on his face. "Wait up! We can all leave together", said Molly.

The time had passed. It was now that Saturday. The band *Manhattan Sound* would be performing later in the dance hall area of *Sissy's Bar*. All the bar staff were informed that they would be on duty. At nine that night the people started to flow into the bar. The place was filling up rapidly. "Holy moly! Tonight is gonna be mad", said Viola. The band arrived at 9:35 in their big black truck. Two roadies brought in all the equipment through the side doors of the dance hall. The band members came into the bar for a quick drink; they were due on stage at10:30. Nick came up to the bar with all the band members to order a round of drinks. Molly came over to serve them. "Welcome to *Sissy's Bar*", she said. "What can I get you?" "I'll have the usual", said Nick. The band members said, "We will have the same." "Okay, Bloody Mary's all round. Don't go getting drunk on me now", joked Molly. "I don't want you falling off the stage." "Don't worry. We are just having one each", said Nick. "Maybe we can have a few later, if that's possible - after they do the gig of course." "We will see how we cope", said Molly. "I will be trying to get them out before 1:00am if I can. The staff and I will have a drink with you then." "That'll do", said Nick. The band brought their drinks next door to the dance area. The two roadies had nearly everything in place. Michael and Jean came in at ten and squeezed their way up to the counter. "Heavens almighty! The place is packed", said Jean. "Yes! I know, Mom. We'll be heading in next door soon to open the other bar", said Molly. "Who is gonna look after this bar?" asked Michael. "Well, nearly all the crowd will be making their way into the other bar soon. There will only be a few locals left in here to tend", said Molly. "Sonia can look after things here."

Molly rang the bell. "The bar next door will be open in ten minutes", she announced, "and the band will be starting up soon." A short while later the crowd made their way next door to the dance area where the bar staff were already behind the long bar. Sonia stayed in the smaller bar to serve some locals. Only a dozen elderly people remained in *Sissy's* with Sonia, among them Michael and Jean. After eleven the dance area was packed to capacity, and the bar staff were working flat out. "This is crazy", said Vicky, but at the same time they were all enjoying themselves; the music was fantastic. Tony said to Molly, "Looks like you know your bands. They are amazing. That girl's voice is out of this world." "I told you so", said Molly. "Flipping heck, I wish I could sing like her." Like all the bar staff Viola was very busy; the only difference was she wasn't enjoying herself. She was feeling bad vibes emanating from the band. They made her feel uneasy.

Next door in *Sissy's* Sonia was having an easy shift. Seven people left to go home, and only five remained - well up until midnight that was. Viola's parents came in to see and hear for themselves the band that everybody were talking about. Michael and Jean were still present. Jenoye said to her husband, "I wonder are there many next door? "I'll take a peep in", said Isaiah. "It is packed", he said. Jenoye took a peep for herself. When she looked inside she could see the massive crowd. She looked up to the stage at the band; her hair stood up on her neck when her eyes made contact with the lead singer. The lead singer's eyes were lit up in a glowing red. Jenoye backed out as quickly as she could, "Drink up, Isaiah. We are leaving." "Why? What's up? You have a full drink here. You haven't even touched it." Jenoye whispered to Isaiah, "That girl singing in there is evil. Her eyes lit up in a glowing red." "You imagined it. It's probably the lighting. I saw their lights - there were red, green, and blue lights flashing everywhere in there. Sit down and relax ... 'evil girl'," laughed Isaiah. "Maybe you're right", said Jenoye, "I just didn't feel good in there. That girl gives me bad vibes."

Michael and Jean decided to stick around as they wanted to make sure that there wouldn't be any trouble next door. On the contrary, the crowd were amazed by the band, and were all out dancing to the sounds of the 50s. At 12:57am the lead singer announced the last song. After they'd performed the song the crowd yelled out "more, more, more." The band rocked out two more songs. At 1:13am they finished up. It was after two in the morning before the last stragglers finally left the big bar.

Molly and the other bar staff came into the smaller bar by which time the roadies had all their stuff packed into the truck. The band had been instructed to give four sharp raps on the window, and that is what Nick did. Vicky opened the door and let them in. Sonia was asked to stay on and serve. Tony sat on the high stool, "My feet are killing me", he said. "Mine too", said Viola. "It must have been really busy in there", said Sonia. "Too right it was", said Molly. The band sat over at a table, drinking together, along with the two roadies. "What time did Mom and Dad go home?" asked Molly. Sonia answered, "They left about one thirty. Your mom and dad were here, too, Viola." "Were they? I never noticed them." "They only had two drinks each and then left." Sonia kept the drinks coming. Before long, the band members and the two roadies came up to join Vicky, Tony, Viola and Molly. The other three members of staff had left to go home after finishing up in the big bar.

It was now after 4am and everybody was getting drunk. Molly was humming one of the songs that the band had performed earlier. Tony was over flirting with Nick. Viola sat at the end of the bar talking with Sonia. She wanted nothing to do with them; they gave her the creeps. Nick kept looking at Viola. For some reason he knew she was spiritual, and this disturbed him a lot. Molly got to talking with the lead singer, "You are so brilliant! You have the most amazing voice." "Well, thank you." "Don't thank her. Thank me", said Nick, with a strange grin on his face. "What does he mean?" asked Molly. "Nothing. Don't mind him", said the girl. "What's your name?" asked Molly. "My name is Lucy Firr." "Well, Lucy, you were gifted with a great voice", said Molly. "Maybe you were too, Molly", said Nick. "Oh, I doubt that" said Molly, "I'd give anything to be able to sing like Lucy. "Anything?" Nick and Lucy looked at each other simultaneously and smiled.

Lucy asked Molly, "Would you give your house?" "Yes, I would - and even the bar, but I don't own any of them." Viola was listening attentively to them talking. "So what do you own that you would give?" asked Lucy. "Shoes, money - not much money though - clothes .. anything really", Molly laughed.

Tony and Vicky were becoming very drunk. Viola had only had a few drinks. "I think we should all go home", she said. "I think you are right", said Tony. "I'm hammered." "Me too", said Vicky. "Let's go home." Viola asked Molly, "Are you coming, Molly? It's nearly five in the morning. Sonia has been behind the bar now for 14 hours - she must want to go home too." Molly muttered, "You can go. I'm staying here." "Very well, we are leaving," said Viola. "Can I go, too?" asked Sonia. "Yes! I'll be okay", said Molly. So Viola, Sonia, Tony and Vicky left the bar. Sonia held Tony up on the way home; likewise, Viola supported Vicky. "Listen. Our apartment is close by", said Viola. "Everybody can crash there until the morning." "That's good thinking", said Sonia. Meanwhile, in *Sissy's*, Molly went behind the bar and put up a round of drinks on the house. When they had all been served Lucy said to Molly, "Now Molly ... where were we? You were saying you would give your shoes, house, money and the bar to have a voice like mine." Nick joked, "Molly doesn't own the bar or the house - that's no good." "Yes! That's no good", said Lucy with a smirk on her face. "Well, all I have are the shoes and clothes then", said Molly. "What more could I give?" Nick said, "If you wanted to have a voice like Lucy you'd need to give your soul ... isn't that right, Lucy?" "Yes", said Lucy. "That's what I made Lucy do", said Nick. Molly said, "What do you mean?" "I made her give me her soul", said Nick, as he produced a piece of paper from his pocket, "All you have to do, Molly, is sign here on the dotted line, and I can do the same for you."

Over in the apartment, Viola and Sonia helped each other to put Tony and Vicky to bed. Then Viola said, "I'm heading back over to the bar, Sonia. I'm worried about Molly." "I'll come with you", said Sonia. "Those two are fast asleep now so let's go", said Sonia, "I've got the spare key for the bar."

Over at *Sissy's* Molly was trying to read the sheet of paper that Nick had taken out of his pocket. It had something to do with a seven year contract and something to do with a soul. Even though Molly was plastered she was kinda freaked out. "What does this mean about seven years fame and fortune? And all you have to do is sell your soul?" she asked. "It's simple, Molly. All you have to do is sign right here. You will have seven years of fortune and a voice that will even be better than Lucy's." "A voice better than Lucy?" laughed Molly. "You must be kidding ... give me a pen quick." Nick became very serious, "No! I'm not kidding. If you sign here, Molly, you will have it all. You will have more money than you could ever imagine." Molly realised that Nick was becoming irate. She became a little anxious. "What happens after seven years?" she asked. "Ask Lucy - her seven years are up soon. Isn't that right, Lucy?" said Nick. Molly looked at Lucy and asked, "Is that right, Lucy?" "Yes. But it won't be a problem. He is a real softy - he will give me another seven, won't you, Nick?" "She knows me too well", said Nick, laughing. "Now, hurry up and sign, Molly. We have to get going."

Molly was feeling pressurised. She didn't even have a clue what she was being asked to sign, but she signed it. Just as she was finishing the last stroke of her name the bar door opened and Viola and Sonia walked in. Viola shouted, "Oh, my goodness, Molly." She ran over to the counter. Molly was barely balancing on the stool with her head on the counter. She appeared to be in a state of hypnosis. None of the band members or the roadies were present. Also, the black truck was gone from outside the premises. It's was if everyone had just vanished into thin air. "Quick! Help me, Sonia." Viola and Sonia helped Molly over to a chair.

Less than ten minutes later Molly's eyes opened. "Are you alright, Molly? What happened", asked Sonia. Viola was in a state of shock as if she knew something strange had taken place. At 5:53am there was a heavy knock at the door. Sonia went over and looked out the window. "It's your mom, Viola", she said. Viola opened the door. Her mom was in hysterics. "What happened here?" asked Jenoye. "Why? What's wrong, Mom?" asked Viola. "Just after 5:00am I woke up in a cold sweat from what seemed to be a weird dream but it felt so real." "What was the dream about?" asked Viola. Jenoye, who was still shaking, said, "I could see a strange demon in the bar. He was negotiating with Molly. He had a paper in his hands, and he was making Molly sign it." "It was just a bad dream", said Sonia, "there is nobody here except Molly." "I'm not so sure", said Viola. "Are you okay, Molly? What happened here?" "Somebody get me a glass of water", said Molly. Sonia brought over a glass of water. Molly had a few sips and said, "I was talking with the band ...then that guy Nick asked me to sign something." "I knew it", said Jenoye, knowingly. "Sign what?" asked Viola. "That's where my mind goes blank", said Molly. "What are you all talking about?" shouted Sonia, "you are freaking me out." "When did the band leave?" asked Viola. "I can't remember", said Molly, "I just remember signing some sheet of paper and the next thing I know, you two are standing in front of me." "Come on, Viola, I'll take you all home", said Jenoye. Everybody got into Jenoye's car. She dropped them off at the apartment. Jenoye helped the girls with Molly who was still in a daze. It wasn't the drink that she had consumed that was making her feel so out of it; it was something more serious. "We need to talk later on, Viola", said Jenoye. "Fine, Mom. I'll come over later after dinner", said Viola. Jenoye got into her car and drove off. On the way home as she was passing by the bar she looked over. She could see a big Rottweiler sitting on the doorstep of *Sissy's Bar*. She jerked the car into a higher gear and sped off as fast as she could.

Isaiah heard the car pull up and he came downstairs. Jenoye came into her home looking stunned. "Where were you?" Isaiah asked. "And what is going on? You look like you've seen a ghost." "Maybe I have seen worse", said Jenoye. "Why? What's going on?" asked Isaiah. "Something terrible has taken place over at that bar last night." "What happened? And where are you coming from?" "I'm coming from Viola's apartment. I woke up earlier in a state." Jenoye told Isaiah all about the dream. Isaiah knew his wife had a gift; he knew she was a powerful medium so he listened to her and believed her. "Viola is coming over for dinner later. I'm gonna talk to her about leaving that bar", said Jenoye. "It's an evil place", and she broke down in tears. Isaiah consoled her, "Come to bed, Honey. I'll bring you up breakfast in an hour or so."

Over at the apartment everybody was fast asleep. At dinner time Viola got up, got dressed, and made her way over to her parents. Viola had the gift of spirituality too. When she came inside she said, "Before you say anything, Mom, I know what you are about to ask me, and don't worry - I'm leaving that bar." "Good, Honey! I think something very bad happened there last night with Molly", said Jenoye. "Me too, Mom. I got a real evil feeling when I went back to check on Molly earlier this morning." "You get out of there as quickly as you can, Viola", said Jenoye. "I will, Mom, just as soon as I work my notice. I have to open up now soon - Molly is in no state to work today. I'll be off at seven tonight, and Vicky and Tony are working later. I'll give in my notice today." "You can find work somewhere nice, Viola. Bar work isn't good", said Jenoye." "I will, Mom, I promise. I must go now. Michael and Jean will be wondering what's going on ... why the bar isn't open." "Okay, Honey, I'll see you later."

When Viola reached *Sissy's* it was already open. Viola went in and saw that Michael was behind the bar. "Sorry I'm late", she said. "This is your day off", said Michael. "Where is Molly?" "She is sick so I'm covering for her. I had to call over to Mom's first as she wanted to see me." "Well, you are here now. That's the main thing. I have to go next door to *Cornie's*. There are quite a few people in for Sunday lunch." A couple of hours later, Molly rose from her deep sleep. Sonia and Tony had already gone. "How are you feeling, Molly?" asked Vicky. "My head aches so much", said Molly. "What time is it?" "It's nearly three o'clock", said Vicky. Molly gasped, "Flipping heck, I'm meant to be working! Where is Viola?" Vicky said, "She went over to open the bar." "Tony and I are working at seven. I'd better get over there", said Molly. "I'll make you a quick cup of coffee", said Vicky. "No, it's okay, Vicky. I'll get one over at the bar."

When Molly came into *Sissy's* after three there were only six customers in the bar. "I'm so sorry, Viola", she said. "I slept in." "It's fine, Molly", Viola said, "It is quiet in here. I think I'll just finish the shift now seeing that I'm here anyway if that's alright with you, Molly." "Yes! I won't argue with you on that", said Molly, as she perched on a bar stool. "Could you please get me a coffee, Viola." Viola brought Molly over a coffee, and asked her, "Do you remember what happened here last night, Molly." "Up until about five in the morning or so - after that, I can't remember a thing", said Molly. "Something bad happened here last night, Molly. I'm not sure what, but I can't work here any more. That's why I'm informing you that as from today I'm working two more weeks, and then I'm finishing up", said Viola. "Aw, Viola! Why? You are my best worker." "Something strange took place here last night. You must try to remember, Molly - it could be serious." "I'm trying to, believe me", said Molly.

While Molly was drinking her coffee she began to experience flashbacks. Viola was at the far end of the bar serving some customers. Just when she had finished putting their drinks up the phone rang. Viola went over and picked up the phone. A man spoke to her. Viola slammed the phone down. Molly - who was still experiencing flashbacks - noticed this and asked, "What was that about? You seem upset." "Some weirdo", said Viola. "Why? What did he say?" asked Molly. He said ... "Now she remembers", said Viola. As soon as Viola said that Molly dropped her coffee on the counter and she fainted. Two men hopped of their seats and helped Molly up. When she came round Molly said to Viola, "I must go. I'll be back later." Viola was feeling freaked out. Molly thanked the two men, and left the bar.

On the way home Molly walked straight into the arms of a man. It was Nick. Molly was completely shocked. "What do you want? Get away from me", she said. "Don't be like that! You and I have a bond now", said Nick. "You and me have nothing", said Molly. "Get away from me, or I'll call the police." "Now, now! Calm down." "I gotta go, I'll be in contact", said Molly. "Okay Honey, God bless you." Molly turned around with a tear in her eye, said "Thanks" and left.

Tony and Vicky arrived just before seven to relieve Viola. "Where is Molly?" asked Vicky. "She will be gone for a few days. She is going to do a bar management course. She had an unopened letter which she only read today, and she had to get a move on." "Surely it's not today", said Tony. "No! Not today but she did have to get a move on. I think she has a long trip ahead of her." "Where is the course?" asked Vicky. Viola answered, "She didn't say. She was in a real hurry. Look, Molly left me in charge for a while. I'll come back in later for a drink. I'll bring in timesheets with me, and work out your shifts, and my own. Right, I'll see you both later". Viola called in next door to *Cornie's* and told Michael and Jean the same cock-and-bull story - about Molly heading off to do a course in bar management somewhere.

CHAPTER FIVE

HEN MOLLY ARRIVED FOR HER rehearsal she was shaking like a leaf.
Nick met her and greeted her with an outstretched hand, "Welcome, Molly!"
A short time later the rest of the band turned up. "What exactly will I be singing?"
asked Molly, "I only know a few songs, and I can't sing." "How do you know you can't sing?" asked
Nick, "I mean ... where did you ever sing? And to whom?" "I sing all the time in the shower, and I
sing around the apartment all the time, but never in a band." "Did you ever get any complaints from
anyone about your singing?" asked Nick. Molly thought hard, then she said, "No!" "There you go
then", said Nick. "You'll be perfect." Nick turned around to the band, "Won't she, guys? "Yes! She
will be great", said all the band members, at almost the same time.

The band started up. They gave Molly a few song sheets. Molly listened to them for an hour
or so while simultaneously reading the words of the songs that they were performing. Nick said
to Molly, "Are you ready to give it a go, Molly?" "Flipping heck! I don't know ... I'm only familiar
with three of the songs." Let's do those three songs then", Nick said to the band. Molly went up
on the stage as the band started up. They played the first of the three songs that she knew. Molly
sang along as Nick sat watching and listening. She sang the next two songs with the band. After
singing the three songs that she knew, the band stopped for a break. Nick said to Molly, "Come
here and sit down beside me. How do you think you did?" "Probably terrible", said Molly. Nick
had a surprise in store for Molly; all the while that she was on stage he had been recording her
voice. "Listen to this", said Nick. He played back the songs that Molly had just sung on a little black
cassette recorder. Molly's voice was fantastic - so much so that Molly exclaimed, "Flipping heck! I
wish I could sing like that". Nick and the band members erupted into a frenzy of laughing. "What
are you laughing at?" asked Molly. "That's your voice, Molly - that's why we are laughing", said Nick.
"Are you serious? No way, it can't be", said Molly. "Well it is. Are you impressed with yourself?"
asked Nick, "the realism of the whole thing." Molly was very impressed.

"Yes! I am shocked! I never knew I could sing. Well, I knew I could sing, but not like that", said
Molly. "That'll do for today, guys", said Nick. "We can resume tomorrow."

The band left their equipment behind them and left. Molly was left alone with Nick. She was
pretending not to be afraid but inside she was petrified. "So, Molly, did you enjoy that experience?"

asked Nick. Now it's worth mentioning here: demons can't read a person's mind. However, they can guess what you are thinking. Not even Satan can read a person's mind; he too can only guess.

"Yes! I loved it", said Molly, even though she hadn't; she was frightened to bits. "I can't believe it", she said, "I can actually sing." "You see! I knew you had it in you", said Nick, "are you all set for tomorrow?" "Yes! I can't wait", said Molly. "Right! I'll see you tomorrow night at eight", said Nick, "don't be late." Before she could say, "Okay, I won't be late", Nick had already disappeared. This really freaked Molly out. She sat on a seat and wept. Then she picked herself up and left the creepy venue. The next evening Molly thought about not turning up. However, she gathered up courage and arrived at the venue at 7:55pm. Nick was already there. He had a big confident smile on his face. "Now, Molly, tonight we are going to do two hours of songs. We need to have them all ready for performing next week at a concert in New York City", he said. "Next week! Flipping heck, how am I going to manage that?" asked Molly. "Maybe you will do better than you think", laughed Nick. The band members came in right on the stroke of eight. They had everything already set up and were ready for action. "We will start with the three songs you already know", said Nick, "and we can try some more then. Is that alright with you, guys?" "Fine by us, Nick", said a few of the boys. Molly went up to the microphone and started to sing. She sang the three songs that she knew, then - as if by pure magic - she kept on singing new songs, one after another, as the musicians played them. After an hour on stage the band stopped to take a break. Molly came down to have a drink of water. Nick said, "That was fabulous. you might be my best singer ever." Molly felt very confused. She knew all the songs that the band were playing ...and yet... she hadn't learned them. "How did I know those songs?" she asked Nick. "Maybe you did know them", said Nick, with a strange looking grin on his face. Molly was thinking to herself, "No! I don't know them and I never knew them, you prat." "What are you thinking?" asked Nick. Molly was surprised with that comment; she had a feeling that Nick could read one's mind, but she didn't reveal her thought. "Oh! I was just thinking ... maybe I did know them after all", said Molly, hiding the truth behind her smile. "There you go! Right, folks, back on stage", said Nick. The band played for another hour. This second hour was passed with brand new songs. Molly, strangely enough, knew them all. At this point, she was feeling scared. She was singing songs, word for word, that she'd never heard before - and had certainly never sung before. She didn't even question herself. She knew Nick had something to do with it.

Nick said, "Right, tomorrow night we will do a full length concert for our rehearsal after which we will be prepared for New York City." "What night are we doing the concert?" asked Molly. "In two nights time", said Nick. Molly bent down to tie an undone shoelace. She was just about to say, "But that's impossible!" but by the time she had her shoelace tied everybody had gone. She was thinking, "It took me three days to travel to New York City. What's he on about? How can we get there in one day by truck?" Once again, Molly was left speechless. She hadn't see one person leave the rehearsal. It was as if they had all vanished into thin air. Things were very strange. Molly began to fear the worst.

Unbeknownst to Molly's parents, the venue where the rehearsals were taking place was just a ten minute walk away from the bar. Molly went over to *Sissy's Bar* where Viola and Tony were on duty. When she came in Tony was excited to see her. "How did your bar management course go?"

he asked. "It went well", said Molly, "thing is ... I have to go away again shortly for a week or so." Just then a customer came up to the counter and Tony went over to serve him.

Viola asked Molly, "Are you okay, Molly? Where were you?" Molly said, "I can't say much right now. You never know who might be listening. Listen carefully to me, Viola. I have to do a concert in New York City in two nights time." "What? How? I mean, how can you do a concert, and in New York, in two nights time ... how?" asked a very confused Viola, "you can't even sing." Molly tried a little humour by saying, "Thanks for reminding me", and managed a hint of a laugh. "Sorry if I'm insulting you, but I hear you singing when you are having a shower - you are brutal ... no offence." "None taken. I don't know how he did it, but I can sing. I heard myself on tape - I'm better than Lucy ever was", said Molly, "and I don't like it. I'm scared."

"You can sing better than Lucy? Molly! Something has happened to you, and I'm afraid it isn't good", said Viola. "I'm petrified, Viola." "Can you remember anything about that night - or should I say morning - at all?" asked Viola. "I'm experiencing flashbacks ... I remember him making me sign a sheet ... it had something to do with a soul on it ... Lucy was talking me into it as well ... I was really drunk." "He can't do that!" said Viola. "I'm pretty sure he can't. My mom is very spiritual. She would know more about it than me." "God! I hope you are right, Viola." "I'm convinced. He can't make you sign away your soul, without your proper consent! You were drunk." "What am I going to do, Viola? I hope I'm not doomed." "Mom is coming over here in an hour or so. If we can get the bar emptied by midnight or shortly after, we can sit and talk with her. I'm sure she will be able to help you", said Viola. Molly said, "I'll be forever grateful to her if she can help me ... I'll be back in an hour, Viola. I'm going over to the apartment for a shower. I feel really dirty." "That's fine, Molly, I'll see you then - and remember ... Mum will help you." Molly nodded her head and left, unconvinced.

On the way over to the apartment Molly was crying. She started to pray. As she was praying, four men walked around the corner. Molly walked right into them. "Hey! Look who it is", said one of the men, "Aha! It's our singer." The four men were from the band. They were on their way for a drink. "Where are you going, Molly?" one of them asked. "I'm going for a shower." "Well! When you have had your shower come over to the bar and join us for a drink." "Oh! I'm not sure", said Molly, "I'm very tired." Just then Nick came around the corner. He said, "It's not a request, Molly. It's an order." Molly had already intended coming to the bar; now she was dreading it. She couldn't believe her bad luck - the band members were going to the bar as well. She wanted time alone with Jenoye and Viola - now her plans were ruined.

As soon as the men were out of sight Molly made a quick dash to a phone box and rang the bar. "Hello", answered Viola. "It's Molly! Viola, the band members are on their way to the bar for a drink! Nick is with them." While Viola was on the phone Nick and the four men walked through the door. Sonia had just finished her shift in *Cornie's* and was now behind the bar. "Are you okay?" whispered Viola to Molly. "They are already there, aren't they?" asked Molly. "Yes!" said Viola. "Don't mention anything to them. As far as they know, nobody apart from myself, knows anything about what happened to me. As far as they are concerned none of my friends knows", said Molly. Viola whispered, "That Nick creep will know! I think he is the devil." "No, no! He can't read your thoughts", said Molly. "Are you sure?" asked Viola. All the time Viola was on the phone Nick kept staring at her. He was wondering to himself, "Who is Viola talking with?" He guessed it was Molly. "Yes!" Molly said, "I'm sure, Viola, trust me. Right! I'd better go." Thinking quickly, Viola said, "Okay, Michael, I'll see you later", and hung up.

Meanwhile, Sonia had all the drinks set up for Nick and the men. Viola came over to talk with them. "How are you all getting on?" she asked, while at the same time she felt like hitting Nick a slap on the face, "I see you are all on the Bloody Marys again." "Why not?" said Nick. "It beats boring coffee any day." "Yeah! I guess you are right ... less of a headache, though, with the coffee, said Viola as she tried her best to act in a lighthearted manner. Viola walked away from them, went over to Sonia and said, "I'll be back in twenty minutes. It's not very busy - you'll be okay until I get back." "No problem", said Sonia, "I'll be alright - unless a bus load stops off."

Viola left the bar through the back door. As soon as she went outside, she sprinted over to the apartment. Viola came into the apartment out of breath. "What are those creeps doing in the bar?" she asked. "Don't ask me", said Molly. "I bumped into them on my way over here." "What were you saying about Nick not being able to read your mind?" asked Viola. "I was thinking about something to myself in his presence and he then asked me what I was thinking about", said Molly. "Maybe we can use this to our advantage", said Viola. "What do you mean?" asked Molly. "I'm not sure yet", Viola said. "I'll think of something. Right, I'd better get back. They'll suspect something if I'm gone too long." "I'll see you over there in half an hour", said Molly. "Remember, mum's the word. Pretend you know nothing." "I won't say a thing", said Viola, and she sprinted back to the bar. She came in through the back door again and went in behind the counter.

Molly came into the bar twenty minutes later. "Ahh! There she is", shouted Nick. "Come over and join us." "I'll be over in a bit", said Molly. "Right, Viola", she said. "I'll be heading off to New York after tomorrow night's rehearsal. Heaven knows when I'll get back. I need you to look after the bar again." "You have another rehearsal first before you go to New York, and then you have a gig the following night! How on earth will you get there in time?" asked Viola. "I haven't a clue", said Molly. Viola said, "Mom will be coming in here shortly. I just hope now that she stays. When she sees those men, she might freak out and leave." "Try and keep her here so I can talk with her", said Molly. "I'll do my best", said Viola. "I'd best get over to them now, Viola", Molly said. "I'll come over and talk with you again shortly."

Molly joined Nick and the band members. About ten minutes later Jenoye and Isaiah came in for a drink. It didn't take too long before Jenoye noticed the strange men. She saw that Molly was with them, and she didn't like the look of them. "Who are those men with Molly?" asked Jenoye. "Is that one of the men who made her sign that paper?" "I'm afraid so", said Viola. Nick was looking over at Jenoye; he didn't like the vibe emanating from her - he sensed she was spiritual. Likewise, Jenoye sensed the evil from the five men. "If you ask me, Viola, I would guess that the most handsome man is an evil spirit", she said. "That's Nick - he is the manager of the band." "Thought as much. He looks cunning", said Jenoye. "Be careful about what you are saying", said Isaiah. "They will hear you." "Has Molly remembered anything about that night yet, Viola?" asked Jenoye. "Yes! I can't say much about it now, though. I don't want them to hear us", said Viola. Jenoye said, "That's good. I'll try and have a word with her later", and continued, "All of those men are evil. We need to get Molly over here to join us."

"That might not be easy, Mom", said Viola. The men were drinking heavily. They were joking and laughing loudly. Molly looked lost amongst them. *Cornie's Restaurant* had just closed for the night. Michael and Jean came into the bar for a nightcap. "Who is Molly with?" asked Jean. "That's the band that played here, isn't it?" said Michael. "Is it? asked Jean. "Yes it is", said Viola. "Why is Molly over talking with them?" asked Jean. "Maybe she is arranging another gig with them", said Michael, "after all, they packed the dance area when they played here." "I don't see the girl with them", said Jean, "wasn't the lead singer a girl?" "Maybe she wanted an early night", said Michael. While Michael and Jean were talking Jenoye tried her best to keep tight-lipped. Nearly an hour later Jean said, "I'm going over to ask Molly to join us - she has been over there with those men long enough."

As it happened, Nick and the band members were getting bored in the bar; it was too quiet. They had asked Molly if she knew any good nightclubs, and she had told them about *The Vixen*. They got up to leave and invited Molly to come with them. Jean came over to the table just in time. Molly was looking for an excuse to get out of going to the nightclub with the men. Molly got up off her seat, and went into acting mode. "Oh Mom! I forgot I was to join you and Dad for a drink", she said as she winked to her mother. "I lost track of time." Molly turned around to Nick. "This is my mom", she said. "Pleased to meet you", said Nick. "Nice to meet you, too, Sir", said Jean. "Look! I have to join Mom and Dad for a drink. I promised them earlier, Nick", said Molly. Nick tried his best to be pleasant, "That's fine! We might call in for a drink later, if you are still here." "I'd doubt that very much", said Jean. "No, no! It's fine. I have to arrange things with the band later, Mum. They can call back for one drink. I have to go away for a few days so I'll do a bit of stocktaking tonight, as I won't get a chance otherwise", said Molly. "Stocktaking tonight? And where are you going?" Molly gave her mom a look; it was a look that meant, "Shut up." "I'll tell you about it over a drink", she said, and then, "Enjoy your night, guys. Call in later if you want." "We will", said Nick, and they left. Nick had a horrible look of disappointment on his face.

When they left Jean said to Molly, "What the hell is going on? Why are you winking and nodding to me?" "You wouldn't understand, Mom", said Molly, "I don't even understand myself." "Why would you do stocktaking in the small hours of the morning?" asked Jean, "and why are you letting those men come back in for a late drink?" Molly tried a white lie: "I'm trying to negotiate a cheaper price with them. I'm booking them to play here again in a fortnight or so. "How come you didn't book them while they were in here drinking tonight?" "Maybe they will sign me a better deal when they are drunk", said Molly. They are good at that, she thought. "You watch out for those boys - I don't like the idea of five men coming back here for drinks, especially when they will be landing back here drunk", said Jean. "It'll be alright, Mom. They are no problem." "I hope so. Now come up and join me and your father for a drink", said Jean.

Molly joined her mom and dad at the bar. Over at *The Vixen* the boys were enjoying themselves. Well, most of them were. Nick was feeling angry towards Molly for not coming to the nightclub with them. He felt betrayed and Nick didn't like anyone betraying him. Back at *Sissy's Bar* Jean and Michael decided to call it a night and went home. Isaiah said to his wife, Jenoye, "I think we should go home, too, Honey. It's getting late." "You go on ahead, Dear. I want to talk with Molly when all the customers have left", said Jenoye. Just before 1:30am, the final customers left the bar. Only

Viola, Jenoye and Molly remained. "We need to talk quickly, Jenoye. Those creeps will soon be back here", said Molly. "Where are they now?" asked Viola. "They went to *The Vixen*", said Molly. "You mean to tell me they are coming back here again? What on earth for?" asked Jenoye. "They wanted me to go to the nightclub with them. When I pretended that I had promised to meet Mum and Dad for a drink they went on without me. However, I knew Nick was angry so I invited them back for a drink after the club closes ", said Molly. "We need to act fast", said Jenoye, "now, Molly, what do you remember about that night?" "When everybody left the bar that night", said Molly, "I was left alone with all the band members. I was complimenting Lucy's voice." "Then what happened?" asked Jenoye. "Lucy or Nick heard me say I'd give anything to be able to sing like Lucy." "Carry on", said Jenoye. "They asked me what I'd give. I said - my house, the bar ... and stuff like that", said Molly. "Keep going ... Nick asked you to give your soul, didn't he?" guessed Jenoye. "Yes!" said Molly, "I said 'No' ... he said I'd be able to sing better than Lucy." "So what happened after that?" asked Jenoye. "All I can remember is signing some sheet ... Lucy and Nick kept pressuring me into it." "I see! He waited until you were drunk", said Jenoye. "He told me I'd have seven years of good fortune", said Molly. "What do you reckon, Mum?" asked Viola. "It's like this, Molly - he has your signature", said Jenoye. "Is that bad?" asked Molly. "I'm not fully sure. The way I see it you didn't sign with your heart in it, did you?" asked Jenoye. "No! Of course not. He made me do it", said Molly. "He can't mess with your free will", said Jenoye. "Will she be saved, Mom?" asked Viola. "He can't force her to sign away her soul without her full consent", said Jenoye. "So! What will I do?" asked Molly. "He mentioned seven years good fortune, didn't he?" asked Jenoye. "Yes! he did", said Molly. "Did you earn any money from this yet?" asked Jenoye. Molly answered, "No. Not yet. We are doing a gig in New York City in two nights time. "I'll probably get paid for that." "Here is what you'll do: don't accept any money from him", said Jenoye. "What will that do for her, Mom?" asked Viola. "If you accept his evil money then you will have succumbed to him", said Jenoye. "How am I meant to refuse the money without arousing his suspicions though?" asked Molly. "Tell him you are doing the first gig for nothing. Say to him that you will accept money for the second gig - a gig that I want you to arrange to take place here in the big bar", said Jenoye. "What have you planned, Mom?" asked Viola. "Tell him that after the gig in *Sissy's* big bar you want to sign away your soul properly, without being drunk this time. Tell him you want a new contract, with your proper signature on it this time", said Jenoye. "What's that going to do for me?" asked Molly. "You get him to rip up the first contract", said Jenoye, "then tell him to be gone." "What if he says he doesn't need another contract?" asked Molly. "He will want a proper contract", said Jenoye. "He knows, without your heartfelt signature, he has to flee. What he has now is just temporary power over you; he wants you to taste stardom, then he will probably ask you himself to sign a new contract." "How do you know these things?" asked Molly. "Let's just say I read a lot. Satan can even make people feel better from illnesses. The only thing is ... his healing powers don't last", said Jenoye. "Wow! I never knew that", said Molly. "Did you, Viola?" "Yes! Actually, I did." "So! What he has now is only temporary?" asked Molly. "Yes, and don't be afraid. We will have you back soon", said Jenoye.

At 2:34am there were two heavy raps on the window. Viola headed over to open the door. Her mom stopped her. "I'll open it", said Jenoye. Molly said, "Don't dare say anything to him, Jenoye! He can't read your thoughts." "I know that", said Jenoye. "Don't worry, I won't say a word." Jenoye exposed her crucifix which was underneath her blouse as she wanted Nick to see it. Then she opened the door. Nick and the four men were standing in front of her. "Can I help you, gentlemen?" asked Jenoye. "Is Molly still here?" asked Nick. "Yes! She is. She is stocktaking", said Jenoye. "Is there something you wanted?" Just then one of the men said, "Yes, we are thirsty." Nick stared with anger in his eyes at the crucifix, and then he said, "Tell Molly not to be late tomorrow night for her rehearsal. Let's go, boys". One of the men said, "What? I'm thirsty." "We have enough drink for one night", said Nick. He turned to Jenoye and said, "Your signature would be harder to get than the president's." Jenoye pretended not to know what he was on about and said, "Huh? Excuse me?" Nick and the men left. Jenoye shut the door and came back to the counter. "Are they gone?" asked Viola. "Yes", said Jenoye. "Thank God", said Viola. "How do you know that he can't read thoughts?" asked Molly. "Demons can't read your thoughts. They can only guess. It's the same with the devil", said Jenoye. "I figured that out for myself", said Molly. "Jesus can read your thoughts though", said Jenoye, and continued, "Right girls! I'm going home. I'll take you both over to the apartment." "You were drinking, Jenoye. The cops might stop you", said Molly. "No! I only drank soda", she answered. "Oh! I thought you were drinking spirits", said Molly.

Jenoye dropped the girls over to the apartment. On her way back to her own house as she passed by the bar she noticed the big black Rottweiler again, sitting on the step, its eyes glowing like fire. Jenoye thrust the car into high gear, and drove home as fast as she could.

When Jenoye came into her house Isaiah was half asleep on the sofa. "It's 3:15am", he said. "What were you talking about to this hour?" "Those creeps came back to the bar. They were looking for drinks. I wanted to stay with Molly and Viola", said Jenoye. "Where are the girls now?" asked Isaiah. "I dropped them over to the apartment", Jenoye said, "I'm so worried about that poor young girl. Why are the blinds half down?" "Oh! I was looking out for your car since after one, then I dozed off", said Isaiah. "I'd better close them", said Jenoye. As she was closing the blinds she saw a Rottweiler looking over towards the window; it was growling. "Quick Isaiah! Come, look at this. This is the third time." "What is it? The third time for what?" Isaiah looked out. He, too, could see the big black growling Rottweiler. "You'd better watch what you're doing, Dear. I think you might be delving into the unknown here", he said. Jenoye said, "I'll take the risk. That young girl was tricked." "Tricked into what?" asked Isaiah. "I'll tell you over a cup of coffee", said Jenoye. Isaiah made two coffees, and Jenoye told him all about what had happened to Molly.

Over at the apartment the girls were asleep. Viola got up to go to the toilet. She heard growling outside, and she looked out the window. There was a huge black Rottweiler looking in their window. It changed into a big black wild boar, then finally it changed into Nick. Viola nearly fainted. She almost couldn't breathe. She closed the curtain, and ran back to bed frightened out off her skin. Molly woke. She heard somebody running in the house, and then sound of crying coming from Viola's room. Molly went in to see what was wrong. "What's up Viola?" "I have just seen Nick change from a dog to some kind of pig or wild animal - then he became himself." Molly paused. She, too, was very frightened now. "I'll sleep in beside you, Viola", she said.

The next morning the girls got up to have breakfast. Vicky asked them, "What time did you two get back last night?" "It was after three in the morning", said Molly. Vicky said, "I thought I heard a pack of dogs outside the window last night, but I was too scared to look out." Viola and

Molly looked at each other with fear in their eyes. "What time did you hear the noise?" asked Viola. "It was around about three in the morning", said Vicky. "That would have been just shortly after Mom closed the door", said Viola. "What would it have been?" asked Vicky.

"They are all demons, Viola", said Molly. "Who are all demons?" asked Vicky. "If I could give you an explanation I would", said Molly. Just after ten in the morning Jenoye came over to the apartment to check on the girls. "Did you sleep alright, girls?" she asked. "Apart from a pack of dogs barking and growling outside our window, yes! We slept great", said Vicky, in a sarcastic tone. "They were outside here last night", said Molly. "Could somebody tell me what's going on?" asked Vicky. Jenoye said, "I saw that big black dog again over at the bar. This time it followed me home." "Me too!" said Viola. "It was Nick." "Are you sure?" asked Jenoye. "Yes! He changed from two different animals outside our window last night into himself." "He appeared as he really is at my house", said Jenoye. "For the last time, what's going on?" asked a very confused Vicky. "We are not fully sure ourselves yet", answered Jenoye. "I'm heading to work", said Vicky. "You lot are crazy."

After Vicky left to go to work Jenoye sat down for breakfast with Molly and Viola.

"What time is your rehearsal tonight, Molly?" she asked. "It's at eight sharp. I dare not be late." "Remember, you will be able to sing like a pro tonight. After tonight you might not be able to sing like that again - that's just my prediction", said Jenoye. "What will happen if she can't sing after tonight?" asked Viola. "That's the thing - I'm not fully sure. He will want Molly to sign a real contract with her heart the next time. That way he will have seven guaranteed years with her voice", said Jenoye. "Don't you dare sign anything, Molly!" said Viola. "Don't worry! I don't intend to", said Molly.

"Are you sure, Mom? Or are you just assuming?" asked Viola. "It's a calculated assumption. I know his power over Molly is only temporary. He needs her signature from free will", said Jenoye.

"So! My singing powers are just for a limited time?" said Molly. "Yes ... which is good", said Jenoye. "Why is it good?" asked Molly. "It means you are not really doomed yet", said Jenoye, "I'm going back to the house now, girls. I'll talk with you tomorrow, Molly." "Thanks, Jenoye, and I'm sorry for involving you in all of this", said Molly.

At 7:55pm Molly arrived for the last rehearsal at the old warehouse. Nick was sitting on a chair with his legs crossed. "Aha! Punctuality, I like that", he said. The band members come in one minute before eight. "Right! Let's get started. We are playing to a massive crowd tomorrow night in New York City", said Nick. Molly went on stage. The band started up. Molly was singing like no other girl on the planet. Her voice was unreal. Nick was recording her again.

After the rehearsal Nick asked Molly to sit beside him again. He played back all the songs, one after another; it took nearly two hours. "Are you impressed with yourself, Molly?" he asked. "Wow! Am I what?" said Molly, lying through her teeth. "I can't believe how good I am." She was putting on an Oscar-winning performance in front of Nick.

"Well, I can make you sing like that for the next seven years", said Nick. "But I am already singing like that, aren't I?" said Molly, continuing to playing dumb. "Oh! I know you are ... thing is.. ahem ..." Nick cleared his throat ... "That's not really you singing." Molly went into acting mode again, "What! Whose voice is it, then?" asked Molly. "It's Lucy's voice. She is singing through you", said Nick. "Lucy? I thought Lucy was gone ... how can Lucy sing through me?" asked Molly. "It's like this. If you sign a contract with me I'll make that your real voice", said Nick. Molly didn't want to push her luck. "What's wrong with the contract I signed?" she asked. "Nothing ... provided you meant it. Did you mean it?" asked Nick. "I can't remember anything about that night", said Molly. "That's what I thought. This is not good", said Nick. One of the band members called Nick over and said, "You will need to get it sorted soon. We are performing tomorrow night. She won't have long left with that voice". Molly could hear what they were saying. It looked like the ball was in her court now. Nick came back over to talk with her. He had an anxious look on his face. Molly knew what he was about to ask her so, thinking quickly, she said, "Flipping heck! It's nearly midnight." "Why, what's wrong" asked Nick. "I have the only key to lock up the bar. I forgot to leave it with Viola. I didn't realise the time - I must dash." "Not so fast. I have to ask you something", said Nick. "Not now", said Molly. "I have to run. Why don't you call over for a drink? We can talk there." Nick shouted after Molly as she was dashing out of the warehouse, "Don't they have a spare key?" Molly shouted back, "Yes, but Viola lost it - I must hurry. Call in for a drink." "Blast! We need to act fast", said one of the band members. "Leave it to me. We will call in for a drink", said Nick. "We'd better get a move on", said another one of the band members. "The bar will be closing soon."

Molly came rushing into the bar, "Will you ring your mom quickly. I want her over here fast." "What's wrong? Are you in trouble?" asked Viola. "No, not yet! Nick was just about to ask me to sign a new contract. I said I had to rush over to the bar, that there is no spare key and I have to lock up." Viola said, "I'll be back in a second. I'll call Mom."

Jenoye answered the phone. "Mom! Get over to the bar quickly." "What is it?" asked Jenoye. "It's Molly - she thinks Nick is about to ask her to sign a new contract. She wants you here", said Viola. "I'll be there in five minutes", said Jenoye. Isaiah asked, "Who was that?" "It's Viola. She wants me to come to the bar. It's for Molly's welfare", Jenoye said. "You be careful! You don't know what you're dealing with", said Isaiah. "I'll be fine - catch you later".

Jenoye sped over to the bar. As she was getting out of the car she saw the band pull up in their big black truck. She rushed into the bar, and went straight up to the counter, "Shut the door quickly. Those creeps are outside." Molly said, "It's fine. I told them to call in for a drink." "Why did you agree to that?" asked Jenoye. "I had to", Molly answered, "Nick was about to ask me to sign a new contract over in the warehouse. I told him I had to rush." Just then the band members came in. "Shush! They are here", said Viola. "So you were using your head then", whispered Jenoye. "Look! That bitch is here", said one of the boys. "I can see that", said Nick. Up at the bar Viola avoided going over to the end of the counter where the men were. Tony, who was working behind the bar with Viola, served the men. "It's the usual - Bloody Marys all round." The men brought their drinks over to a table. Viola, Jenoye and Molly were talking at the counter. They were whispering as they didn't want Nick and the men to hear them. "How did you know that Nick was about to ask you to sign a new contract, Molly? Did he mention it to you?" asked Jenoye. "He mentioned my voice. He said I didn't have long left with it. He said the voice I have now is Lucy's. She is singing through me." "How can that be?" asked Viola. Molly said to Jenoye, "It would appear Lucy isn't yet doomed. Is that right?" "She must be in some sort of limbo. She is looking for a new host", said Jenoye. "How do you mean", asked Viola. Jenoye said, "It's hard to explain... it's like this.. Lucy had seven years of good fortune. Her time was up. However, through her singing and good looks, she can brainwash spectators. Nick realises this, so he is probably giving her another seven years. This is where Molly comes into the picture." "If what you are saying is correct, then if Molly signs Lucy will be able to possess her body?" asked Viola. "That is correct", said Jenoye. "What will happen to me?" asked Molly. "You will still have your own body. It will be the spirit of Lucy, though, that will possess you", said Jenoye.

Nick came up to the counter again and ordered more drinks from Tony. "Tell Molly to come over and join us", he said. "I'll send her over now", said Tony. "Nick wants you to join them, Molly", said Tony. Jenoye answered, "She is talking with us. We have things to discuss." Tony went over and told Nick. Nick was furious. "We will sit here to the bitter end tonight", he said.

One of the band members comes over to Molly on Nick's instructions. "You'd better get some rest. We have to be in New York City by seven o'clock tomorrow evening. "I'll be going home soon now", said Molly. The man went back and told Nick. Two more hours passed by. Nick was starting to lose his patience. Jenoye was still in the bar. It was now approaching 3:30am. Nick was really infuriated now. He wanted to talk with Molly alone. He didn't have much time left; in fact, Molly might have already lost her newfound voice. Jenoye was determined to stay, however long it took for Nick and the men to leave. Only fifteen more minutes passed. "Come on, let's get out of here. That bitch will never leave us alone", said Nick. "What are we going to do now? We are playing that gig tomorrow night. Molly's voice could be gone by then", said one of the men. "We will wait for her outside her house", said Nick.

The men got up to leave. Tony came over, opened the door and let them out. When Tony was just about to shut the door he noticed Nick's eyes turn to a fiery red. Tony turned a pale white; it frightened the life out of him.

With the men gone Jenoye invited Molly and Viola to stay with her at her house. "Any room for me?" asked a very pale Tony. "What happened to you?" asked Viola. "His eyes were like fire! His eyes were actually like fire", said Tony. "Whose eyes?" asked Viola. "Nick's eyes turned into fire", said Tony. With Tony shaking like a leaf, Jenoye said, "Okay, there is room for you too. You can sleep on the sofa." "Who was that?" asked Tony. "You don't wanna know", said Viola. "Believe me, you don't wanna know." Viola and Tony collected the empty glasses, and Molly gave them a hand to clean up. A short while after, everybody got into Jenoye's car and headed over to her house. It was now after four in the morning.

Outside the apartment a brutal noise erupted which woke Vicky. She opened the window and looked out. There were Rottweilers and wild boars in the driveway. They had fiery red eyes and they were going mad. Vicky closed the curtains as quickly as she could and crawled in under the blankets, sobbing with fear. The horrific noise went on for another half hour, then all of a sudden it stopped. Vicky was still trembling with fear. Over at Jenoye's house everybody had gone to bed, except for Tony who was on the sofa. Several minutes later the big black truck pulled up outside the house, and a furious Nick stepped out. He went up to the door and gave it three heavy raps. Jenoye and Isaiah come down the stairs. Isaiah opened the door. "Where is Molly?" asked Nick. "She is asleep. What do you want her for?" asked Jenoye. "Tell her we have to get a move on. We have to be in New York City for tonight", said Nick. "I'm afraid I can't let her travel with drunk men", said Jenoye. "I'm not drunk! Now tell her to get a move on", said Nick. "I think differently

- you were drinking Bloody Marys all night", said Jenoye. The noise had woken Molly. Through some divine intervention she came down the stairs singing, and her old voice was back; the singing was awful. Nick heard her. He was shocked. He realised his time with Molly's new voice was up. He did have her signature though. If he wished, he could plague Molly for seven years. However he couldn't claim her soul - without her true free will signature. He was thinking fast, "I'll be back in three hours after we get some sleep. You'd better be ready, Molly, or else." Nick and the men left.

"What does he mean? Or else?" asked Molly. "He has a hold on you with that signature, like it or not. The thing is he can't claim your soul. He will be able to torment you though", said Jenoye. "What can I do?" asked Molly. All the noise has woken Tony and Viola as well. Viola came down the stairs. "What's going on?" she asked. "Those creeps were here", said Jenoye. "What did they want?" asked a half asleep Tony. "They were looking for Molly." "What for?" asked Tony. "It's a long story", said Molly, and added, "Tony, you can go up to the bed. I'll lie on the sofa as I'll be going in a few hours", said Molly. Tony didn't argue; he went upstairs into the bed. He was in too much of a daze with sleep for things to register. Jenoye said to Isaiah, "You should go up to bed too, Honey. I'll make the girls some coffee".

Meanwhile, in a motel, Nick was pacing up and down the floor in a state of pure anger. He knew that Molly's new voice was gone and the spirit of Lucy was beginning to weaken. She needed a host body soon or she would be lost in the underworld. Nick had to act fast. They would be leaving for New York in a few hours.

In Jenoye's house the girls were drinking coffee. Molly asked Jenoye a question, "What did you mean when you said Nick can torment me for seven years." "He will still have a grasp over you. He has your signature." "But you said he tricked her", said Viola. "I know. He can still torture her though, even though he can't claim her soul", said Jenoye. "If he gets her to sign a new contract - and it will need to be before tonight - then he has complete control over her", said Jenoye. "Let's pray", said Molly. "Not a bad idea", said Jenoye. "The girls got on their knees and started praying. They prayed nonstop for two hours.

Over at the motel Nick was grinding his teeth in anger. This anger was just about to be multiplied. There were two heavy thuds on his door. One of the men answered the door. A motel worker asked, "Is Nick in?" Nick answered, "Yes! I'm here. What is it?" "Chantelle from *The Periwinkle Hotel* telephoned.", the man said. "What does she want?" asked Nick. "She said they had a fire in their ballroom, and she asked me to tell you they have to cancel tonight." "What! Is she still on the phone?" asked Nick. "No. She asked me to give you the message", said the motel worker. Nick exploded into a ferocious anger, throwing things around the room. One of the men said something that calmed his anger, "This will give you more time to work on Molly." Nick put both his hands on the man's face. He slapped both sides of his face and said, "True, true" with a big sly grin on his face.

It would appear that the prayers were working in Molly's favour. After 11:30am Jenoye said, "It looks like they aren't coming for you, Molly." "Maybe our prayers have worked", said Viola. "God! I hope so", said Molly. Just then the black truck turned up outside Jenoye's house. "Flipping heck! This is it", said Molly. One of the men came over towards the house. Jenoye answered the door. "We had a cancellation tonight", said the man. "Tell Molly we will meet her for a rehearsal instead this evening at eight o'clock sharp. Usual place." "Very well", said Jenoye. The truck pulled away. "Where are they going? Why aren't they taking me?" asked Molly. "They had a cancellation tonight. They want you for a rehearsal instead at eight, at the usual place", said Jenoye, and continued, "That's not too bad. It gives us time to come up with a plan."

"What sort of plan?" asked Molly. "I don't know just yet ... I need time to think." "Well, at least we have a bit of time to work on one now", said Molly. Viola cleared the atmosphere, saying, "I see your usual voice is back, Molly." Jenoye and Molly, although they found it difficult, managed to laugh. "If you sing like that tonight at rehearsal, Molly, Nick will run back to New York City", laughed Viola. "If only it were that simple", said Jenoye. "No matter what he says to you tonight, Molly, do not sign anything." "I won't. Better still, I'm going to sing in my usual way. If that doesn't annoy them then I don't know." "That's the thing, Molly. He knows you can't sing. He will have some plan up his sleeve - you must be prepared to counter attack", said Jenoye. "Do not be threatened into anything, Molly", said Viola. "We'd better get over to the bar", said Molly, "I am doing the early shift." Viola said, "I'm off today. Vicky is working with you." "Oh my goodness!" said Molly. "What is it? asked Viola. "Vicky was in the apartment all by herself last night! I hope nothing happened to her. I hope those creeps didn't go round there", said Molly. "That's right. We forgot all about Vicky", said Viola. "Come on", said Jenoye, "I'll drive you over to the apartment. We can pick her up."

In the apartment Vicky was still in shock. Jenoye and the two girls went inside. She wasn't in the sitting room. Molly rushed upstairs. She could hear Vicky sobbing. "What's the matter, Honey?" she asked. Vicky pulled the blankets down from over her face and said, "Thank God it's you." "What happened to you? Why are you crying?" asked Molly. "There were wild dogs and animals howling outside our window in the early hours this morning. I was frightened for my life", said Vicky. "My poor dear!", Molly said, "well, we are here now. I'm so sorry. This is all my fault." "Where were you all last night? I was too afraid to even go to the toilet", said Vicky. "You might not understand if I tell you", said Molly. Viola came into the room and said, "Look, if you want me to work your shift, Vicky, then it's not a problem." "No!" Vicky said. "I'm not staying in here on my own ever again! I'll work my shift. I'll just grab a quick coffee first." "I'll head on over to the bar and open up", said Molly. "Fine, I'll see you over there in ten minutes", said Vicky. "You can get a ride over with me. I will wait for you", said Jenoye. "Thanks!", said Vicky. "I'm still shaking with fear after last night." Molly went over to open the bar. However, Michael had already opened it. "Well, look what the cat dragged in", he said. "Sorry I'm late. It was a late night", said Molly. "I guessed that", said Michael. "Who is working with you today?" "Vicky. She is running a little late as she got her times mixed up. Jenoye will be dropping her off here in ten minutes", said Molly. "That's fine. I'll head in next door here now to the restaurant", said Michael. "Thanks for opening up for me, Dad, and I'm sorry I was late", said Molly. "Not to worry, there aren't many people about. I'll catch you later", said Michael.

Back at the apartment Vicky asked, "Where did those animals appear from last night? They looked so fearsome." Viola said, "We really don't know. We will never leave you on your own ever again". "I hope not!" said Vicky, "I thought they were going to push the door in and eat me." Nick came in to the bar for a cup of coffee. Against her will Molly went over and served him. Three more customers come in for a drink. Molly was pleased to see them as she didn't want to be left alone with Nick. Three minutes later Vicky came in to work her shift with Molly. Shortly after, when he had finished his coffee, Nick got up to leave. Before he did he went over to Molly and said "Don't be late tonight! Eight sharp. Make sure you turn up," and he left the bar.

Jean came in for a coffee. "I hear you were open late again last night", she said. "There were a few locals in. I didn't want to refuse them. They are good customers", said Molly. "Just be careful. The cops might come down on you. The time limit is 2:00am. Don't push it too much", said Jean. "I know. You are right", said Molly. "I'll ease up on the hours from now on." "Are you okay?" asked Jean. "I don't see much of you these days." "Nothing a few prayers wouldn't cure", joked Molly. Jean got a flashback of the days when she and Cissie always went to Mass. As she thought of Cissie, she said, "You will have plenty of prayers said for you. That I'm sure of."

At seven o'clock Tony and Sonia come in to relieve Vicky and Molly from their shift. "Flipping heck! Is it that time already?" said Molly. "You can stay on and do my shift if you want", joked Sonia. "Don't tempt me. I'd love to stay on", said a very uneasy and nervous Molly. "Wish I had your love for work", Tony laughed.

Molly left the bar and headed over to the apartment for a shower. After her shower she got on her knees in front of a little statue of Saint Martin - a statue that Cissie had left in her pram years earlier. She never really knew who gave it to her; she assumed it was her dad or mom. Anyway, Molly prayed for guidance, her prayers coming from deep in her heart. At 7:45pm, she set off walking over to the warehouse for her rehearsal.

When Molly arrived at the warehouse she found it empty. At 7:57pm Nick turned up. "You are here. Good. The band will be here shortly", he said. "What exactly are we going to be doing tonight? My voice is back to its old self", said Molly. "That's entirely up to you, Molly. I can give you the best female voice in the world. You will have more money than beyond your imagination", said Nick. Molly said, "I want to keep my own voice, thank you very much." At eight sharp the band turned up. "Well? Is she ready?" asked one of the band members. "No, she isn't", answered Molly herself. "Here is the deal, Molly", said Nick. "Either you agree to my terms or I'll plague you for seven years." "What is your deal?" asked Molly.

Just then Molly was transported to some other dimension; it was like she was in a sort of weird dream. Nick was with her. He showed her a big mansion of a house ... a handsome man who seemed to love her ... she owned a sports car, and she appeared to have money beyond her imagination. In the weird dream she heard Nick say to her, "This can be all yours. All you have to do is to say you want it, and I'll give it to you. I won't betray you." For some reason, even though Molly was very impressed with what she was seeing, from within the depths of her being her conscience was pulling at her heart. Her inner voice was telling her, "No! It's not real, it's evil." She kept saying "No, no, no" ... then, all of a sudden, she was back in the warehouse. When she found herself back in the warehouse, she was still saying, "No, no, no." Nick erupted, "Listen to me! I'll torment you day and night unless you sign this contract." "You are already tormenting me", said Molly. "I have your signature", said Nick. "I can either torture you or I can give you a life that would leave every girl of your age jealous. You will have them begging you for your autograph." "Yeah! At what price?" asked Molly. "It's only a soul. You can't see it, you can't touch it - what use is it to you?" said Nick.

"I want to keep my soul. I'm not giving it away", said Molly. Nick changed tactics. "You are not like your mother."

Meanwhile over at *Sissy's*, Jean came in. "Where is Molly?" she asked, "Michael and I are taking her out to dinner." "I don't know. Maybe Viola knows", said Sonia. "Where is Viola?" asked Jean. "She is over at the apartment", said Sonia. Jenoye came into the bar. She was concerned about Molly. Jean asked her, "Do you know where Molly could be?" "Yes!" Jenoye said. "We'd better get a move on."

Back at the warehouse, Molly was saying, "What do you mean? I'm not like my mother? You leave my mother out of this!" Nick said, "You want to keep something that you don't even know about? Your mother didn't want to keep you." "What are you on about? My mother and father love me", said Molly. "Your father is on my side. Your mother, though, she thinks she is on the other side. She didn't think twice about giving you away", said Nick. "I love my mother and father and they love me", said Molly. In a flash Molly was once again transported into a weird lifelike dimension … she was taken into the past. In this weird dimension she could see a child being born. Jean and Michael were standing there. The girl having the baby resembled Molly … she looked so much like her. It was Cissie, Molly's real mother. Nick then showed her as a baby being taken away in a car by Jean and Michael. In another phase Cissie was in her flat laughing and joking with Kathleen … she looked happy to be rid of the baby and was saying to Kathleen, "Good riddance to Molly." Nick had distorted this phase.

Over at the bar Jean didn't hesitate. She followed Jenoye quickly out to her car. On the way in the car Jean, now panicking, cried out, "What is going on? Where is Molly? Is she in some sort of trouble?" "She could be", said Jenoye, "I need to call over and collect Viola. She might know the location." "What location? What's going on?" asked Jean. "We will explain on the way", said Jenoye. The car pulled up outside the apartment. Jenoye beeped the horn repeatedly. Viola came running out. "Get in! We need to get a move on", said Jenoye.

"Do you know where Molly is?" asked Jenoye. "Yes, she is in a warehouse not far from here. I'll direct you", said Viola. "Could you please tell me what's going on?" asked Jean. "I'll tell you", Viola said, "I really don't think you will understand though." Then Jenoye blurted out, "She is being pressurised by the devil into signing away her soul. We need to hurry." Jean cried out, "What? How can this be? How do you know? Are you sure she isn't taking any drugs." "I said you wouldn't understand", said Viola. "What do mean? Devil? Soul? That's a load of rubbish", said Jean. Jenoye was driving fast with Viola was directing her on the way.

Back at the warehouse Molly asked Nick, "Who is that girl having the baby?" "It's Cissie, your mother." "That baby is me?" asked Molly. "Yes", said Nick. "Where is my father then?" asked Molly. Nick laughed, "Ah! He is out doing my work." Just then Molly was transported back to the present. Nick pulled out a paper which was a new contract for signing. "Now! Are you going to sign this or not?" he asked. Molly exploded with anger, "No way! My mom might have given me away. I'm not giving myself away, you bully. Now flee from me."

Just then the car pulled up outside the warehouse. Jean, Jenoye and Viola rushed over and pushed the door in. Nick was shouting angrily, "I'll torture you for seven years, you little bitch." Jean yelled out, "Molly! Come here to me." Molly ran to her, crying as she ran towards her, shouting

"Mom, Mom, Mom", and ended up in her arms. Nick roared at Jenoye, "This is your doing! You couldn't keep your religious nose out of it." Jenoye held a crucifix in front of his face; she said, "Jesus died on the cross for us. You gave up your free will; you can't force anyone to give up theirs. Now be gone - in the name of Padre Pio, Saint Francis and Jesus." When Jenoye spoke these words a sheet of paper fell at her feet. It was the sheet that Nick had forced Molly to sign while she was drunk over at *Sissy's Bar*. At the exact moment the sheet fell at Jenoye's feet Nick and the band members disappeared into a cloud of white smoke and were gone. Witnessing this with her own eyes Jean collapsed. She soon came round and got back up on her feet and managed to mutter, "What - or who - was that?" "You have just met the evil one himself", said Jenoye. Then she called Molly over, "Look at this paper. Is this your signature?" "Yes, it is", said Molly. While all the women present were looking at the paper the ink slowly faded away in front of their eyes, until eventually Molly's signature was completely gone. Molly dropped to her knees in prayer, "Thank you, Lord Jesus! Thank you. Lord Jesus." Suddenly, a fire broke out on the stage area of the warehouse. "Quick! Let's get out of here", yelled Jenoye. Everybody ran to the door as fast as they could. While they were outside the warehouse rapidly went up in flames. The whole building was burned down by a rampant inferno. The fire brigade arrived but it was too late; the building was beyond saving.

The four women had left before the fire brigade arrived. They didn't want to face them - or any cops. Heaven knows, if they had stayed around to be interviewed by the police and had to tell the truth, then all four of them could have been sent to an asylum.

The women went back to Jenoye's house. "What was all that about? What in Heaven's name just happened?" asked Jean. "I'll try to explain", said Molly. "Please do", said Jean. "Do you remember that band that played in our ballroom one Saturday night?" "Yes, I do. How can I forget? The noise of them was brutal", said Jean. "Well! After they finished playing that night the band members came in for a drink to the small bar in *Sissy's*", said Molly. "And what happened then?" asked Jean. "We drank into the small hours. I commented on the lead singer's voice. I remember saying, "I'd give anything to be able to sing like her." "Nick suggested that she give her soul", said Jenoye. "So! You did, Molly?" asked Jean. Jenoye interrupted, "No! She didn't. Nick tricked her into signing it away in a false contract - while she was drunk." "Then how come he didn't take her away?" asked Jean. "He knew he couldn't take her, without a proper complete free will signature", answered Jenoye. "That's why he wanted Molly over at that warehouse tonight. He wanted to talk her into signing a new contract", said Jenoye. "Is that right, Molly?" asked Jean. "Yes, I only went over there because he threatened that if I didn't he would torment me for seven years", said Molly. "How do you know he was the devil? Maybe it was some prankster", said Jean. "Did you not see what happened over there?" asked Jenoye. "I did. Maybe he is a magician", said Jean. Molly became annoyed, "He knew my mother. Can you explain that? Jean was gobsmacked. She froze and said, "What do you mean?" "Does the name Cissie mean anything to you?" asked Molly. Jean felt weak. She had to sit down, "My God! How do you know about Cissie", she asked. "I didn't know about her", said Molly. "That Nick creep told me about her. He just laughed at me when I asked who my father was." "Now do you believe her?" asked Jenoye. Jean didn't know what to say. She held her head in her hands and said, "I'm sorry, Honey. I meant to tell you a few years back. I just couldn't find a way ... I love you, I always did, and I always will." Jean was crying her eyes out. Molly came over and hugged her, "It's okay, Mother. I love you too." Viola said, "I could do with a drink. Anybody coming with me?" "Not a bad idea - we can celebrate having Molly back with us", said Jenoye. "A drink sounds like a good idea", said Jean. "Let's go over to *Sissy's*, and we can talk more about this, Mom", said Molly. "What am I going to tell your father? He won't understand what happened to you", said Jean. "We will find a way. You didn't believe me at first", said Molly. The girls went over to the *Sissy's* where Sonia and Tony were working. It was a very quiet night in the bar as most of the customers had gone over to the bar across the street where there was a drinks promotion as it had just reopened. Jean said, "Let's have a lock-in drink for the staff. There are only a few customers left in here and they will be leaving soon." "It's a bit early to close up", said Sonia. "No. Not just now. You can flick the lights at midnight", said Molly.

The restaurant had just closed for the night. Michael came in to see how the night was going in the bar. "Gosh! It's quiet in here tonight. Where is everybody?" asked Michael. "The bar across the street has opened up again - they are having a drinks promotion", said Tony. "Ah well, I suppose they could do with a good night too", said Michael. "Don't be heading home just yet. We are having a lock-in drink after midnight", said Jean. "What's the occasion?" asked Michael. "We have the best reason in the world", said Jenoye. "Very well, if it's going to be a special occasion", said Michael, "but I'd need to go home and have a shower first." "I'll go home and bring Isaiah over. He is sitting in the house, expecting me back soon", said Jenoye. Michael said, "I can get a ride over to the house with you. It'll speed things up." "No problem. Let's go", said Jenoye. When they reached Michael's house Jenoye said to him, "We can leave the cars at our houses. Isaiah and I will give you a knock in twenty minutes. We can all walk over together." "You're making this occasion sound like a real drinking session", said Michael. "Believe me, when you hear what has to be said tonight you will want a good stiff drink", said Jenoye. "Is everything alright?" asked Michael. Jenoye said, "All will be revealed over at the bar. Now go and have your shower. We will call for you shortly." Jenoye came inside her house, "Isaiah, go and get cleaned up." "Why? What's going on?" asked Isaiah. "We are going over to *Sissy's*. We are having a lock-in drink", said Jenoye. "Are we celebrating something?" asked Isaiah. "Yes, we certainly are. We are celebrating the return of Molly's soul", said Jenoye. "Now I can't refuse that then. I'll put on my suit", said Isaiah. Half an hour later Isaiah and Jenoye called over to Michael's house. He was ready to go. All three set off walking to the bar.

In *Sissy's* only two customers were left. Tony was now on the other side of the bar. It was too quiet for two bar staff so Sonia could cope on her own, no sweat. Isaiah, Jenoye and Michael come in. Just as they were walking in the door Vicky arrived also. They started drinking. "What are we celebrating?" asked Michael. "We can't say just yet. We will wait till we have no strange ears listening", said Jean. "Let's talk about the future", said a very happy and relieved Molly.

Back in Ireland in the town of Mulldish, Agnes was now married to Tommy Murphy. Cissie has kept her surname of McGinley. Hardly a day passed without them both thinking of Molly. They didn't have a clue as to what part of the world she was in. Before long this was all about to change.

In San Francisco in *Sissy's Bar* the staff were just about to have the bar to themselves. The last two customers - who were good local regulars - were about to leave. Sonia had just dimmed the lights down. Molly went over to the two customers, "Sorry for dimming the lights. We are going to have a lock-in staff night - you are welcome to stay if you like". "We understand. We were actually going home anyway. I have to get up early for work", said the lady.

When they had left Michael said, "Right! Can somebody tell me what the occasion is?" Molly tried to remember everything. She started with the first time she met Nick in the university in New York City. She then recalled the concert in the arena where she first heard *Manhattan Sound*, and the thoughts she had about Lucy's voice. She then talked about the night the band played in their big ballroom and once again she mentioned the thoughts she had about Lucy's voice. She then tried to explain what happened in *Sissy's Bar* - the signature and the contract and how Nick tried to trick her into signing away her soul. Michael was listening intently. He couldn't believe his ears.

He believed Molly, though, after she mentioned the transportation into the past - seeing Cissie having the baby, then seeing Cissie giving away the baby, and the baby being taken by Michael and Jean. Michael was left with his mouth wide open. He was so shocked he could barely speak. Then he began to cry. He tried to explain everything. He was just about to go into the details when Molly stopped him, "It's okay, Father. I couldn't ask for two better parents. I love you both. I'm so glad to get a second chance."

With the revelations out of the way the staff, along with Jenoye and Isaiah, started to relax and get down to drinking. Michael and Jean told Molly all about Cissie, and how she and Kathleen used to work for them in *Jean's Restaurant*. Molly was full of questions. She was amazed that she was from a traveller bloodline. She was saddened about the rape of her biological mother, Cissie. Equally, she was proud of Cissie for not having an abortion. And she was pleasantly surprised when they mentioned that they knew Cissie's address. They told her about her granny and they told her that Cissie was the oldest of six siblings. After talking about Cissie for a few hours, Michael suggested, "What about sending Cissie and your grandmother tickets for San Francisco?" Molly was overwhelmed with excitement. "That would be brilliant", she said. "Now! Let's welcome our girl back from the grasp of the devil", said Jean. "I'm going to church every Sunday from now on", said Molly. "I'll make it my business to go on my days off work too." Jean laughed, "Ha ha, You and Cissie will get on great. She is very devout." "I can't wait to see her. She sounds like a great woman", said Molly. "She is indeed", said Jean. "Michael and I will purchase tickets tomorrow. We will post them to Cissie and your grandmother first thing - they can stay with us for a few weeks", and then she said, "Alright, raise your glasses!"

The folks raised their glasses. "To Molly - welcome back to us, and to the side of our Lord", said Jenoye. "To Molly", they chorused. Then Molly said, "I'd like to raise my glass to the woman and her daughter who helped me through all this." Everybody raised their glasses once again, "To Jenoye and Viola." "Thank you both ever so much", said Molly.

The next day Michael and Jean paid a visit to the travel agency. "We would like to buy two tickets for two women living in Ireland. We want to bring them over here to San Francisco. Could you arrange that for us?" asked Jean. "Certainly", answered the agent, "I'll just take a few details from you. I'll have it sorted in no time." After buying the tickets Jean dropped Michael off at the restaurant. She headed on home as she wanted to write Cissie a letter to accompany the tickets. She wanted to apologise for the past, and how her departure was cunning.

Eight days later, over in Ireland, Agnes and Tommy had just finished their breakfast when the postman came along on his black bicycle. He put three letters through the letterbox. Agnes went out to the hallway and picked up the letters - one was for Cissie and the other two were for Agnes. "Any good news?" asked Tommy. "Probably just bills - I'll open them ... yes, as I thought, one for the electricity, and one is a dental appointment", said Agnes. "When is your dental appointment?" asked Tommy. Agnes answered, "It's in three days. There is a letter here for Cissie, too. I'll have to ring her at work as she would probably just head on home after work, without calling here." Cissie was now living in her own little cottage. Tommy and Agnes were living in her homestead. Cissie was working in *The Oyster Bar*. The manager answered the phone in *The Oyster Bar* and said, "Cissie, it's for you. I think it's your mother." "Hi Mum. How are you?" Agnes answered, "I'm fine, Honey. There is a letter here for you. It has American stamps on it." "Oh really! Okay, I'll call over to you after work. I finish at six", said Cissie. She was wondering, "Who in America knows me? Ah, I'll just have to wait until after work to find out." Cissie was in a curious mood all day at work. She kept wondering about the letter. The thought of Jean and Michael did enter her head. "I wonder ... did they go to America? Or, maybe they are in Australia. Aww! What the heck - I'll find out when I go over to Mum's house", she thought. The day dragged on. Finally, six o clock came round. Cissie finished her shift, and headed on over to her mother's house.

Tommy was out feeding the cattle and sheep. Agnes was in the kitchen making the evening tea. Cissie came inside the house, "Hello, is there anybody here?" Agnes heard her and came out of the kitchen, "Hello, my dear, how are you?" she asked. "I'm fine, Mum", Cissie answered, "Where is the letter." "I'll just go and get it ... it's in the sitting room." Agnes brought out the letter and handed it to Cissie. When she opened the letter the first thing Cissie noticed were the tickets. "Who are these for?" she asked. She switched to the letter and started to read it out loud, so her mum could hear. "Dear Cissie, I hope you have forgiven our quick departure, all those years ago. I have sent tickets for you and Agnes. Molly knows about you both, and she wants to see you and her granny. I'm keeping the letter short. I have included my phone number. If you can't make it please ring and let me know. Best Wishes, Jean and Michael." Agnes was in shock, "My Lord! Are we getting a chance to see Molly?" she asked. "Looks like it", said an equally shocked Cissie. "Open the tickets! See where they are for", said Agnes. Cissie opened the tickets, "They are for San Francisco. I thought they might have gone either to the USA or Australia", said Cissie. "When are we to go?" asked Agnes. "The tickets are open for three months. We need to use them before that", said Cissie. "Are they airline tickets?" asked Agnes. "Yes. I've never been on a plane before", said Cissie. "Neither have I", laughed a very excited Agnes. "This is amazing! We are going to see Molly ... after all these years. I can't believe it. I haven't stop loving her - I think about her every day", said Cissie. "Me too! I can't wait to finally meet my grandchild", said Agnes. As she burst into tears Cissie started to cry also. Tommy came in for his evening tea. and saw both women crying. "What's wrong? Did we get bad news?" he asked. "On the contrary, we have just received the best news possible", said Agnes. "Then why are you both crying?" asked a very confused Tommy. "We are crying with happiness. We have received news about Molly", said Cissie. "About Molly? Where is she? And what sort of news?" asked Tommy. "We have tickets for America. We are going to San Francisco. That's where Molly lives. We got a letter from Jean and Michael. Oh, my heart is beating with joy", said Agnes.

"You never know what the day will bring", said Cissie, "I mean, I never thought I'd ever see her again. Then we receive news like this." "I'm happy for you both - I know how much you both love her. This will be great for you", said Tommy.

"We need to get passports", said Agnes. "You mean, you have to. I have mine. It is valid for another two years", said a very happy Cissie. "Really! Well, I need to get on the ball", said Agnes. "Can I use your phone, Mum? I think we should ring Jean to let her know we are both coming", said Cissie. "Of course", said Agnes, "I wasn't thinking. Yes, certainly! Ring her now." Cissie rang the number and got through to *Cornie's Restaurant*. Michael answered the phone ... "Hello, is this The Smiths?" Cissie asked. "Yes! I'm Michael Smith", he said, immediately recognising Cissie's voice. "Is that you, Cissie?" "Yes!", she said, "I got the tickets. I'm just ringing to let you know we are both very grateful, and we are accepting your kind offer." "I'm so glad to hear that. It's great to hear your voice again", said Michael. "It's great to hear you too. It's been a long time", said Cissie. Michael said, "I'll tell Jean that you are both coming. She will be so excited. Molly is beside herself with excitement. She is hoping you will both come." "Is she there? Can I talk to her?" asked Cissie. "Not at the moment. She and Jean went to the shopping mall. They will be back in a few hours", said Michael. "Okay, maybe I'll ring at the weekend again", said Cissie. "That would be great. I'll arrange it with them both. I'll let you know the best time to ring. It's awkward with the different time zones ... let's say, if you ring at 4:00pm your time on Saturday", said Michael. "That's brilliant", said Cissie. "I'll ring you on Saturday. I have to hang up now - I'm on Mum's phone." "Okay Cissie. I'll hear from you soon. God bless", said Michael. "Bye. Take care - catch you soon", said Cissie.

Molly and Jean come into the restaurant. "You will never guess who rang", said Michael. Molly hopped with excitement; it was as if she knew straight up. She shouted, "Cissie!" Tell me it was Cissie." "Yes! It was", Michael said. "Are they coming? Please say they are!" said Molly. "They are indeed", said Michael. Jean and Molly bounced up and down like two mad women, holding each other. "Fantastic news", said Jean. "This is so beautiful", said Molly. "They will be ringing here on Saturday", said Michael. "Are they?" said Molly. "I can't wait to hear their voices."

A couple of weeks passed by. "I wonder when my passport will arrive", wondered Agnes. "The girl at the post office said it could take up to four weeks", said Cissie. It didn't take four weeks. On the Wednesday of week three Agnes received her passport. Tommy asked Agnes and Cissie, "Now that you both have your passports and tickets when will you be going to San Francisco?" "I think I'll ring the restaurant again. We can arrange to go on Saturday", said Cissie. Cissie rang the restaurant again. This time Molly answered the phone. "It's Cissie. I'm ringing to let you know that Mum and I will be flying out on Saturday." Molly was so excited, "That's great! I'll let Mom and Dad know. We can go and pick you both up at the airport."

After talking for ten minutes the two women said their goodbyes for the moment.

In the early hours of the Saturday morning Tommy drove Agnes and Cissie up to Shannon Airport. Their flight out to San Francisco was at 8:00am. They arrived in good time and checked in at the airport. A few hours later they were told that they would be boarding the plane in ten minutes. "I'm so excited I feel like my heart is gonna burst out through my chest", said Cissie. "Mine too! If it weren't for the fact that I'm going to see Molly, I'd probably be frightened to death of the plane", said Agnes. "We will be safe. It will be like sitting on our own sofa", said Cissie. "Hope you are right - I'm terrified of crashing", said Agnes. After two long flights, with a connection in New York, the plane touched down in San Francisco Airport.

Michael, Jean and Molly were running a little late as they were stuck in heavy traffic. Agnes and Cissie waited for their luggage. When they finally lifted their bags off the conveyor belt the realisation of meeting Molly kicked in. "This is it. I can hardly breathe", said Cissie. "Let's make our way to the arrivals hall", she continued, "Michael said he would meet us there." "I hope he recognises you now", laughed Agnes. Cissie and Agnes were waiting for twenty minutes. "Gosh! I hope they remembered the time. I hope they haven't got it mixed up - they might think it's twelve hours later", said a concerned Agnes. "No! Not at all. They are more than likely just running late, or they could be stuck in traffic. It's a big city", said Cissie. Two minutes later, Michael pulled up outside the airport. The three of them made their way over towards the entrance. "Look! I can see Cissie", said Michael. "Oh my God! You are right. She is standing with her mum", said Jean. "Where? Where?" shouted Molly. "There! She is beside the blue door, right opposite the woman wearing the red suit", said Michael. As they made their way over towards Cissie and Agnes, Cissie recognised them, "That's them! That's them, Mum. I see them - they are walking towards us." Molly was hyper excited, "Is that them?" she asked. "Yep! It sure is", said Michael. After all these years the reunion between Molly and Cissie was finally happening. "You must be Cissie", Molly said. "It's so unbelievable to see you again!" said a very emotional Cissie. "Come here and give your granny a hug", said Agnes. "You two haven't changed much", said Cissie. "Thanks very much", said Jean, "and you haven't changed too much yourself. Has she, Michael?" "She certainly hasn't", said Michael. After a lot of tears and a serious amount of hugging all five got into the Smiths' car and made their way to their home. For the next three weeks Molly and Agnes spent time getting to know Molly.

Agnes and Cissie went to a little cafe. They were having a few hours to themselves while Jean, Michael and Molly were preparing the bar for an eighteenth birthday later on in the evening - one of their locals girl was having a party. While working side by side in the bar Molly asked Michael and Jean not to mention one word about what happened between her and Nick. "You know, Cissie would understand - she is very holy", suggested Jean. "That's the reason I don't want them to know. I don't want them thinking I'm unholy", said Molly. "You are not unholy. Remember, you were tricked", said Jean. "Nevertheless, I never want to tell them. I'm getting a second chance - not just with my life - I'm getting the chance to know my biological mother, and my granny", said Molly. The three weeks had nearly passed. Cissie and Agnes were spending the last day of their holiday with Molly. Over the course of the three weeks Molly had told them almost everything about her life. Likewise, Cissie and Agnes shared their life stories. Cissie invited Molly to come to Ireland to celebrate her twenty first birthday which was only three months away. She wanted Jean and Michael to come, too.

On their last day Cissie, Agnes and Molly said their goodbyes. "You have a job waiting for you in *Sissy's Bar*, if you want", said Jean. "That's for sure. I'll have no need to interview you", said Michael. "Maybe if you change the spelling", joked Cissie, and they all laughed. "We will look forward to seeing you all again - in Ireland next time", said Agnes. After more tears Cissie and Agnes got ready to fly back to Ireland.

On Christmas Day 1968 Molly was in Ireland along with Jean and Michael. Not only was she celebrating Christmas but it was the day of her twenty first. Cissie and Molly had bonded; the past was behind them. Meanwhile in San Francisco Vicky, Viola, Tony and Sonia were taking care of things. Back in Ireland, everybody was on their way to Mass. They would come back later to enjoy Agnes's cooking; she had stayed behind to prepare dinner. The folks arrived back to the house and they all enjoyed a big feast together. Cissie and Agnes would be holding a twenty first birthday party for Molly on the 28th of December. Over their two week stay in Ireland Molly and Cissie were now bosom pals; so much so that Molly wanted her to move over to San Francisco to live. Cissie knew that Jean and Michael would always be Molly's parents. The best she and Molly could be was true friends for life. Cissie told her mum, Agnes, "I'm going to rent out my house. I'm going to San Francisco to live. I don't want to be apart from Molly ever again." "Are you sure? Is this what you want?" asked Agnes. "Yes! Molly and I can come and visit you twice a year. You can come visit us, too", said Cissie. "Well, I suppose if you rent the house, at least that way if you get homesick you can always come home", said Agnes. "Exactly", said Cissie. "The house will be left to Molly one day. After all, it is money that I got paid for her that bought it in the first place."

On January 7th 1969, Molly, Jean and Michael left Ireland. Once again they had an emotional goodbye, not nearly as bad as before though. Cissie would be coming over to live in San Francisco just as soon as she got the tenancy of her house sorted out. On the flight Molly was chatting happily. "What an amazing family. I love their accent", she said. She had met all of Cissie's siblings. "We are so happy for you, Molly. We always wanted Cissie to love you. It turns out she always has", said Jean. "Well, I understand everything. It must have been hard for her. Ah! You know what? I'm not going to dwell on the past. Cissie is part of my life now and that's all that matters", said Molly. Michael and Jean just smiled. "You two are my parents, though. You always will be - I love you both", said Molly, then she rested her head on her mum. Molly slept in her mum's arms for up to three hours of the flight. Jean was running her fingers through Molly's hair and crying with joy until eventually she herself fell asleep.

After the Christmas and New Year's celebrations Cissie got on the ball. She put an advertisement in the local paper advertising her house for rent. Molly and Cissie phoned each other once a week, usually on a Saturday. A few months passed by. Eventually, Cissie received a phone call. A couple with a little six month old baby wanted to rent the house - it would be two more weeks, though, before they had the deposit money. Cissie opened up her heart, "Come ahead. Forget the deposit money - you can just pay the rent weekly to my mother." The couple arrived two days later with their baby and moved into the house.

Cissie rang Molly to tell her the good news. She told Molly she would be coming to San Francisco within three weeks. Molly was overwhelmed with joy. Meanwhile, Cissie would stay with her mother for the three weeks.

In the spring of 1969 Cissie arrived in San Francisco. Once again Jean, Michael and Molly picked her up from the airport. The months passed by. Cissie had settled in to working in the restaurant, and in the bar. She kept her promise to her mother. She visited once that year, during the summer, and Molly was with her for the holiday in Ireland. The following year, they visited twice. The years passed by. Cissie had been living in San Francisco five years now. She was getting married soon to a man from Chicago. Molly had three years completed in a convent; she has chosen to become a nun, something that Cissie had always wanted to do.

Molly never mentioned a word about Nick to Cissie. She made everyone who knew promise never to mention her ordeal. Jenoye became good friends with Cissie; she loved her spirituality.

After Cissie got married she and her husband decided to open up their own business, a little coffee shop. Less than a year later Cissie gives birth to a baby boy. She named him Francisco, after one of the little visionaries of the Lady of Fatima, in Portugal. She had a baby girl the following year, and one more the year after that. She named the two girls Lucia and Jacinta after the girl visionaries of Fatima. Molly was now entering her eighth year in the convent. She thanked Jesus daily for giving her a second chance.

One day in the convent one of the girls decided to leave as she couldn't focus any longer. Molly tried her best to talk her out of leaving. The girl, named Lorraine, had said, "I can't do this anymore. I only entered the convent because a man broke my heart. It's not a good enough reason for becoming a nun".

Molly was saddened. She got on well with Lorraine. However, she accepted her choice. "If it's not meant for her then I suppose I'll have to carry on without her", she thought.

The following year - year nine - Molly was taking her final vows. Agnes and Tommy had flown out for the occasion. Cissie was crying with joy. Her true vocation was to become a nun, but seeing her biological daughter making her final profession made her very happy.

Everybody was present for the occasion. Jean and Michael didn't feel sad. They wouldn't become grandparents, but seeing their daughter safe in the hands of the Lord gave them great peace of mind.

Molly did mention her dark experience to one more person. That was Father Desmond. That same priest was celebrating Mass that day; in his homily he quoted from that day's gospel reading, "What profit would there be for one man to gain the whole world and forfeit his life? Or what can one give in exchange for his life?" Matthew 16:26. After saying that Father Desmond looked benignly upon Molly.

Printed in the United States
By Bookmasters